THE HOUSE OF ATTILA

THE HOUSE OF ATTILA

Ernie Hasler

Book Guild Publishing
Sussex, England

First published in Great Britain in 2010 by
The Book Guild Ltd
Pavilion View
19 New Road
Brighton, BN1 1UF

Copyright © Ernie Hasler 2010

The right of Ernie Hasler to be identified as the author of this work has been asserted by him in accordance with the Copyright, Designs and Patents Act 1988.

All rights reserved. No part of this publication may be reproduced, transmitted, or stored in a retrieval system, in any form or by any means, without permission in writing from the publisher or the author, nor be otherwise circulated in any form of binding or cover other than that in which it is published and without a similar condition being imposed on the subsequent purchaser.

All characters in this publication are fictitious and any resemblance to real people, alive or dead, is purely coincidental.

Typesetting in Baskerville by
Nat-Type, Cheshire

Printed in Great Britain by
CPI Antony Rowe

A catalogue record for this book is available from
The British Library.

ISBN 978 1 84624 394 3

Contents

1	Descent into Hell	1
2	The Journey	4
3	Nico	9
4	Maria	13
5	The Kitchen	19
6	The Farm	25
7	The Hotel	29
8	Charlie	32
9	Team Building	41
10	The Boilers	46
11	The Preparations	56
12	The Gathering	67
13	Warlords	82
14	The Manhunt	87
15	Dominance	92
16	Reunion with Prince	100

17	The Challenge	109
18	The Football Team	113
19	The Award	126
20	Reunion with Maria	135
21	Prince is Sold	150
22	Strategic Mistake	170
23	Nataša Disappears	177
24	Shoemaker Reports Back	184
25	Football Play-offs	189
26	The Second Gathering	205
27	Elimination	214
28	Visit to Grandmother	233
29	Journey to Oban	242
30	Freda Pays the Price	261
31	The New Hotel	268
32	The Boat	275
33	International Football	289
34	The Escape	301

1

Descent into Hell

It was the first, dark hours of the morning of New Year 1992 when Nico and Maria Sokota, brother and sister, were dragged across the snow and bundled roughly into the back of a lorry along with thirteen other children by the ruthless soldiers.

The children cringed as they heard the terrible cries and screams of terror issued by their parents and neighbours in the burning barn, trapped by the cunning leader of the raiding squad who had sprung the perfect and unexpected attack while the residents of the little hamlet were still celebrating the New Year with music and dance. The leader of this raiding squad was not carrying a gun like his soldiers, but instead he carried a curious sword. He had an obsessive belief in this sword and the inscription on one side of its blade, which read, 'Sword of Attila – Ruler of the World'. On the other side of its blade was a more curious inscription: 'You will rule from a town sitting under a crown beyond the Pillars of Hercules'.

Claiming the first casualty of war is a bitter dispute between Serbs and Bosniaks. However, unrecorded by history, this tiny mountain hamlet in the hills above Sarajevo has a silent claim to being among the first casualties of the war. But there are no significant witnesses in a position to proclaim this cruel massacre.

* * *

In the months leading up to the war, the Yugoslav People's Army (JNA) in the region began to mobilise in the hills surrounding the city. One small unit was led by Harold Szirtes, an extreme nationalist eccentric carrying a sword instead of a gun.

In April of 1992, the Bosnian government demanded that the government of Yugoslavia remove these forces. Milošević, who headed the Serbian government, agreed to withdraw the individuals who originated from outside of Bosnia's borders. An insignificant number of those Bosnian Serb forces in the army were transferred to the VRS (Vojska Republike Srpske), which had declared independence from Bosnia a few days after Bosnia itself seceded from Yugoslavia.

On 5 April, the day of the declaration of independence, marches took place in Sarajevo, with the largest group of protesters moving towards the parliament building.

At that point, Serb gunmen fired upon the crowd from the Serbian Democratic Party headquarters, killing 200 people. These people, Suada Dilberovic and Olga Sučić, are considered by Bosniaks to be the first casualties of the siege of Sarajevo; today, the bridge where they were killed is named in their memory.

Armed conflict broke out after the European Community recognised Bosnia and Herzegovina as a sovereign state on 6 April, 1992. The Yugoslav People's Army attacked the Old Town district with mortars, artillery and tank fire, and JNA units seized control of Sarajevo's airport.

The JNA expanded its control of approaches to the city by establishing road blocks along key roads. By the end of April, the contour of Sarajevo's siege was largely established. On 2 May, 1992, a complete blockade of the city was officially established by the Bosnian Serb forces. Major roads leading into the city were blocked, as were shipments of food and medicine. Utilities such as water, electricity and heating were cut off. The number of Serbian forces around Sarajevo, although better armed, was inferior to the Bosnian defenders within the city. Hence, after the failure of initial attempts to take over the city by JNA's armoured columns, the besieging forces continuously bombarded and weakened the city from the mountains. They were fortified into at least 200 reinforced positions and bunkers.

The second half of 1992 and first half of 1993 was the height of the siege of Sarajevo. To counterbalance the siege, the Sarajevo airport was opened to the United Nations (UN) airlifts in late June of 1992; Sarajevo's survival became strongly dependent on them.

Reports indicate an average of 329 shell impacts per day during the course of the siege, with a high of 3,777 shell impacts on 22 July, 1993. The shell fire caused extensive damage to the city's structures, including civilian and cultural property.

The shelling of the city took a tremendous toll on lives. Mass killings due primarily to mortar shell impacts made headline news in the West. On 1 June, 1993, fifteen people were killed and eighty injured during a football game. On 12 July of the same year, twelve people were killed while in line for water. The largest of these killings, however, was the first Markale market-place massacre on 5 February, 1994, in which sixty-eight civilians were killed and two hundred were wounded.

In response to the Markale massacre, the UN issued an ultimatum to the Serb forces to withdraw heavy weaponry beyond a certain point in a given amount of time or face air strikes. Near the end of the given time, Serb forces complied. City shelling drastically decreased at that point, which could perhaps be seen as the beginning of the end of the siege.

The eccentric sword-carrying Harold Szirtes was one of the beneficiaries of the conflict.

2

The Journey

As the children lay on the floor of the lorry, the screams and shouting were suddenly overwhelmed by long, loud bursts of automatic gunfire from many guns.

'If we are separated, do not give up hope that we will find each other,' Nico whispered.

One of the soldiers kicked Nico hard in the stomach and shouted at him to stop talking. Niko rolled over, gasping for breath and sorely winded by the cruel kick.

After a journey of about an hour, the lorry stopped beside another parked lorry. The children were roughly kicked and pushed out of the back of the lorry. The girls were separated from the boys and reloaded into the back of the original lorry, which immediately drove off, with four female, gun-carrying soldiers guarding the frightened and now tearful human cargo, most of whom were hardly into their teenage years.

The boys were loaded into another lorry, which also immediately drove off following the first lorry with four male, gun-carrying soldiers guarding the young and powerless victims.

Both lorries were now heading through the bleak, cold, winter darkness of early morning along the road to Belgrade.

On entering the outskirts of the Serbian city, the lorries with their headlights switched off and running on just side lights, slowly approached an industrial area of the city and drove through the open gates of a factory yard. The gates were immediately quietly closed behind them.

The girls were again roughly kicked and pushed off the lorry and into a corrugated, steel-clad industrial shed about twice the size of a double domestic garage. The boys were similarly incarcerated in a similar shed at the opposite side of the yard and both sheds were locked with two heavy padlocks. The children were left locked in the sheds for all of the next day. When one of the boys started banging on the door and shouting to be let out, one of the soldiers unlocked the door and immediately hit the boy full in the face with the butt of his rifle, breaking the boy's nose.

Fortunately each of the two sheds had a flushing toilet with a hand basin, and cold water from the basin was used by some of the other boys to eventually stop the resulting nose bleed.

One of the girls in the other shed started to shout and scream to be let out. The door of the shed was unlocked and four female soldiers rushed in and grabbed the girl, stripped her clothes off and three of them held her face down on top of a table, while the other female soldier thrashed her buttocks hard with a thick piece of electric cable until she was reduced to a sobbing, quivering object of misery, which they roughly dumped on to the floor. They left the shed, locking the doors behind them.

Later that evening the doors of the sheds were opened briefly and several loaves of bread were pushed in to each shed; the doors were then closed and securely padlocked.

Although each of the sheds had an old wood-burning stove with a metal chimney pipe leading the smoke up and out through the corrugated steel roof, and a plentiful supply of logs, the sheds were very cold, particularly during the night as the outside temperatures plunged to well below freezing.

As Nico and Maria tried to find sleep in the cold of their

separate prisons, strangely they both had roughly the same thoughts. The terrible scenes and sounds of the attack on the village were deeply etched in their young minds. They were both previously aware of the ruthless cruelty of the conflict and both knew in their hearts that their parents were now dead.

The same thought crossed both their minds, that their parents would have tried to escape from the burning barn and would probably have died together quickly in a hail of automatic gunfire. The thought of their parents dying cruelly wrenched and screwed deeply at their hearts and brought silent tears to their eyes. They both gained some comfort in their almost certain knowledge that their parents, led by their father, would have tried to flee and that their end would have been swift under the furious hail of bullets. The thought that their parents probably did not suffer helped them in their own helplessness and insecurity.

Both Nico and Maria found themselves thinking about their mother and father and how they had taught them most of what they knew. Although Nico and Maria had been taught appropriate boy things and girl things respectively, both had also been taught common Christian things; some of these important bible stories came to both of their frightened little minds in the stark wilderness of these dark, cold sheds. One favourite scripture their mother often used when things were difficult repeated over and over again in their minds: there are some things that people cannot do, but God can do anything.

For some reason in the midst of all their grief and trouble their mother's image and voice resonated in their memories. Both thought about that short scripture and it caused Nico to think 'Wherever Maria ends up I will find her.' And it caused Maria to think 'I know that however long it takes, Nico will find me.'

* * *

THE HOUSE OF ATTILA

The next morning, before it was light, the girls were roughly loaded on to their lorry with their female soldier guards and the lorry doors closed and locked. Then the boys were loaded into their lorry. The gates of the yard were quietly opened and the two lorries drove slowly and quietly out and on to the road. The lorries came to a junction with a major road and one lorry took the road to the south and the other lorry turned on to the road leading north.

Both lorries were actually cattle transporters and the children could see through the ventilation slits and were immediately alarmed at the fact that the lorries were going in different directions.

Suddenly Nico felt very cold, not just the effect of the winter air temperature, but a coldness caused by an inner fear for himself and his young sister. He suddenly realised that they were now in the hands of people traffickers or modern day slave dealers.

He, better than most, knew the seriousness of their predicament, as he had just in the last year won a significant bursary prize at school for an essay he had researched and written on the subject of modern day people trafficking. He recalled the main elements of that prize-winning essay with a cold chill.

Contrary to popular belief, slavery didn't end with William Wilberforce's bill passed in 1833 in Britain or by Abraham Lincoln's initiative in 1863 in America. In fact, as Nico had discovered in his research, there were anything up to 27 million people enslaved around the world.

Nico had asked in his essay if people could try and grasp the extent of the misery and cruelty experienced by these millions of individual souls, cruelly exploited in the most primitive conditions until they were of no more economic value.

It was happening in countries on all six inhabited continents. And yes, that included the United States of

America and the enlarged European Community. At the time the CIA estimated that 14,500 to 17,000 victims were trafficked into the so-called 'Land of the Free' every year.

Why wasn't more being done to end this universally condemned practice? Perhaps it was advantageous to the rich that this massive, invisible population and huge unofficial economy existed in all countries including sophisticated countries?

Nico knew that many of the professions – the civil service and regulatory authorities – benefited from undeclared gifts and inducements from the extensive underworld. It was clearly visible and felt by the community everywhere, yet in practice strangely invisible to the regulatory authorities.

One excuse that was often used by the authorities was that slavery now took on myriad subtler forms than it had during the crude Atlantic slave trade – including sex trafficking, debt bondage, forced domestic or agricultural labour, and chattel slavery, making it tougher to identify and eradicate.

However, cruder forms including drug dealing, protection and murder, each highly visible on the streets, seemed to go on regardless of the effect on the law-abiding communities.

The underworld or criminal economy was growing faster than officially admitted and was becoming intermeshed with legitimate business and even governmental organisations. Criminal networks were now worldwide and penetrated international boundaries with relative ease. Organised crime could accurately be described as one of the major economic globalisations of the late twentieth century.

Nico remembered precisely his definition and summary on modern slavery, which he had written and rewritten many times in the process of refining the large and complex subject to its essential elements.

3
Nico

Nico felt very cold and small as he silently thought about these things and his little sister speeding away from him. The tears rolled down his cheeks.

With his face hard up against the side of the lorry, he again remembered his mother's often quoted scripture and silently offered up a prayer to his great God and eternal Father, explaining their predicament and asking for help, somehow quietly confident in the promises that Jesus had made.

As Nico dozed and woke between the hard bumps and jolts of the lorry, although he did not know it fully, mentally he was growing up very fast. It was quickly dawning on him that he was now head of the family and responsible for his sister Maria.

Regardless of how weak and powerless he was in relation to their adversaries, his commitment to his sister was absolute and greater than the power of guns, and this was becoming the predominant thought in his head.

The boys in the lorry were running a fever, shivering and huddling closer together, trying to keep warm on the floor of the lorry, which mercifully had a good deep covering of new straw. Nico was running a fever, too, and time had no meaning as the lorry travelled on and on, night and day, making very slow progress due to stopping frequently and making long detours to avoid areas of conflict and groups of soldiers whose alcohol-fuelled actions could be very unpredictable.

He began to mildly hallucinate and his imagination took him back into the recent past.

He remembered his mother, father, his young sister and he all living a happy family life in an idyllic small farm in the hills overlooking the city of Sarajevo, where his father worked as a designer in an architect's office and his mother worked in a local nursery school.

They all worked in their spare time running the small farm as an assurance against harsh winds of change so often experienced in this volatile corner of Europe. However, the family had been unable to foresee the terrible changes that lay ahead and the fiendish hatred stirred up in the hearts of previously good friends, neighbours and customers.

Nico's main job on the family farm was driving the old tractor and working various farm implements – ploughing, harrowing, fertilising, seeding, spraying and harvesting the sixty-three acres of good, fertile land.

Nico's family nickname was 'Action Man' and his mission statement was 'nothing is impossible'; anything that needed moving, lifting or transporting on the farm was Nico's job. He enjoyed working on the farm all the year round and it also built up his muscles and strength.

Nico's father was a regular churchgoer and his church pastor taught fathers to be leaders within the family. Consequently he had taught his whole family well, especially that good fortune doesn't just come to you. He taught them by example that you have to work for good fortune and play hard for your luck in every situation you find yourself in.

Nico's father knew and took great delight in quoting proverbs from the Old Testament, and especially those supporting his pet philosophy, by far his favourite subject:

THE HOUSE OF ATTILA

'All hard work brings a profit, but mere talk leads only to poverty,' he would expound, reciting chapter and verse.

This was often rewarded by family members with 'Oh! Here we go again.' But they knew he was right and they all really respected his example, for he certainly showed all these beliefs as he worked hard at building up the family farm.

At the end of harvest season the family held and greatly valued their own private thanks giving service at the dinner table, where they formally reminded each other and gave thanks for God's many blessings. They also recognised and gave thanks for the individual contributions each family member had made to the year's farming. Their father was very good at this. He kept a diary of the year's farming events and would recall some of these highlights amid great laughter, as the family remembered struggles and dramas, many of which were not so funny at the time, but this teamwork resulted in deep family bonding.

This principle of sticking to it and winning through had ingrained itself and become part of Nico's character even at his young age. This strong personal characteristic had made him captain of the school football team, and his determination, physical strength and leadership had been significant in winning many a difficult game for the team and the school. Football was his greatest personal preoccupation; Nico would get up early in the mornings to get his farm work done before going to school. This gave him free time to join the local informal football games played almost every evening during the summer.

Nico just loved playing football; it was where he was totally alive and in his particular element.

Suddenly the lorry stopped and the back door was opened. The guards ordered the boys to get out and roughly pushed and prodded them out. They were in the enclosed cattle sheds of a cattle auction market. There was a small auction ring with about twelve men around the edge and each boy was paraded in front of these twelve who engaged in serious bidding for a boy as they were inclined.

Nico, with his good physique, raised quite a bit of bidding and was finally bought by a big, burly character with long black hair in an army officer's uniform. A label with Major Szirtes printed on it was tied round Nico's neck and he was returned to the enclosed shed. After the auction the big, burly character came to the shed with his young teenage son to collect his newly bought property. Nico thought, it's a bit strange seeing an army officer with long, unkempt hair.

Szirtes looked at Nico straight in the eye and said, 'You are a displaced person without any identity and without any human rights. You are my property now, you work for me, you depend on me and without me you will die. If you work hard for me on my farm, life will not be too bad and you may enjoy a little free time. However, if you give me cause for anger your life will be short and painful. Do you understand?'

Nico nodded and quietly said 'Yes.'

The man smiled a cold, mechanical smile and said, 'My name is Harold Szirtes and this is my son Imri Szirtes. Come, we have a long drive in front of us.'

4
Maria

Maria was very frightened as she sped along the road in a similar lorry to that Nico was in, but she too had noticed the lorries driving in opposite directions at the road junction and she now felt very alone.

She was in a state of shock after what had happened and could not really comprehend the loss of her family. Maria was a real family girl; the farm her father had built up was a haven of security, where she and her mother spent many happy hours together keeping alive and practising the old country domestic skills, winning many awards for their farm produce at local country shows and festivals.

Maria was good at school work and achieved good marks in all subjects, however, she had special talent in music where she played the harp and sang. She had a natural, ringing voice that was very pleasant on the ear and seemed the perfect match for her harp. Maria often sang at the country shows, festivals and concerts and was popular with the locals.

These highly honed skills were all part of her father's philosophy: you have to work hard developing your skills to win your luck. Though there is no doubt that she had been gifted with a rare talent to start with.

The great love of Maria's life was her beautiful horse Prince, a large white stallion, a present from her father on her twelfth birthday for doing well at school. She spent time with Prince every morning and every evening and they both took part in many pony club events together.

When they were together Prince responded to every thought that Maria had, sometimes almost before she formed the ideas in her mind. He also visibly responded to everything she said with absurdly comical expressions made with his big eyes, ears and noisy expulsions of his breath, including impatiently nudging her forcibly with his muzzle especially when he expected a piece of carrot.

Maria experienced deep pain worrying about what had happened to Prince during the terrible ambush and she wondered where he would be now.

The tears rolled down Maria's face. She was so miserable she began to think she would be better dead, however, she knew that her mother and father would expect her to make the best of whatever circumstances she found herself in.

The Old Testament, Book of Ruth, came to Maria's mind. In the story when bad times fell on the two women, Ruth had been loyal to her adopted mother-in-law and to her mother-in-law's God; Maria took Ruth's example to mean that she too should be loyal to the memory of her own mother and her mother's absolute faith in Jesus the anointed Son of God, as her mother had so lovingly taught her. Oh! How Maria pined for her mother at this moment and tears again ran down her cheeks.

Maria thought about the story of how Ruth attracted the attention of the ruler of the nation, because he noticed that she went about her business in a quiet modest manner in contrast to the other loud and coarse gleaners scavenging the fields after the harvest. One of the ancient laws of the nation of Israel was for landowners to leave some of the crops in the fields after the harvest for very poor people to scavenge. There were very strict social taboos against the ruler marrying a foreigner. Ruth was a Moabite, a race particularly reviled by the Israelites.

Boaz, the ruler, disregarded these rules and took Ruth as his wife.

Maria therefore resolved to put her faith in God and all that her mother had taught her and make the most of whatever situation she found herself in.

Suddenly the lorry stopped and the back door was opened. The guards ordered the girls to get out and roughly pushed and prodded them; this time they were submissive and there was no resistance.

They were in the enclosed backyard of a country hotel; the girls were herded through the back door of the hotel and along a corridor on the ground floor and into a small dining-room. One by one each girl was escorted to a shower room by one of the female soldiers and ordered to strip and shower. The hot water was luxurious after the long journey in the cold lorry. After the shower each girl was ordered alone into the next room, still naked for selection. The guard did not explain what selection meant. There were two men and two women in the room and they proceeded to examine the girls in a quite offhand way, making jokes and laughing a lot. The two men and two women were suppliers of illegal hotel workers and prostitutes to the international hotel and brothel trade. None of the girls had any form of identification or proof of nationality.

Fortunately Maria was a slow developer and still looked like a young girl, so she was initially destined to be one of the many illegal hotel workers.

The two groups of girls were escorted into two separate rooms and were told to select two complete changes of clothing and wear one set and pack the spare set in a travel bag.

When the girls were dressed and ready with their packed bags, two female guards came in to the room. One of the guards announced loudly, 'listen very carefully to what I am telling you. You are now displaced persons with no means of identification or human rights, you are illegal immigrants in whatever country we place you and most local people passionately hate illegal immigrants. You now belong to and are totally dependent on a very powerful international organisation that does not tolerate dissent from any of its people; anyone who does not cooperate with the organisation will be severely punished and anyone who goes against the organisation will be killed. These are the basic rules and there are no exceptions allowed.

'You are now being taken to a local hotel to work for a while where you can be assessed and trained for work in other countries.

'Although you will never have any normal freedoms and you may not particularly like what you have to do, if you apply yourselves and so long as you are useful life can be tolerable. For your own sake understand clearly your absolute powerlessness and your dependence on pleasing your immediate supervisor, otherwise your life will be full of pain and possibly very short.

'The choice is yours.'

The now severely shocked girls were led out and loaded into two minibuses, with six girls, two guards and a driver in Maria's vehicle. It was only four o'clock in the morning as the vehicle drove along the deserted road and headed towards the lights of a built-up area just visible in the distance.

As they drove along, Maria noticed a road sign that indicated that the vehicle was heading south east. The minibus stopped at the rear of a medium-sized hotel and adjoining leisure complex where the girls were quickly and quietly ushered inside.

An elderly woman greeted the girls with words softened by a smile.

'Welcome to the world of lost and anonymous people.' She led them to a crowded bedroom containing six single beds with an *en suite* lavatory and shower; there was little room for anything else. The elderly woman said simply, 'This is your bedroom and it is up to you to make the best of it for each other. Leave your things here and come with me and I will explain what you have to do.'

The woman led them into a large laundry room where there was a large work table with eight wooden chairs around it; this clearly doubled as the staff room and equipment store. She pointed to some mugs hanging on hooks above a marble work surface and said. 'Make yourself some tea with boiling water from the urn and there is sugar and bread in that cupboard and milk and cheese in the fridge.'

When they had all had tea and sandwiches they sat round the table. The woman said, 'My name is Freda and I am the housekeeper. My job is to run this hotel's cooking and cleaning smoothly, your job is to help me do that, if you don't help me, you will be immediately taken away and I do not wish to think about your fate if that happens.

'Let us try to find out who is good at what. There are basically two areas of work: cleaning and cooking.

'First of all, who is good at cooking?' Maria was the only girl to put her hand up: Freda said, 'You are very young, what experience do you have?'

Maria said, 'My mother.' She nearly broke down as she remembered her mother; however, she gathered herself and said, 'My mother and I won many awards in the local country shows and exhibitions for our farm food.'

Freda smiled. 'Well that's settled, you go to the kitchen and tell the cook that I sent you to work in the kitchen and the rest of you report to the cleaning supervisor Karl, and I warn you, girls, you do not get on the wrong side of Karl, he can be very cruel.' She picked up the phone and dialled a number and said, 'Karl, the five new replacement cleaners for those who left yesterday have arrived, we are lucky to get them so quickly.'

Karl entered the room. 'Right, come with me and I will show you where you will work today and I will tell you what I expect, Karl was a lean, tall man with long black hair tied in a pony-tail. Karl had a black goatee beard. 'Come on, come on, move it out of here, there is a full day's work to be done.'

Freda looked at Maria and said, 'You go to the kitchen and report to the cook, the kitchen is through that door and along the corridor.'

5

The Kitchen

Maria followed the corridor to a door marked with a sign. It read:

Kitchen Private – Authorised Persons Only

She could hear a man's voice from within the room beyond the door; Maria pushed the kitchen door open and peeked in. The hotel chef, a big man with a red complexion looked at her and shouted, 'Can you not read? The sign says, "Authorised Persons Only".'

Maria walked towards him and said very quietly, 'Freda said I was to work in the kitchen.'

The chef exploded. 'I keep asking Freda for women not schoolgirls.'

'Milo, Milo, that's enough,' Freda shouted loudly as she pushed past Maria. 'This is Maria and she will be your new assistant and this one has to last a lot longer than all the rest. You and your drinking have caused me and several good girls more trouble than you are worth; if you cannot work peacefully with the staff I give you, then it is you who will go the next time, do you understand me? This is your last warning, Milo.' Freda turned and quickly left the kitchen.

Milo picked up a big glass jug of milk and hurled it at the stone fireplace, letting out a stream of curses clearly describing his opinion of Freda. The milk ran down the wall and collected in a puddle in the empty fire hearth. Milo slumped onto a chair, leaning his elbows on the table, cupping his face in his hands and saying wearily, 'What can I do? What can I do? I am surrounded by incompetents.'

Maria went over to the sink and filled a basin with hot water and squirted in some washing-up liquid. She washed a kitchen cloth and began to clean the milk from the stone fireplace. When she finished cleaning the wall she turned to Milo and asked him, 'Please show me where you keep the shovel and brushes.'

Milo pointed to a door and Maria opened the door, which led into a large storeroom with a sluice sink and lots of shelves containing all the cleaning materials and equipment. Maria selected a brush and dustpan, returned to the fireplace and swept up the broken glass, then finished cleaning the fireplace. She looked at the clock and noticed that it was six o'clock.

When she finished she went over to Milo, and asked him what needed to be done: Milo smelled heavily of drink and stale sweat, however, he was now subdued and a bit ashamed after the reprimand from Freda. He said, 'We need to prepare for the guests as they come down for breakfast starting at seven o'clock and continue through to nine o'clock and it can get frantic if they all come at the same time.'

'Please show me how you like to work and I will be able to help you, although I look young I am a good cook,' Maria said quietly.

Milo got up a bit unsteadily and started laying out some plates. He said, 'You concentrate on slicing and peeling the cucumbers, tomatos and apples and put out cheese and salami slices. I will concentrate on the toast, tea and coffee.' Fortunately the orders came in a nice steady stream that first morning and things flowed very smoothly. When the orders stopped, Milo slumped into the chair and said, 'You eat some of the food that was not used and help yourself to a cup of tea or coffee, you have to eat when you can in this job. I don't feel like food this morning, I stayed up too late last night, I will just have a cure from the cooking brandy bottle,' which he produced like a magician from under the table, accompanied by a half smile as though looking for a signal of approval.

Maria did not show him any visual signal, instead in a businesslike manner she said, 'What do we need to do next?'

Milo said, 'We need to wash up all the dishes and clean the kitchen ready for coffee and biscuits between ten o'clock and eleven o'clock and then we need to get ready for lunches.'

Maria said, 'I will wash up if you tell me where everything is and keep me right about what we need to do next.'

Milo did not argue – he just sat watching Maria working and taking an occasional small sip from the brandy bottle.

Coffee and biscuits were served, followed by midday lunches and then all the washing-up was done. Maria tidied up the whole kitchen area and put everything in its place, with some guidance from Milo who seemed quite pleased with her, and she felt a sense of confidence from her increased familiarity and proper organisation of the kitchen.

Freda came into the kitchen with a big smile and remarked, 'I have received compliments about the food from one or two guests.' She then said, 'Maria, you should lie down in your room for at least a couple of hours before the evening meals are required. We start at six o'clock.'

Maria made her way up to the bedroom where several of the other girl cleaners were lying on top of their beds complaining about the work they had to do and the difficulties they had experienced during the day. One of the girls also spoke loudly about the men guests in the hotel and some of the sights that she had seen as she entered bedrooms. She also began to talk about sexual favours that may be required during the night and laughed how it might be better than this crowded bedroom with a lot of miserable women, little knowing how soon that prophecy was to overtake two of the cleaning girls.

Maria quietly lay down on her bed and withdrew into her thoughts. She remembered her mother regularly saying to her, 'When things seem difficult count your blessings.' So she started to list her blessings. Freda, the boss of catering and cleaning, seemed a nice woman. Milo, the chef, clearly needed help and she could provide that help, even if she had to put up with his drinking and volatile behaviour, yes, it made her useful and that must be a blessing. She came to the conclusion that her skills in the kitchen gave her some tenuous security and she thanked the Lord for the skills her mother had taught her. With these last thoughts Maria drifted into a fitful sleep.

She woke to the sound of the telephone ringing, with the receptionist reminding them that it was time for staff to attend the restaurant to serve evening meals.

Maria entered the kitchen to find Milo already preparing some steaks by bruising them with a mallet. He greeted her with a cheery smile and said, 'Are you ready for the main shift?'

Maria responded with a smile and said, 'Yes I am ready and keen to help if you tell me what to do.' This response seemed to please Milo who seemed to have recovered his energy, which was clearly lacking earlier.

With Maria and Milo working well together, the evening meals were completed successfully and they cleaned up the kitchen on the stroke of midnight. Freda came in and said, 'You have run the kitchen well today. Maria, go to bed to be ready for an early start in the morning.'

Milo, meanwhile, headed for the bar for a night cap.

Next morning when Maria entered the kitchen, Milo was nowhere to be seen. As she was up fairly early she thought nothing of it and started cooking a special soup for lunch called Mecsek 'Highwaymen's Dumpling Soup' (stuffed dumplings with soup poured over them). This soup was a highly prized speciality in Serbia and Maria had won several awards for her particular version. She left the soup pans cooking and as there was still no sign of Milo, Maria started preparing the breakfasts. When the orders started coming through, she worked hard and just managed to keep up with the demand. When the rush stopped she started cleaning up and Freda came in and said, 'Well done.' Milo came into the kitchen at that point looking very rough and started shouting about the state of the kitchen. Freda went ballistic and shouted at him, 'You drunken bum, where have you been all morning? You are absolutely useless in that state. You are fired, get your things packed and get out of here before I send for Karl to see that you are out of the hotel within the hour. Milo, please go quickly, you know what Karl is like and what he will do to you if you are still here when he comes.'

Milo said, 'Freda, give me another chance, I will stop drinking, I promise you.'

Freda said, 'I am sorry, Milo, but that's what you said the last time and the last and the last time. I can't risk it; you know very well Harold Szirtes doesn't take excuses from anyone. If the customers had not been able to get their breakfasts this morning and complained to him about it, it would be me that was leaving, and I am not going to risk that because of *your* drinking. Please go before Karl comes, I do not want to be responsible for what may happen if Karl finds you here after I tell him you are fired.'

Milo in his hungover condition was very volatile and he suddenly exploded in a tirade of verbal abuse aimed at Freda as he began to move towards her. 'Who do you think you are?' He screamed. 'You jumped up skivvy. I … I …' and his voice suddenly faded away as the atmosphere in the kitchen suddenly changed and he saw the dark and menacing figure of Karl framed in the doorway.

Karl's icy voice pierced the silence. 'Freda, take the girl out of here for ten minutes.'

Freda quickly put her arm round Maria's shoulder and led her out of the kitchen, closing the door behind her. Freda and Maria waited in the sluice room for ten minutes, neither of them saying anything, each weighed down by a cold fear for what may be happening to Milo.

Freda said, 'Come, we need to prepare for the ten o'clock coffee and biscuits.'

The kitchen was empty when they returned but there was quite a lot of blood on the floor with a smeared trail leading to the kitchen door as if someone bleeding had been dragged across the floor. Freda said, 'Maria, quickly get the mop, bleach and a bucket of water and let's clean this up before anyone comes.'

Working silently, they quickly and thoroughly cleaned up the blood, including the trail that led out of the kitchen into the yard.

When they finished cleaning, Freda held Maria's hands and, looking into her eyes with tears streaming down her cheeks, said, 'You know that you must never say anything about this.' Maria just nodded with tears streaming down her cheeks also.

6
The Farm

Nico was taken to work on a large farm in the region in the north of Serbia and Montenegro, close to the Hungarian border.

The large agricultural estate was owned and run by Harold Szirtes, a significant member of a fanatically close-knit community. This ethnic faction became a significant player in the terrible events led by Slobodan Milošević and Radovan Karadžić.

Harold had a great admiration for Attila the Hun, the fifth-century warrior who helped unite the Hun kingdom in what is now Hungary, through a series of conquests, looting and pillaging. Attila acquired a vast empire that stretched through parts of what are now Germany, Russia, Poland and much of south-eastern Europe.

He came to be known as the Scourge of God, because of the devastation he brought on the Roman Empire.

Like his fifth century hero before him, Harold Szirtes was an opportunist. The resulting conflicts and ethnic cleansing of the current Balkan war had provided opportunities for ruthless people like Szirtes to grab power where significant population change had occurred and he took possession of drug and people trafficking networks that extended well beyond the borders of Serbia.

Harold had acquired through marriage a large agricultural

estate extending to 2,000 hectares during the conflicts. He was grooming his son Imri for political leadership in this peculiar mediaeval cultural backwater at his large country house and well protected estate. It was suitably named the House of Attila.

His son Imri was born six months after his marriage and his wife disappeared one year later. Herr Shoemaker, his batman, in the army unit he commanded, moved into the mansion house shortly after his wife's disappearance. Local rumours were rife at the time.

As it began to get dark Szirtes turned off the main road on to a single track road which was blocked by a huge steel gate with a nameplate bearing the words:

HOUSE OF ATTILA.

'Everyone get out,' ordered Harold Szirtes as the car approached the gate and stopped.

Harold, his son Imri and Nico approached the gate and Harold addressed a camera above the left-hand gate-post. 'It is me, Harold, and my son Imri and, ah, another replacement farm worker; I hope this one gets on better with the dogs.' Harold laughed at his own joke with a steely mechanical sound.

He placed his thumb on a small glass lens in the middle of a panel with the words Biometric Security printed on the casing. The red light on the panel turned to green and the large steel gate blocking the road silently opened.

'Back into the car,' ordered Harold.

As they drove up the driveway to the large mansion house Nico noticed that there was a television camera on each of the lampposts. They got out of the car and Harold said to Nico, 'Come with me and I will show you where to sleep.'

As they walked towards the stables Harold said in a steely voice, 'Do not even think of escaping from this place, this is hunting country and my neighbours and I are always looking for opportunities to exercise the horses and the hunting dogs. We always keep the dogs hungry.' With that remark Harold burst into a fit of laughter, repeating to himself, 'We always keep the dogs hungry.' He laughed even louder. Nico suddenly realised that this man was serious about the implied threat and was probably insane.

As they reached the stables Harold said, 'You make yourself at home with the horses – at least you will be dry and warm, which is more than most displaced persons without any identity deserve. Remember we love a man hunt and we always keep the dogs hungry.' He turned and walked away laughing insanely to himself at what appeared to be his favourite joke.

It was now quite dark and Nico opened the stable door and entered the long, narrow building. There seemed to be a number of horses in individual stalls and they moved restlessly, some snorting and blowing as he passed. Then his eyes were drawn to a white horse in the end stall and as he walked towards it the horse seemed to respond to his approach and it let out a low whinny. He began to run towards it, exclaiming, 'Prince, Prince, how did you get here?' He hugged the horse's neck, pressing and rubbing his face against Prince's face with his tears streaming down his face. Then the chilling realisation dawned: if Prince was here he must have been brought here by the people who attacked the hamlet that awful night. Major Harold Szirtes must be one of the murderers who killed his parents.

After Nico got over the shock of the realisation of who these people were and also the pleasure of finding Prince, he found the hay and straw store.

He suddenly realised that the stables were quite warm and as it was the middle of winter there must be some heating system. He noticed two large pipes just above floor level running along the full length of the back wall of the stable.

He found an empty stall and felt that the pipes were hot. He followed the pipes to the far end of the stable where they went through the end wall; there was a door in the wall so he cautiously opened it and found himself in a suite of changing rooms equipped with toilets and showers.

Beyond the changing rooms there was a large kitchen. Nico opened the fridge. He quickly made himself a cheese sandwich and washed it down with a cup of milk.

Following the pipes again, they disappeared through the end wall of the kitchen: However, Nico remembered the chilling words of Harold Szirtes. 'We always keep the dogs hungry.' So Nico decided not to go outside in the dark.

Nico crashed out exhausted on the straw and immediately fell asleep but not before mentally preparing himself to rise early in the morning.

He now fully realised that as a displaced person without identity he was completely powerless; it was almost as though he only existed by permission of his captors. He now knew that he would have to do whatever they told him no matter how disagreeable it was. He also knew that he would need to be very careful and not give these ruthless people any idea that he knew about them and their part in the heinous crime against his parents and other friends.

7

The Hotel

'Come now, wash your face and I will help you with the ten o'clock coffee and biscuits,' said Freda. The two of them worked well together and served the customers for the mid-morning break. As soon as the dining-room emptied Freda sent for two cleaners and instructed them to do exactly what Maria wanted. She said to Maria, 'I am making you the cook as I believe you can quickly grow into this job and make a success of it; these two girls will be your assistants and I expect them to help you raise the standards of this restaurant.'

Maria followed the short corridor to the kitchen doors: she pushed it open. She forced all thought of Milo and his bloody end out of her mind. She whispered, 'Dear Lord Jesus please help me in my helplessness.'

Maria went over to the sink and filled a basin with hot water. She began to clean the work surfaces, and the two women came into the kitchen and Maria said, 'Hello, my name is Maria and I am the cook, what are your names?' One girl said, 'I am Lette, pleased to meet you.' The other girl said, 'I am Mary and I am pleased to meet you.' Maria said, 'Let's work together as a team. Get a cloth each and help me get this kitchen clean.' The three girls made short work of the task and Maria said, 'Well done, Lette and Mary, let's have a coffee before we start preparing for lunch.'

The kitchen operations ran well and there were no disasters or complaints. Maria congratulated them again and suggested they clean the kitchen then have something to eat. 'Let's see if we can come up with ideas to make things better in the kitchen.'

Lette said, 'I will wash up if you tell us what we need to do next, we are so relieved to be away from Karl and we want to work with you.'

They soon tidied up the whole kitchen area and put everything in its place, with some guidance from Maria who seemed pleased and they all felt a sense of confidence from their joint ownership and proper organisation of the kitchen.

Afterwards Maria made her way up to the bedroom where again several of the other girl cleaners were lying on top of their beds, seemingly exhausted. Once again Maria lay down and withdrew into her thoughts. Lette and Mary had immediately accepted her authority and had worked hard to help her. Freda seemed to be her friend, which was a huge blessing. Once again she came to the conclusion that her skills in the kitchen were the key to her new job and she thanked the Lord for the skills her mother had taught her. With these last thoughts Maria drifted into a fitful sleep.

She again woke to the sound of the telephone ringing with the receptionist reminding them that it was time for staff to attend the restaurant to serve evening meals.

Maria, Lette and Mary entered the kitchen with a sense of satisfaction about how clean and tidy it looked. Maria gave the two women a cheery smile and said, 'Are we all ready for the main shift?' Mary responded with a smile and said, 'Yes I am ready and keen to help if you tell me what to do.'

'Mary, please prepare the first ten steaks by bruising them with a mallet,' said Maria. 'Lette, will you please clean and prepare the soup. This will be the chef's special tonight.'

Lette and Mary made an 'Ooh!' sound and they all laughed.

With the three girls working well together the evening meals were completed successfully and as they cleaned up the kitchen Freda came in with a well inebriated Karl and Harold Szirtes. The latter said, 'My compliments to the chef for the food particularly the soup. I want to enter the hotel's soup into a national hotels association chef's competition.' Freda, Maria, Lettie and Mary smiled and nodded at everything he said, thinking that he wouldn't remember anything about it when he woke up in the morning.

8
Charlie

Nico woke while it was still dark. Though he did not have a watch he knew the sunrise was about 6.30 a.m. and he thought he could see just a glimmer of light in the eastern sky so he estimated it to be about 5.30 a.m.

He quickly got up and went to the sluice room at the end of the stable, giving Prince a rub as he passed. There was a big sink with hot and cold water and a couple of bars of soap so he quickly stripped off and had a good wash. There were roller towels mounted on the wall and he roughly dried himself and dressed. Clearly the way the stables were well equipped indicated that the horses were an important feature of the estate.

Nico made his way to the back of the big mansion house where he saw a light on through a window and he could see a girl working at a sink. He waved at her and she opened the door. He said, 'My name is Nico and I was brought here last night to work on the farm, I slept in the stable last night.'

'Come in and I will give you something to eat, my name is Valda, I am the assistant cook and I am preparing breakfast for the staff.' She quickly filled a plate with sliced raw tomato, cucumber, apple, cheese and two thick slices of buttered bread and passed it to Nico. She then poured and passed him a large mug of steaming tea. 'Eat it all, it may be evening before you eat again.'

THE HOUSE OF ATTILA

Nico was really hungry and quickly finished the food, making him feel so much better. Two men came into the large kitchen, selected and filled a plate of food and sat at the table and began to eat. Then three women came in and did the same.

None of these people spoke to Nico; however, it was not long before another man came into the kitchen and selected a plate of food and sat down beside Nico. After chewing and swallowing his first mouthful of breakfast, he said, 'You are the new worker, are you?' Nico said 'Yes.'

The man then forked in another mouthful of food and began to chew. When he had finally swallowed the food, he said, 'I am the estate manager, you will call me Herr Shoemaker and you will do exactly what I tell you to do. You look to be too young to have any skills. However, you do look quite fit and strong, and so you may be useful as a labourer. Valda, show him where the clothing store is and get him sorted with good boots and work clothes.'

Valda motioned to Nico to come and led him to a very large storeroom full of horse-riding equipment and clothing; at the far end there was a large selection of work clothing and footware. She said, 'Put your old clothing in this polythene bag, find new work clothing and make sure it is all a good roomy fit. There is nothing worse than working in tight clothing and boots. You will need to hurry as Herr Shoemaker will not take long to finish his breakfast.' Nico quickly selected two heavy shirts, four pairs of football shorts, two pairs of football socks, two pairs of moleskin trousers, two good belts, a pair of working boots, a pair of wellington boots, a donkey jacket and a waterproof jacket and trouser suit.

He quickly took off his old clothing, discarding it in a waste bin that Valda brought over from the corner of the room. He dressed in one set of the new clothing.

Valda said, 'You will be working outside and you need

warm clothing in this cold weather – take this army surplus great coat, this furry hat with the ear flaps, leather work gloves and two pairs of these cotton under gloves. Finally take this warm sleeping-bag: you will need this more than anything else. Put all the stuff you are not wearing today in this bag to keep it all together. I have made up a bag of supplies to keep you for a week out at the log cabin. It is in the kitchen; do not forget to take it with you.'

Herr Shoemaker was the only one in the kitchen when they returned and he was just finishing his mug of tea.

He stood up and said, 'Let's go to work. Bring all your work clothing, your sleeping-bag and your food with you as you will be sleeping at the work site for a week.'

Herr Shoemaker led the way to a small flat-back rough-terrain lorry. Nico put his bags in the back of the lorry, covering them with a tarpaulin sheet. He then joined Herr Shoemaker in the cab of the lorry.

Herr Shoemaker started the engine and began to drive along a rough road leading to a large forested area on the far side of the estate. Herr Shoemaker said, 'Your first job at the House of Attila is to cut firewood to keep the big mansion house warm through the cold winter. You will live there six days a week. You will be brought back to the mansion house on Sundays to do your laundry and get new supplies for the next week.'

'The last worker tried to run away but the hunting dogs soon found him; there wasn't much left of him when the hunt riders caught up with them.' Herr Shoemaker laughed and said, 'The hunting dogs are always hungry.' He laughed again as though it was a delicious thought and something to savour. Nico felt chilled but it was not the cold morning that caused it.

They finally arrived at a log cabin, obviously constructed from the local timber. There was a big pile of cut logs, each about two metres long, stacked at the roadside.

Herr Shoemaker said, 'Get your gear, your bag of supplies, the petrol and oil and put it in the log cabin and then come back and we will load up some of the logs on to the lorry.' They both worked hard and the lorry was soon loaded.

Herr Shoemaker said, 'Now come with me and I will show you how to do your job.' They went round to the other side of the log cabin where they found a stable and a workshop with a horse in one of the stalls. Herr Shoemaker pointed to a number of petrol chain-saws and said, 'Have you ever used one of these?'

Nico said, 'Yes I have used chain-saws.'

Herr Shoemaker said, 'Good, let's try you out. Bring the horse out and harness one set of the drag chains you will find at the back of the workshop.'

Nico quickly made friends with the horse. He found the leather harness and fitted it carefully to the horse and led him out of the stable. He found the drag chains and, quietly talking to the horse, fastened them to the harness.

Herr Shoemaker said, 'I see you know your way around horses, bring a chain-saw, a can of petrol and a tin of oil, put them in the pick-up truck and I will drive them to those trees over there; you lead the horse with the drag chains and I will show you what you need to do.'

Nico followed the pick-up truck, talking quietly to the horse as they walked. 'What name do you like?' he said. 'Dobbin, Trigger, Fred, Charlie?' The horse snorted and looked round at Nico when he said Charlie. Nico smiled and said, 'Charlie it is then, good, that's settled. Your name is Charlie.'

Herr Shoemaker was waiting at the edge of the trees with the chain-saw in his hand; he had filled it with petrol and oil and had started the chain-saw to ensure it was working. He switched the engine off as Nico approached and said, 'This plantation of trees needs thinning, so your job is to take out the smaller trees to make room for the best ones to grow. You will cut them into two-metre lengths and then drag them out to the roadside where a tractor and trailer will pick them up every day and take them back to the mansion house. You will help the tractor driver load the trailer at the end of each day and you must not let the supply of logs fail as the mansion house needs about one tonne per day in winter. With the last worker running away and then being killed by the hunting dogs there is only two days' stock of logs left at the mansion house.

'Now let me see you cut down a tree, chop it into lengths and drag the first length out to the roadside.'

Nico selected one of the smaller trees and quickly cut it down, stripped it of its branches and cut it into four two-metre lengths. He began to chain the four logs together when Herr Shoemaker stopped him and said, 'Just drag one at a time, you will find that the end of the log will catch in roots, shrubs and drainage ditches and the horse will not manage to pull more than one through all the obstacles and undergrowth.'

Nico removed three of the logs, chained the remaining one and, leading Charlie, they slowly dragged the single log out to the roadside, stopping and starting several times to clear the end of the log stuck firmly in the undergrowth.

Herr Shoemaker seemed to be satisfied and said, 'You will find it is hard going and you need to stack twenty-four similar logs by the end of the day and repeat that each day until Saturday night when you will return to the mansion house to do your laundry and get some sleep to recover your strength.'

With that Herr Shoemaker climbed into the pick-up and drove off.

Nico looked at Charlie the horse and said, 'Charlie, we need to do this better than one log at a time or we will spend most of the day freeing and dragging them out of that terrible undergrowth.' Charlie looked at Nico and he seemed to nod. Nico continued, 'Well that's agreed then; let's go back to the cabin where I noticed some galvanised corrugated steel stacked at the back of the workshop and I think I can make a strong sledge.'

They quickly walked back to the cabin workshop where Nico found a heavy hammer. He took a two-metre log, about 150 mm in diameter, from a pile of logs and he pulled out a corrugated steel sheet from the pile. Putting one end over the two-metre long log, he stood on the steel sheet and hammered it until its end curved round the log.

He then did exactly the same at the other end of the steel sheet; the sheets were originally four-metre lengths, which left more than two metres between the ends as a kind of metal sledge.

Then, with a hand saw, he cut two lengths of log that exactly fitted along the sides of the sledge, forming retaining sides to the top platform. He then cut two further lengths of logs about 100 mm in diameter and used these to nail the retaining sides together and attach them to the end logs holding the whole sledge strongly together.

When he finished he said to Charlie, 'Now we have a nice flat sledge with a large curved front which will ride over all the undergrowth and will make our dragging job so much easier.'

Nico then attached the chains to each end of the log, which were protruding from the curve of steel. He took two very large nails from some he found in the workshop and used them to secure the chains in place.

Nico then led Charlie back to the forest plantation, easily dragging the sledge behind them. They worked together as a good team, felling and trimming trees and dragging four logs at a time on the sledge, which rode up over all the undergrowth and the snow.

When they finished dragging out twenty four logs they went back and hid the sledge back at the tree-felling site.

Nico then felled and trimmed a further five trees, cutting them into four two-metre lengths to give them a good start the next day. As there was no sign of the tractor and trailer they went back to the stable to get out of the cold wind. Nico found a grooming brush and scissors and began to brush and cut out all the tangled bits of Charlie's tail, mane and coat, which had clearly not been attended to for some time. He then carefully lifted each of Charlie's feet and inspected his hooves and lower legs for any sign of damage or sensitivity. He finished by having a good look in Charlie's mouth, ears and eyes, completely satisfied with Charlie's condition. He said, 'Charlie, you'll do for a few years yet.' Charlie gave Nico a sideways look, almost a frown.

Suddenly Nico noticed through a window the lights of the tractor coming in the distance. He put his great coat on and he went back out to the pile of logs at the side of the road. Nico greeted the driver with a friendly smile and a loud 'hello'. But the tractor driver quickly replied. 'Never mind the chat, let's get these logs loaded and I can get out of this freezing wilderness.'

The two men worked individually and silently, quickly loading the trailer. As Nico pulled down tight the timber hitch knot on the final retaining rope, the driver suddenly let out the clutch and the tractor leapt away. Nico had to jump back to avoid the wheel of the trailer. He looked at the driver who appeared to be laughing as he sped away.

Nico went back to the stable and found some oats and hay and put them in two separate troughs that Charlie could easily reach. He then found a large bucket, filled it with water and placed it next to the troughs and said, 'That's you OK now, Charlie, I'll see you in the morning.'

Nico picked up some dry hay and straw and walked into the log cabin. He soon had the log-burning stove going. He went outside and returned with another bag full of logs just to make sure he had enough.

He looked in the bag of supplies: there was plenty of basic food wrapped in a number of polythene bags to keep it fresh, and Valda had made up a toilet bag with all the essentials.

He found a heavy blackened kettle obviously well used to being boiled on the fairly large ledge built into the front of the stove. He half filled the kettle and placed two eggs in it and put it on the ledge of the stove. He found a bread knife and cut four slices of bread from one of four loaves, carefully wrapping the loaf tightly in its polythene bag to keep it fresh. He then cut several slices of cheese and used these as filling for the sandwiches. Nico then began to eat them hungrily as he had not eaten since breakfast. When the kettle boiled he eased it back from the fire until it was only simmering. After it had simmered for about five minutes he took the eggs out and made a mug of black tea with some of the water. There was no milk in the supplies, but black tea was fine. He cut the eggs in half and scooped out the inside of each with a tea spoon, savouring their satisfying taste.

He sat back with his mug of tea and started to count his blessings just as his mother had taught him. She always said that positive thoughts tend to bring positive outcomes and negative thoughts tend to bring negative outcomes.

The log fire was warm, Nico's stomach was full and the mug of tea was good. The Old Testament story of Joseph came into his mind, how almost four thousand years ago Joseph, at age seventeen, had been betrayed by his brothers and sold as a slave, just like Nico and his sister had been captured and taken into slavery. However, even in his distress, Joseph had trusted God and He had blessed him, just as Nico trusted God and received His blessings even in this situation. He thought specifically of Valda who had been kind with the supplies and clothing, dependable Charlie, the horse, this log cabin with the log stove, the isolation and peace to think, the type of work he had been given – yes, he had many blessings to count at this moment.

Nico dropped to his knees and prayed with thanks for his blessings and asked that his sister would also find blessings wherever she was and that the Lord Jesus would bring them together again soon.

Nico found his sleeping bag and spread it on a bed in the corner of the room, leaving the curtains open so that he would wake at the earliest sign of light. He stripped off and snuggled into the warm sleeping-bag.

9

Team Building

Maria went up to the bedroom. Several of the cleaning girls were crying. Apparently Harold Szirtes and Karl had very violently raped Ramana and Lillie. The two girls were bleeding, one from the nose and one from the mouth and both were badly bruised where they had been tightly held and beaten.

Maria took the two girls down to the kitchen and found Freda in her room and told her about the injured girls. Freda put on a dressing-gown and came to the kitchen. She said, 'Dear Ramana and Lillie, come let me clean you up as best I can.' She led the girls to a sluice room that was fitted with a hot and cold water shower, which she turned on and adjusted the temperature. She said, 'Strip off these soiled clothes and stand under the shower.' She took off her dressing-gown, which was all she was wearing and began to gently soap the two girls down. She said to Maria, 'Go to the kitchen and you will find a filling funnel with a rubber tube fitted to it. Bring it and a large jug and a packet of salt.'

Maria went to the kitchen and found all the items and brought them back to the sluice room. Freda took the jug and filled it with water cascading from the shower; she gave the almost full jug to Maria and said, 'Put plenty of salt in the jug and stir it well.' When Maria had done as she asked Freda said to Ramana, 'We will wash all that filthy sperm out.'

Ramana did as she was asked. Freda held the funnel up about face height and said, 'Maria, pour all the salt water into the top of the funnel.' They repeated the process for Lillie. Freda said, 'Maria, find three towels and two kitchen work coats and bring them back here.' When they had dried off and put on their coats and Freda her dressing-gown, they all went back to the kitchen. Freda found a bottle of brandy and poured all of it equally into four cups. Holding one for herself she gave the others to the girls. Maria said, 'I don't drink.'

Freda said, 'Make an exception tonight.'

Freda held up her cup and said, 'Curses on these male bastards.' She swallowed the cupful in one gulp. The two other girls followed her example and Maria took a small sip then handed her cup to Freda.

The three women finished the bottle with Maria watching and then they retired to their bedrooms.

Eventually Maria fell asleep after giving up a short but silent prayer for comfort and healing for the two girls, for Freda, her boss, and the blessings of her work in the kitchen She also asked for protection and blessings for her brother Nico wherever he might be.

All too soon the telephone rang as the night porter gave the hotel staff room calls to wake them up and tell them to get to work.

Maria quickly washed and dressed and went down to the kitchen. She began bringing out the various items of food required for the breakfasts. As she worked she thought, We must improve the kitchen and the standard of food. She decided, although I am the youngest of the three girls I have been given the cook's position, I can only improve the quality of the kitchen by team work.

Lette and Mary arrived and Mary blurted out, 'Did you hear what happened to Ramana and Lillie last night?'

Maria said, 'Yes, but you need to be careful what you say, we are prisoners in this place, we have no rights and our captors are very ruthless, so please take great care for yourself.'

'Do not let anyone hear you speak about these things or you may be next.'

Mary put her hand over her mouth with a little cry of 'Oh!'

Maria forced herself out of the negativity and said brightly, 'Let's focus on today and try to help each other to make a success of it. I have been thinking and the best plan for our own security is to be very good at what we do and to try to become known for the best food in town. Let's agree to that and shake hands on it.' The three girls solemnly shook each other's hand, saying with big smiles, 'To the best kitchen in town.'

Maria said, 'We each need to think of what type of cooking we are best at. Mary immediately said, 'I am good at cooking vegetables; as I was the oldest sister to three brothers and three sisters we seldom had any meat, so I became very good at cooking vegetables.'

Maria said, 'That's great, you can specialise in our vegetables. However, we need first to get on with the breakfast orders.'

The breakfast session passed smoothly and quickly. At the end of the rush Freda came in and said, 'Well done, the kitchen seems to be much better under your control.' Maria took the opportunity to tell Freda. 'Lette and Mary are working well and we hope to improve the quality of food from the kitchen and to make it the best in the town.'

Freda looked at Maria without speaking for what seemed an age. 'I believe you are serious.' She said. 'If you think you can do it, I will give you all my support. Meanwhile please excuse me, I have to get the hotel cleaners back to work, they went on strike this morning in protest about Ramana and Lillie who are sick and still in bed.'

'When Karl hears about them striking at least one of the strikers will pay terribly for their rebellious actions. I have seen this many times before and I am so fearful for these silly girls. There is nothing I can do except to try to get on with it regardless of the difficulties; I do appreciate you taking on and running the kitchen.' Freda left the kitchen wearily as though heavily laden.

Maria and the girls coped with coffee and biscuits and with the lunches, taking the opportunity to add chef's specials at lunchtime. Those who chose them commented favourably. With their successes behind them, the girls went up to their rooms to rest before the big evening effort.

However, their rest was not enjoyed for long before there was a pounding on the bedroom door. 'Get downstairs to the dance hall immediately,' A voice shouted through the closed door. 'Oh! Except the kitchen staff. Repeat, kitchen staff are not included.'

All the cleaning staff hastily dressed and quickly made their way down to the dance hall. The fourteen cleaning staff were all there including Ramana and Lillie. There was an air of tense expectation when Karl and his constant companion Felix walked into the room.

Karl stood on the low stage and started to speak. 'It has come to my attention that there has been a rebellion in this hotel.' He hesitated for a long pause before going on. 'The organisation we work for does not tolerate rebellion.' Again he hesitated. 'You will tell me who instigated this rebellion or you will all suffer very badly.'

'I will be in the office, Felix will be in the hallway, speak to Felix and he will arrange for you to speak to me discreetly. Believe me, if I do not find out today who initiated the rebellion you will all entertain the guests at the Gathering of the Huns on Friday evening. I hope you understand what entertain the guests means; I hope you also understand that there will be a hunt on the Saturday, which may feature some or all of you, if necessary, as the quarry. I will leave you to consider what I have just said, but do not underestimate what I have said. I expect to know who the instigator of the rebellion was by five o'clock today and I am never wrong.'

Karl abruptly left the stage and he and Felix left the room. Some of the girls immediately broke into tears and began wailing.

Maria had fallen asleep while the other girls had left the room. She woke suddenly and looked at the clock. It was going on to half past five. She jumped out of bed, quickly dressed and ran down to the kitchen.

Lette and Mary were already working. Maria said, 'Sorry, I nearly slept in, thank you for starting without me. Lette and Mary were strangely subdued. Maria said, 'Is there something wrong?'

Mary said, 'I don't think we should talk about it.'

Maria said, 'If it is something I have done or said please tell me.'

There was a long silence. Lette suddenly said, 'Do you not know about Karl and Felix's visit and the threats to all the cleaners and that just before five o'clock Jenna and Rebecca were carried out unconscious and taken away in the back of the van?'

10

The Boilers

Nico woke to the faintest increase in light as the morning dawned through a heavy sky. He extracted himself from his sleeping-bag, poked the log fire into life, put a couple of new logs on and opened the baffles to let the air through.

Now able to draw air, the fire quickly sprung into life. Nico felt the side of the kettle; the water was warm enough to wash with. He put the plug in the sink outlet and poured the kettle of warm water into the sink. He filled up the kettle and put it back on the stove. He quickly washed, dried himself and dressed.

He looked in the cutlery drawer and found a long-handled toasting fork. He cut four slices of bread and proceeded to toast them, buttering them as each one was ready to let the butter melt in. When the four slices were toasted he opened a tin of beans and poured them over two of the slices of toast on a large plate. He placed the other two slices on top and squeezed down on each, making two nice thick toast and bean sandwiches, and began eating them.

The kettle began to boil and Nico made a mug of black tea. Looking out of the window at the dark clouds as he drank his tea, Nico thought, 'It could easily snow today. Although it is still quite dark I think we will try to get an early start.'

Nico got Charlie out of the stable and they made their way

to the area of forest where they had last worked. He harnessed Charlie to the sledge and then started the chain-saw and cut down five trees, cleaning them and cutting them into two-metre lengths as he went.

He then cut a number of thin straight poles from some of the branches. He loaded four logs on to the sledge, put the poles on and the heavy hammer.

At this point it began to snow.

As they progressed out of the trees towards the road, Nico hammered in marker poles in a straight line along the route taken by the sledge. They worked all morning, cutting trees and bringing the logs out until they had twenty-four piled up at the roadside. By this time the route of the sledge was well marked with thin poles and the snow had been compressed into a nice flat surface by the constant compression of the sledge with its load of logs.

Nico said to Charlie, 'We have done well this morning, let's go back to the cabin and get some heat.' Nico installed Charlie in the stable with food and water and then went into the log cabin. He livened up the fire with more logs and opened the air baffles a little; he made a single cheese sandwich and a cup of tea. Nico sat in the chair and rested for a good half an hour, he then decided to go back out and cut more logs.

They worked away in the forest for a couple of hours with the snow falling quite heavily. Then Nico became aware of someone approaching. As the figure became more visible through the falling snowflakes Nico recognised it as Herr Shoemaker.

Nico stopped the chain-saw and greeted him. 'Hello, Herr Shoemaker.'

Herr Shoemaker said, 'Yes, I am very impressed, the sledge is a very good idea and I see from the piles of logs here in the forest that you have worked very hard, I am very pleased.

'You will have to come back to the House of Attila; there is a big gathering tonight for weekend celebrations. The boiler man has betrayed his trust and will be severely punished; you will be needed to keep the boilers going through the whole weekend until we get someone else as a replacement boiler man. You are too valuable here in the forest to use you permanently as a boiler man as you are by far the best worker we have had in this job. Come now, let's stable the horse and then I will explain a little about the House of Attila.'

Once they had stabled Charlie and Nico had made sure that he had enough food and water to last for at least three days, he and Herr Shoemaker went into the log cabin. 'Make some coffee and I will try to briefly explain the background to the House of Attila.'

When they both had a mug of coffee Herr Shoemaker said, 'Where do I start to try to explain such a complex story? I know, let us start in mediaeval times and I can also practise my speech for tonight on you.

'A tribe known as the Xiongnu existed in western China at the time of the Han Dynasty, which was the last two centuries before Christ. The majority went north west in search of new homes. They found their way into the valley of the Volga and, in the second half of the fourth century, attacked the Alans, a people related to the Samarians, who lived between the Volga and the Don. After routing the Alans, they then went on to conquer the Ostrogoths and drive the Visigoths westwards. Early in the fifth century, they seem to have been reinforced by fresh hordes, and had become so powerful that, by the time of the Emperor Theodosius the Great, the Romans felt obliged to pay them a substantial tribute. Still, the Hunnic Empire could not pose a serious threat to the Roman Empire; its economy was too primitive, its internal divisions too great and Hunnic skills in strategy and siege-craft too lacking to defeat a sophisticated, organised opponent.

'By about 420 AD, however, a Hunnic confederacy had

been established, enriched by plunder and tribute, by the hiring out of mercenaries to the Romans and by the extortion of what can only be called protection money. Their Empire stretched from the Baltic to the Caspian when, in 445, one of their two joint-rulers, Attila, murdered his brother Bleda and seized control of the confederacy.

'Attila reinforced his position by, it is said, digging up a rusty old sword he claimed he saw in a dream and proclaiming it to be the Sword of Mars. The Empire he inherited was built on and sustained by booty; without a continual flow of plunder and tribute it could not survive. So it was that the God of War's chosen one launched an immediate invasion of Eastern Europe. This was in 447 AD, a time when the empire was already suffering a series of natural catastrophes: earthquakes, pestilence and famine, and it is little wonder that the by now Christian Romans saw the Huns as the very Horsemen of the Apocalypse.

'The victories of this period may have more to do with Roman demoralisation than any inherent military superiority of the invaders. The Huns fought as horse archers, though their forces were much bolstered by the heavy cavalry of their Germanic subjects. In fact, the composition of the opposing armies would have been remarkably similar, with large numbers of Germans and even Huns to be found on both sides. The Roman army of the time was little more than an assembly of allied or mercenary tribes, with barely an Italian amongst them.

'During the next three years, Attila's men lived off the booty and tribute of the eastern empire before turning, in 450 AD, to the West. The western empire at this time was nominally ruled by the Emperor Valentinian III, but was effectively controlled by the warlord, Aëtius. It was Aëtius who assembled a confederacy with which to confront the Hunnic threat. This was composed of Franks, Visigoths and his own Romano-Germanic army.

'The two forces met in 451 at the great battle of the Catalaunian Fields, near Châlons-sur-Marne. It was a brutal battle of little tactical subtlety, barbarian against barbarian, and by the end of the day Aëtius had the upper hand. He could have finished Attila once and for all but he did not. Knowing that with the Huns destroyed, his Visigothic allies would overrun the whole of Gaul, he let the Huns escape. It was a judgment which the citizens of Italy would bitterly rue.

'For Attila now led his horde across the mountains to Mediolanum, the ancient Roman capital now known as Milan. He spread devastation across the whole of northern Italy and came to the walls of Rome itself. There is a story that Pope Leo persuaded Attila to spare the city and that the great king, in terror of the Cross, retreated. This, however, is Christian propaganda. The truth is that Attila had heard of a threat from the eastern empire and turned back to deal with it.

'He planned to destroy Constantinople, and ensure that the Romans would remain in thrall to him forever. But in 453, lying in a drunken stupor, Attila suffered a nose bleed. The blood trickled down the back of his throat and choked him to death. For a man who had boasted that "Where my horse has trodden, no grass grows" it was a curiously anti-climactic death. The empire he had created did not survive him.

'With Attila dead, the Huns ceased to be a mortal threat to the Roman Empire though the West never recovered and soon passed into the hands of the barbarians. Yet such was the mark left on men's minds that every subsequent wave of Asiatic invaders in the centuries to come were known to westerners as Huns. So that the realm they founded is known to this day as Hungary.

'The remnants of Attila's Huns regrouped in south-eastern Europe, ruling over the Slavs of that region. These peoples were to found a new empire which troubled the

Byzantines for hundreds of years, and were known as the Bulgars.'

Herr Shoemaker paused with a big smile. 'What I have told you is my party piece, which I will recite without notes tonight at the gathering this weekend; they are coming from hundreds, no, possibly thousands of miles away to hear me perform what I have just told you.

'The important thing for you to know is that Harold Szirtes has discovered the long lost Sword of Mars that gave Attila the Great his authority. This sword has curious inscriptions on each side of its blade – "Sword of Attila – Ruler of the World. You will rule from a town sitting under a crown beyond the Pillars of Hercules."

'The first empire was built on and sustained by booty; without a continual flow of plunder and tribute it could not survive. So too the second empire is being built by Harold Szirtes on plunder and booty, and to partake in its rewards requires absolute loyalty, and if anyone betrays the House of Attila, even in the slightest way, their time is short, very short indeed.' Herr Shoemaker revealed a sense of venom as he finished this last sentence.

'The boiler man and his tractor will come for the load of logs you have stacked at the side of the road. When you have loaded it you can ride back to the House of Attila on it to take up your duties as boiler man for the whole weekend. One other important thing is close and lock the doors of the stable, the log cabin and the store before you leave. The hunting hounds will be out over the entire estate on Saturday and we do not want to provide any place of refuge for their quarry.'

With that Herr Shoemaker left. Nico closed up the baffles on the fire and then went round to see Charlie, quickly double-checking that he had enough food and water for three days. He said, 'Goodbye, Charlie, you need to look after yourself for a few days.' Finally he locked all the doors and went to the log pile to wait for the tractor and trailer. He did not have long to wait before it arrived. He again greeted the driver with a cheery hello. But he received the same surly reaction as before.

They soon had the trailer loaded and strapped down, and the driver started the engine. Nico shouted to the driver, 'Just wait a moment until I get my coat on.' The driver suddenly drove off and disappeared.

Nico was momentarily shocked at this behaviour, but the four mile walk was not really a problem for a really fit boy like him, so he just buttoned up the great coat and started walking along the wide tracks in the snow left by the tractor and trailer.

With the snowy conditions it took Nico about an hour and a half to reach the House of Attila. He approached from the back of the house and made his way to the stables. He saw the still loaded tractor outside what he assumed from the smoking chimney to be the boiler room.

Herr Shoemaker appeared in the doorway. Following close behind was the tractor driver and behind him another man holding a long pointed knife, which he used to prod the tractor driver when he wanted him to move. 'Hello, Nico,' said Herr Shoemaker. 'I am afraid you will have to unload the logs yourself; this foolish boiler man has been defiant and obstructive for the last time.'

'Come inside and I will show you what you need to know to run the boiler.' Herr Shoemaker began his instructive tour. 'This is a large but very simple wood-burning boiler, there are no complicated bits to go wrong, it is very robust and it is not really hard work, but you have to feed it with timber fairly constantly, especially this weekend when we have many guests staying in the mansion house who will be using lots of hot water.

'It consists simply of a steel outer casing containing water pipes, all completely protected with a very thick lining of refractory bricks. The main fire bed of the boiler consists of replaceable cast-iron pipes, which are water cooled with a small gap between each for the burnt ash to fall through into an ash chamber, which is easily raked out from time to time. There is also a series of hinged side doors giving access to rake out any non-combustible debris that may get onto the fire bed. The rate of burning is controlled simply by opening or closing the front door of the fire chamber, letting in more or less air, which you also open to feed logs into the fire from time to time. When you open the fire door more air rushes in and the fire burns hotter and much faster. As the door is a fairly loose fit, when it is fully closed enough air gets in round the edges of the door to keep the water supply hot and the logs just smouldering away. Above the combustion chamber is another chamber used only for incineration purposes, however, you will not be required to use that. Let me show you how logs are fed into the furnace.'

Herr Shoemaker opened the furnace door and, lifting a two-metre long log from the pile in the boiler room, pushed one end of the log into the furnace about three quarters the way in. He then took a piece of steel tube with a T-shaped handle and used this as a tool to push the log right into the furnace. Each log weighed about fifty kilos and burned for a long time if the fire door was kept closed.

Herr Shoemaker said, 'You can burn up to six logs at a time but normally you will only need two. You know how fast to burn by the temperature difference of the outgoing water and the returning water. The outgoing water should be about eighty degrees centigrade and the returning water should be about seventy degrees.' He pointed to the thermometers on the outgoing water pipe and the water return pipe. 'As you can see, there are two thermometers on each pipe just to be sure.' He continued in this vein for another five minutes.

When he was done Nico said, 'Thank you, I can handle this job through the weekend, but do you think I will have enough logs here for the whole time?'

Herr Shoemaker said, 'Yes you should have enough logs in the boiler room stack to last through to Monday, but you also have the trailer full outside, which is far more than you will need. I have asked Valda to clean out Fredrick's room in the boiler house and change the bed sheets. She will also bring you some food to last you through Friday night and Saturday.

'It is important that you keep the doors shut and do not go outside the boiler room on Saturday, because the hunting hounds will be released on Saturday morning and they will be hunting across the whole estate until possibly late Saturday afternoon. It is most important that you stay inside on Saturday.'

He paused and added. 'I must go and get washed and dressed for my performance tonight, I know that you will manage the hot water system faithfully.' With that he quickly walked out of the boiler room.

Nico quickly checked the thermometers and looked in the furnace fire chamber – the temperatures were perfect and the logs were still nearly full size.

Valda appeared in the doorway and handed him a bag and said, 'Herr Shoemaker asked me to make you some food. How are you, are you all right?'

Nico said, 'Yes thank you, I am fine.' With that Valda left and closed the door behind her.

Nico looked at the door connecting to the stables and thought, 'I will just have a look to see how Prince is.' He tried the door but it was locked. He then opened the boiler room door and went into the yard to go round to the stable's main door. He noticed that the very large yard in front of the stables had a few vehicles parked with people circulating among them as though they had just arrived causing a significant babble of greetings and conservation. As he approached the stable door the man who had been previously prodding the boiler man with a knife stepped out and said, 'You must stay inside your boiler room this weekend. It is dangerous for you to be outside, do you understand?' Nico nodded and retreated back to the boiler room, closing the door behind him.

11

The Preparations

The Thursday had been a long day for the hotel, in light of what had happened to Jenna and Rebecca and the uncertainty about their fate.

Freda came through to the kitchen at the end of the day after the kitchen had been cleared up at fifteen minutes past midnight and the girls were just leaving to go to bed.

Freda said, 'Maria, can I speak to you for a moment? Let's have a cup of tea before you go to bed.' Maria quickly made two cups of tea and the two of them sat facing each other over the table.

Freda started by telling Maria, 'Harold Szirtes who owns this hotel has a great country estate with a huge mansion house about twenty kilometres from the town and he is holding his monthly gathering this weekend.

'I have to take half of the cleaners to these events along with other staff from other local hotels that he owns to serve and clean up after the guests. This means that you will have to manage the kitchen and dining room with a skeleton staff this weekend.'

Maria said, 'We will manage, Freda, are you all right, you are looking very tired?'

Freda momentarily broke into tears; however, she quickly got a grip on herself and said, 'I am sorry, that's not like me.' She said, wiped the tears away. 'It's just that I am so worried about Jenna and Rebecca; I have seen this happen so many times before and other troublesome girls have just disappeared.

'There are stories, some say they are taken away and get forced into prostitution. There are other stories about orgies at the estate where the girls suffer beatings and multiple rapes.

'There are other stories about the girls being set to run for hunting dogs to bring down and kill; these are the most terrifying wolfhounds that Harold Szirtes breeds on the estate. Oh! Forgive me, I have said too much, please do not repeat this to anyone for your own safety as well as mine.' Freda started to cry again, only this time she let it happen until she had exorcised her grief.

Maria let her recover and then said, 'Do not worry about the hotel, we will muddle through as best we can until you come back, but we must get some sleep as the work will be hard over the weekend, both for you and for me, so let's get to bed.'

The following morning everyone was given an early call to assemble in the dance hall. When all the hotel staff had gathered Freda stood on the small stage and said, 'I am taking half the staff to the House of Attila for the monthly gathering and the remaining staff will need to run this hotel while we are away, this will require everyone to help each other and I am leaving Maria as the person in charge. She is very reasonable and I expect you all to help her as much as possible. We have had enough trouble this last week and we need to help each other to prevent more trouble coming to our girls. Quickly, get yourselves something to eat and drink as we are all going to have to work hard over the next three days. Remember what I have said, girls, the only way we can keep each other out of trouble is to help each other.'

A little time later the bus arrived to take the work party to the House of Attila.

* * *

Maria quickly addressed the seven girls left in the kitchen. She said, 'There are eight of us all together, Mary and I will try to run the kitchen, that leaves six of you to try and cope with all the cleaning and also serving tables.

'As Freda said we are all displaced persons in the same boat, no one will help us; we only have each other, so let us try to muddle through as best we can until the rest come back.'

Fortunately all the girls accepted the situation without complaint, partly because they realised that what Maria said was the stark reality of their unfortunate lives and partly because they were all very scared of what had happened to Jenna and Rebecca.

The weekend at the hotel was a real slog for all of them, but they managed quite well and on the Sunday lunch session a large family party arrived with a brother who was on leave from a very lucrative job in Dubai. So enthusiastic was his appreciation of the Mecsek Highwaymen's Dumpling Soup, which he said was nearly as good as the soup his mother used to make, that he asked to see the chef. Maria came out to the table and he presented her with 5,000 Czech crowns along with his business card as his appreciation tip. She was completely shocked with the amount and tried to refuse it, but he would not take no for an answer and more or less forced it into her hand. Maria retreated into the kitchen; she did not know what to do so she decided to leave it until Freda came back.

She looked at the business card and read the words: Dmitar Hrvat, Breeding Manager, Al Quoz Stables in Dubai. Telephone number and e-mail address.

Freda and her eight girls were picked up and transported the forty kilometres to the House of Attila by a hired coach. She had done this trip so many times before and although it was hard work it had become routine. As the coach drove along she mentally prepared for what she had to do.

Her job was to help supervise the domestic arrangements of the mansion house under the direction of the estates manager Herr Shoemaker. Her duties were similar to those of her day job at the hotel, the only difference being that she and the domestic staff were kept out of the secret goings on of the men guests; in fact there were guards with swords posted outside all the doors leading to the great hall when the ancient ceremonies were taking place. When food was required it was transported to one of these guarded doors and left there, and only when the domestic girl had retreated back to the kitchen was the door opened and the trolley of food or drinks taken into the great hall by a man who came out for it.

All the domestic staff including Freda were carefully instructed that if they saw, even by an unfortunate mistake, the ancient ceremonies going on in the great hall, they would immediately forfeit their life by the swords of the gatekeepers; they were solemnly told that this was the ancient law of Attila. The way that this was theatrically presented to the girls by Herr Shoemaker using a sword to enact the imaginary deed left them in no doubt that if they did happen to cast their eyes on the ancient ceremonies their remaining time would be short and gruesome.

When the bus arrived they were all shepherded to the great kitchen. They deposited their small personal overnight bags in a side room and then they were assembled with another eight girls who were already in the great kitchen for their induction training.

As they waited for what was now very familiar to Freda, she thought to herself, 'The House of Attila could put many world class companies to shame the way they attended to the instruction of employees, albeit enforced and unpaid employees.'

Herr Shoemaker strode into the great kitchen dressed in a formal morning suit consisting of a grey tailcoat and matching trousers, grey top hat, white shirt and cravat. Around his waist was a sword belt and scabbard containing a sword with a pearl encrusted handle, which was clearly visible. Freda thought, 'You have to hand it to the man the way he dresses for every occasion. Who else would dress up to impress a bunch of displaced persons most of whom, including herself, were illegal immigrants?'

Herr Shoemaker stood and carefully surveyed the now hushed audience; he looked at them carefully one by one for what seemed to be an age.

He began. 'Welcome to the House of Attila for this very important weekend for our guests who will be staying here. You all have a very important role to play in this weekend, for you will manage the domestic arrangements to make this weekend a most memorable one for the guests. Your job is to keep the mansion house absolutely clean and sparkling throughout the weekend and also to prepare and provide food and refreshments as required.

'You will be instructed exactly where, when and how to do your work, and if you obey those instructions exactly everything will be OK. However, the great hall, the minor hall and their annexes will be used for the ancient ceremonies of Attila the Hun. While these ancient ceremonies are being held your eyes must not see, or your ears must not hear what is taking place.

'Armed gate keepers are posted at every door leading to these rooms and they are sworn to kill by the sword anyone who intrudes upon the ancient ceremonies.' With that he drew out his sword and raised it high diagonally across his body and above his left shoulder. Then he drew it quickly downward as though slicing through an imaginary foe. The girls all let out a shocked exclamation, some even letting out a scream.

With that Herr Shoemaker about-turned and strode out of the open door, leaving a shocked silence behind him.

Freda thought to herself, 'Follow that if you can.' She quickly rose, went to the front, faced the girls and said, 'For those of you who don't know me, my name is Freda. What you have just heard, unfortunately, is the hard facts of life here at this place, this weekend, but I am the domestic supervisor and I have been here many times before so if you follow my instructions you will be OK.

'First let us form into our strengths. Who has good experience in the kitchen, cooking food?' Four girls held up their hands. 'Good, you will work in the kitchen. Have any of you worked as head chef?' One girl held up her hand. 'Are you happy to take charge of the kitchen?'

The girl nodded and said, 'Yes.'

'Then the three of you shake hands with the chef, and say, "Chef, I am happy to work for you."' The three girls each shook hands with the chef and confirmed their 'happiness'. Freda said, 'Well that's the kitchen team settled.'

She then faced the remaining twelve girls and said, 'The cleaning team have the most delicate job in this situation and I will lead the cleaning team; you must remember what Herr Shoemaker said about the serious danger of accidentally intruding on these ancient ceremonies. If you do exactly what I tell you, we will all be OK. Have any of you been supervisors before?' Four girls put their hands up. Freda said, 'In that case we will form four teams of three, each of you supervisors pick one girl at a time in turn to make your teams.' When that was done Freda said, 'Each of the teams including the kitchen team shakes each other's hands and say: "One for all and all for one." I will say that again,' said Freda. '"One for all and all for one." What that means is that you have to work together for the team and also look after each other. Let's do it.'

Starting shyly, but quickly becoming more confident as

they progressed, the teams all shook each other's hands in orderly turn, repeating each time, 'One for all and all for one.' By the time they had finished, they were all smiling brightly.

Freda said, 'Now, team one, you are responsible for the ground floor, go and check out the ground floor and make out a list of what has to be done and meet back in the kitchen at eleven o'clock with your list.

'Team two, you are responsible for the first floor, go and check that out and make a similar list. Remember, back here at eleven.

'Team three, you get the picture.

'Team four, you are responsible for the great hall, the minor hall and their annexes.' The girls in team four let out an audible gasp! However, Freda carried on speaking. 'For that very reason I will be in overall charge of team four, come let us go and check them out.'

Freda took the girls of team four through to the great hall. Herr Shoemaker was standing in the middle of the hall surveying the scene and visualising the evening to come. He was now dressed in a white T-shirt, blue jeans and white trainers.

When he saw Freda and the girls, he said, 'Ah! Dear Freda, I am glad you are here, first we need to clean the whole hall before we put the tables and seating in place.'

Freda said to Mattie, the supervisor, 'Take the girls into that corridor where there is a sluice room and get floor brushes, mops, mop buckets, cleaning cloths, polishing cloths, hot water, soap solution and furniture polish.'

Mattie quickly did as she was told and soon the girls were cleaning the hall and all the wood-panelled wall surfaces, which were just the right height to be reachable without having to get ladders.

When that was done Herr Shoemaker said, 'Now, we have seven new franchises tonight so we will need two tables with a total of seven chairs all facing into the hall, spaced equally along that wall of the great hall. We will need a similar number of tables and chairs along each of the adjacent walls for the fourteen invited existing franchises. We will need one long single table in the centre of the stage for Harold Szirtes, his son Imri, Karl, Felix and myself, which requires the four best chairs with the throne in the middle.' The girls went into one of the annexes and brought the appropriate tables and chairs and positioned them according to Herr Shoemaker's instructions.

The girls quickly washed and polished all of the furniture items until they shone.

Herr Shoemaker stood contemplating the scene, it was five minutes to eleven and Freda was about to ask if they could take a break, when he said, 'Freda, leave me in peace for a little time until I think of how we will arrange the evening. Bring the girls back in thirty minutes.'

Freda and the girls returned to the kitchen where the others were already gathered. Freda said, 'Quickly now get something to eat and drink while we can, and then we will hear a report from each team.'

All the reports were reasonably good, revealing that there was not a lot of preparation required before the guests arrived and that there was plenty of clean bed and table linen if required. The kitchen larder, refrigerators and freezers were well stocked and the wine cellar was full. Freda said, 'Well that's a relief; I will try to get a timetable of what is expected over the weekend.'

Freda went back to the great hall and asked Herr Shoemaker. 'Could I have an idea of what is expected over the weekend?'

He said beaming with pleasure, 'Freda, I can do better than that, I have prepared a list of what I want done and times of exactly when I want the work done.' He walked to a table in the corner of the room and picked up six A3 sheets of paper. 'Here is the dining schedule and menus for the whole weekend: evening meal tonight, Saturday morning breakfast tomorrow, Saturday lunch, Saturday evening dinner, Sunday breakfast and Sunday lunch.'

He then went back to the table and picked up four more sheets and said, 'Here are the cleaning schedules and times for cleaning the great hall, the minor hall and their annexes; I know I do not have to tell you the importance of keeping to these schedules precisely.'

Freda said, 'Thank you, Herr Shoemaker, you make it so much easier with your great attention to detail.'

Herr Shoemaker actually blushed and laughed in a peculiar high-pitched way, making a very camp gesture with his left hand as though fending off the compliment.

Freda turned away and said, as much to cover his embarrassment as to gain time to study the schedules with the team leaders, 'I will bring the girls back in thirty minutes if that is all right with you.'

'Yes, yes,' he replied very hastily. 'Thirty minutes will be fine.'

Freda returned to the kitchen and gave the appropriate schedules to each of the team leaders and said, 'Take ten minutes to study these with your team and then we will discuss them.'

Freda joined team four and explained. 'It is very important to keep to the schedule; it is not really demanding in terms of work, but the times are very important.'

The other three teams were quite happy with their cleaning schedules and the kitchen team seemed to think that their schedules were reasonable.

Freda said, 'OK, each team prepare as best you can then take every opportunity to eat and rest between your big work periods; keep your work schedules somewhere safe and refer to them often. May God be with you.'

Freda put team four's work schedule in an empty vase on a

THE HOUSE OF ATTILA

high shelf and returned with team four to the great hall. Herr Shoemaker said as they approached, 'There is a new carpet and a roll of rubber underlay in the corridor; get the girls to bring them in and lay them precisely in the middle of the floor.'

Using the whole team including Freda, the girls managed to lift and carry the heavy underlay, then the deep-pile carpet, and roll them out one on top of the other in the middle of the floor. The carpet rolled out like this covered a huge area of forty-nine square metres and with its deep pile it looked very impressive. With Herr Shoemaker directing operations it was eventually positioned to his complete satisfaction. Freda said, 'Herr Shoemaker, this carpet is new, you only had the wooden floor last time.'

'Yes this is my idea; I have been given much more creative authority to improve the franchisees' gatherings. However, it is not finished, take the girls into the other corridor and bring the roll of PVC to cover the carpet to protect it from body fluids.' Freda did not ask what he meant; she did not want to know as she had heard enough disturbing rumours about what went on behind the heavily guarded doors.

Herr Shoemaker then said, 'Freda, get the girls to set out and dress the dining tables and chairs for twenty-six dining places in the minor hall.'

When they had finished, he was satisfied and dismissed Freda and the girls, saying, 'That will be all for this afternoon, rest and freshen up ready for the guests arriving at about five o'clock.'

Freda and the girls returned to the kitchen where they found the other teams. Freda asked each team leader to report and when all reported that all preparations were satisfactory Freda looked at the clock on the kitchen wall and said, 'It is half past two. We have to be available to show guests to their rooms from five o'clock onwards. Come get your overnight bags and I will show you where we will all sleep.'

Freda then led the girls to the large and spacious attic where twenty single beds were arranged in two rows with a corridor up the middle. There was a kitchen area in one corridor with a table and eight chairs. In the opposite corner was a row of three classic toilet pans fitted with water cisterns. In the adjacent corner was a shower area with three shower units. One of the girls said, 'There is not much privacy!'

    Freda replied, 'Let us count our blessings that we have these facilities and make the best of them. Rest now while we have the chance.'

12

The Gathering

The few vehicles parked at the rear of the mansion house had now grown to about thirty. The time was half past six in the evening and all of the guests had signed in and been shown to their rooms where they were preparing and dressing for the meeting and dinner. At the same time as the guests were arriving, three men in the stable toilets had stripped Fredrick, the boiler man, and had laid him face down on a table and were administering an enema. When they completed the procedure, they seated him on a lavatory to ensure that his bowels would be completely evacuated before his forth coming trial.

The guest list comprised of seven new franchises and fourteen recent and now well established franchises. Dress was formal dinner suit and black tie.

The guests came down from their rooms as the time approached half past seven. They were led to one of the annexes off the great hall for a drink of traditional rakija. A few of the established franchisees recognised each other from the last gathering and they clustered together, while those who did not know anyone tended to stay on the edges of the room. When they were all assembled they were led into the great hall where they found their places at seats marked by an individual name card.

When they were all assembled Herr Shoemaker strode

into the middle of the hall and ascended the small stage and announced loudly, 'Please be upstanding to receive our leader.'

A fanfare of trumpets sounded through the hall. When it died away a roll of beats on a single drum began, then it changed to a regular slow beat and the drummer appeared through the door marching in time to the beat followed by Karl, Felix, Imri and finally Harold Szirtes.

The procession marched in time to the drum round the three sides of the hall then ascended the small stage where they each stood in front of their respective chairs on each side of the throne with Harold Szirtes taking the centre.

On the stage about two metres in front of the throne a large sword was mounted by the hilt on a polished wooden stand with its blade pointing to the ceiling.

Harold Szirtes sat on his throne and Herr Shoemaker announced loudly, 'Please be seated.' Everyone sat down. He waited a few moments, carefully looking at all the faces. 'Welcome to the House of Attila,' he said with slow emphasis on the words House of Attila. 'My name is Martin Shoemaker, I am the estate manager and I manage everything that happens in this great house and the surrounding estates. Let me first introduce you to the people sitting on the stage.

'On my extreme left is Felix Hienmann, he is in charge of intelligence.' Felix stood and bowed. 'Next to Felix is Karl Stonier, our head of security and enforcement.' Karl stood and bowed. 'On my right is Imri Szirtes, heir to the great House of Attila.' Imiri stood and bowed.

'Finally and appropriately on his throne is Harold Szirtes, head of the House of Attila and the source of your future prosperity. Gentlemen, I give you the head of the House of Attila, Harold Szirtes.'

Everyone in the room faced Harold Szirtes, bowed and then sat down.

Harold Szirtes stood up and began to speak. 'Gentlemen, I

invite you to drink a toast to the ancient Attila the Hun who could have ruled the then known world, but for his tragic and untimely death.' He called out in a firm and confident voice. 'Provide our guests with the means of drinking the ancient toast.'

At that command three men appeared, each carrying a tray of glasses containing a good measure of rakija. They served the glasses to each person, whispering, 'Don't drink yet, wait for the toast.'

Harold raised his glass and announced, 'Gentlemen, to the memory of the great Attila.'

Everyone followed, by raising their glasses and saying, 'The great Attila.' And proceeded to drink the large measure in one gulp.

Harold Szirtes said, 'Thank you, gentlemen,' and sat down.

Herr Shoemaker came down into the centre of the carpet and proceeded to recite in very theatrical fashion the story of Attila as he had practised on Nico at the log cabin in the forest.

At the end of his performance Herr Shoemaker sat down well pleased with his theatrical performance. A ripple of applause started and then quickly became a standing ovation. Herr Shoemaker stood up and bowed to the three sides of the hall and then turned and bowed to Harold Szirtes.

When the applause died down Harold Szirtes stood up and began speaking. 'Attila the Hun. Or, "The Scourge of God", as he was known by the Romans, had a reputation for cruelty that was deserved, but not unusual for the time. In possession of a mysterious sword, which seemed supernatural by the circumstances of his receiving it, he killed his brother and co-ruler, Bleda, to gain absolute power. A lesson for us in the twentieth century. That lesson is: You cannot share power in your locality, you have to quickly eliminate competition and become the dominant force or you will be at war all the time.'

Harold beamed as he announced, 'Gentlemen, the secret I am going to share with you is that this very sword that we have been speaking of has been found. The sword you see before you is the very Sword of Attila the Hun. This sword, it is said, gave mysterious power to Attila. Attila dreamed of this sword and when a certain shepherd beheld one of his flock limping and could find no cause for this wound, he anxiously followed the trail of blood and at length came to a sword it had unwittingly trampled while nibbling the grass. He dug it up and felt compelled to take it straight to Attila, who rejoiced at this unusual gift with its curious inscriptions.

'Being superstitious, he thought, "I must believe in it and use it to become ruler of the whole world and through the Sword of Mars I will have supremacy in all wars."'

Harold lifted the sword out of its mounting and said, 'Inscribed on one side of the blade are the mysterious words: *Sword of Attila – Ruler of the World.* On the other side of its blade is a more curious inscription: *You will rule from a town sitting under a crown beyond the Pillars of Hercules.*

'Who can tell me the meaning of these inscriptions?'

Harold became stern as he said, 'However, gentlemen, this reference to the Sword of Mars is a historical error introduced by the Romans to try and justify his successes by attributing his power to one of their gods. The Huns would never give credence to a Roman god; its true name is Sword of Attila the Hun and it was supernaturally delivered into his hand.

'However, as Herr Shoemaker described in his historical account, Attila died prematurely by misadventure to put it kindly and did not realise the power of his true destiny. That is history, however; the sword has been found and the House of Attila is rising again in this present time, only this time we will rule the world and you will be part of this success and share in its bounty.'

Harold continued. 'Gentlemen, you have all bought a franchise from the House of Attila, the seven of you sitting across from me are about to begin your businesses, the fourteen of you sitting at the sides of the hall are all very recent franchisees and have already tasted the beginnings of success, so you have returned to the source to learn again the basic principles of success.'

He raised his voice at least three decibels, 'To be part of the House of Attila you must learn the facts of life. Charles Darwin was absolutely right. This world is about the survival of the fittest. However it may be dressed up by the propagandists, it is still the jungle, the survival of the fittest and the most ruthless. Many families, social groupings at local level and organisational structures in companies are all pecking orders of dominance.

'So they are too within nations and also between nations at international level. Look at the United States, the United Kingdom, Germany, France, Japan, Italy and Canada. They are called the G7 and they rule the world by the might of arms and power of money.' Harold paused for a few moments as though these last significant words had exhausted his mental capacity. Then he continued. 'These powerful bodies are not benevolent but they are singularly ruthless, carving up the resources of this world between them in proportion to their individual financial muscle. Yes it is true, money rules the world.'

He continued. 'What is so fascinating is that no one really knows who rules the world. Some people think it is now George Bush, the American president, but the reality is that the capitalist shareholders are so diverse, spanning the continents that circle the globe, that they are unknown to each other. Some may only have a few shares and some may have billions, but generally they all act in selfish unison almost like a biological organism dividing and stratifying like the hierarchies in the food chain.

'In fact the world does not know how much money is in circulation, for much of the underworld does not keep its money in banks. So the so-called world economy is just a measure of what is actually known, and only a fraction of the *total* world economy. However, we will leave that to the economists, bankers and politicians and get on with our business.' He laughed at his impressive sounding analysis and joke, and the great hall responded with loud laughter.

'I think we will pause here to have a comfort break, gentlemen, please return to your seats in fifteen minutes.'

Harold turned to Herr Shoemaker and said, 'Martin, how do you think it is going?'

Herr Shoemaker replied, 'You are doing very well, it is almost perfect, I have been watching their faces and their attention is riveted on you and every word you speak.'

The franchisees started to return to their seats. Harold Szirtes said, 'Martin, another toast, this time to the success of the franchisees of the House of Attila.'

Herr Shoemaker signalled to a hidden attendant, and two men appeared with trays of glasses containing a good measure of rakija. He then stood up saying, 'Gentlemen, please be upstanding for a toast to the successful franchisees of the House of Attila.'

When they were all standing Herr Shoemaker raised his glass and said loudly, 'To the successful franchisees of the House of Attila.' The assembled company followed suit.

When the company was seated Harold Szirtes stood up and started to speak.

'Welcome back.' He paused. 'Having decided that money rules this world and that dominance and pecking order is the mechanism for success, we now need to cover the next most important fact of life.

'All human beings have weaknesses and are fallible. Herein lies the key to our power. People lust after all manner of things; all people have an Achilles heel. Knowing these things and exploiting these weaknesses under the surface is the core business of the House of Attila. Our franchise will span the globe, no one and no place will be beyond our reach.

'At this stage I call upon Felix Hienmann, who is in charge of intelligence, to outline the strategy you need for your local situation.'

Felix stood up on centre stage. 'Good, good, good evening,' he said nervously. 'Please excuse me, I am not used to, nor do I like being, in the limelight.' Trying to make a joke of his poor start, he said, 'I much prefer to be creeping about in the shadows. Oh no! Is that what they call a Freudian slip?' The audience erupted into laughter, thinking this was contrived.

He gathered himself and said, 'Let me tell you how to control your local area using good intelligence as the basis of your operations. Every local area comes under the jurisdiction of various layers of regulatory authority, however, all human structures are composed of ordinary people with all their weaknesses. The higher in the organisation you go, the bigger the egos you find. This is important to you, because the bigger the ego, the more susceptible the person is to temptations, particularly those involving vanity and subtle flattery.

'How do you use this? You make up a list or better still a database of all local politicians, including all regulatory enforcing officers, including police, taxation, fire, health, safety, environmental, licensing and so on.

'Local competitors need to be included in this strategy as they may pose an even greater threat than the regulating authorities.

'Research, identify and record all their individual interests, weaknesses, obsessions, known offences, rumours and dubious friends.

'Create opportunities to exploit these tendencies,

collecting and recording as much compromising photographic evidence as you can.

'Individuals and their families are very susceptible to blackmail and as a last resort people can be eliminated if necessary.

'Thank you, thank you,' Felix said as he shuffled back to his seat, and a round of applause rippled through the audience.

Harold Szirtes stood up and started to speak.

'The final fact of life that you need to learn is that no one goes against the House of Attila and gets away with it. In this regard every franchisee must be absolutely ruthless. One act of mercy by you in your local situation could result in your downfall. In some cases we need to join together against a powerful foe when they arise. That is the strength of the federation of the House of Attila. No one is beyond our reach or control; even the highest in every land have secrets, lusts and fears. You must learn to recognise these opportunities and exploit them in your local area.

'Finally, gentlemen, the biggest resource the House of Attila has is illegal immigrants. The poorest countries in the world or where ethnic tensions prevail cause a constant stream of people into our organisation. The main part of our business is providing them transportation and a safe place to live and work.'

Harold Szirtes let a grin escape as he delighted in the way he had described the awful business of people trafficking and exploitation.

He sat down well pleased with his performance and the audience immediately rose to their feet applauding loudly.

Herr Shoemaker rose and announced, 'We will have a comfort break before you return to learn how to be ruthless and dominant. I leave you with this thought. What you will see in the next session is the punishment of a displaced, illegal immigrant, who has been obstructive, refused to clean our leader's hunting boots and tried to undermine our organisation for personal gain. Please return to this great hall in twenty minutes.'

The room emptied amid a babble of animated conversation.

Slowly the great hall filled again as the franchisees returned. They were visibly more relaxed and making relationships.

Herr Shoemaker stood up and called them to be seated, saying, 'Please be seated, the next part of the induction process will begin in two minutes.'

He continued: 'Order, order. Let me introduce Karl Stonier, our head of security and enforcement. He will now explain the code of conduct expected of all franchisees and employees.'

Karl walked forward on to the carpet, which was now covered with a large plastic sheet tucked under all the way round, and in a loud and confident voice said, 'The underworld as the media calls us, succeeds or fails by the loyalty of its members or the lack of it. The regulatory authorities do not discover crime by their detective work, they discover crime through informers.

'What sets the House of Attila apart is our policy to deal with informers, even the merest suspicion must be followed through. The House of Attila demands absolute loyalty and is ruthless in this respect. You as franchisees will only be as secure as the loyalty of those who work for you. The first thing you must learn is to be totally ruthless. Let me demonstrate this to you on Fredrick, our boiler house man. We gave Fredrick, a displaced person, an illegal immigrant, a nice job, food, board and clothing. But Fredrick was not happy with all these comforts, he became obstinate and began to rebel and then offered sensitive information about us to the local police for personal gain.'

The lights around the room first dimmed, then went out

completely. A spotlight came on, illuminating the centre of the plastic-covered carpet.

Suddenly a blindfolded naked man stumbled on to the carpet area; his thumbs were tied together behind his back.

The shocked audience let out a loud and startled gasp.

Karl stepped off the carpet to lift a large whip, consisting of a wooden handle with nine heavy thongs of leather, the ends of which were enhanced with large metal rivets. A replica of a cat o' nine tails said to have been used by Attila the Hun.

Karl stepped back on to the plastic-covered carpet and said in a loud voice, 'This is Fredrick, our boiler man. We were concerned when we saw Fredrick's signs of rebellion, so Felix arranged for a police officer who owes us many favours for his indiscretions to visit the stables and accidently meet Fredrick. He suggested to Fredrick that it would be financially worth his while to obtain information about when the next gathering would take place at the House of Attila. Felix had previously let Fredrick hear him speak about the next gathering. Felix, being suspiciously minded and not trusting anyone, gave false information by saying that the date for the next gathering was last weekend. The policeman passed this information on to Felix.'

Karl approached the still blindfolded Fredrick, saying, 'Why did you betray us Fredrick?' He suddenly lashed him across his bare buttocks. Fredrick let out a long and mournful cry and fell to his knees whining and whimpering like a wounded dog with blood oozing from several lacerations.

Karl silently circled the edges of the carpet looking intently at Fredrick. He then walked towards the sorry kneeling figure and shouted in his face. 'Why did you bite the hand that fed you, Fredrick? Get up, you traitor, get on to your feet.' He lashed Fredrick across the back.

Fredrick almost jumped up screaming. 'Don't hit me, don't hit me.' He staggered about the carpet, dripping blood from his now scarlet back and buttocks.

Karl watched him as he staggered around, still whimpering and twitching at imaginary threats. Karl was now intently focused like a big cat stalking his prey. He watched until Fredrick staggered sideways, opening his legs wide, trying to regain his balance. Karl drew the whip viciously upwards in a whipping motion, much like when a towel is whipped to make a cracking sound. The ends of the thongs struck Fredrick full in the genitals. Fredrick collapsed like a burst bag with a long moaning sound and curled into the foetal position.

Karl could not restrain the smile of satisfaction he felt as he signalled two men to switch off the spotlight and come and drag Fredrick off into a small ante room where he would be attended to.

Two men quickly cleaned the blood off the plastic carpet cover and the floor leading to the side room. The only illumination came from the great hall side lights. When they finished cleaning the main lights were switched back on.

The delegates looked shocked – in fact some looked decidedly white faced.

Karl walked into the middle of the plastic-covered carpet and said, 'There is no place for weakness in our organisation, your security and success depends on your ruthlessness. Even if you suspect a traitor you must weed them out immediately. If you fail to act the traitor will bring you down.

'To embed the importance of this, you will take part in a hunt to the death tomorrow; the quarry will be the traitor Fredrick.

'We are now going to dinner and will finish the evening with some musical entertainment before you retire to bed. We have a very busy day tomorrow and you need to be fresh.'

* * *

One of the annexes had been set out as an elegant dining room with all places set with individual name cards. The menu included a selection of classic Serbian dishes including a cassoulet of snails, Russian style rabbit and cherry strudel. All washed down with bottles of Serbian beer.

Herr Shoemaker brought the room to order by announcing, 'The waitresses will visit the tables to take orders for the meals and I hope everyone enjoys their selection of food.'

The dining-room settled to a quiet babble of conversation with classical background music playing through the public address system.

Everyone expressed satisfaction with the quality of food and the excellent service from the waitresses, so Harold Szirtes rose to his feet and said, 'Bring all the cooks and waitresses into the hall.' He stayed standing until they were all assembled and said in a loud voice, 'Thank you, ladies, the meal and the service were outstanding and we wish to show our appreciation.'

The entire company responded with a vigorous round of applause.

When the ladies retired he said. 'The next hour will be a question and answer session. I appoint Martin to be the master of ceremonies to ensure that things do not get bogged down in detail, but to keep things moving along.'

Herr Shoemaker stood up and asked, 'Gentlemen, are there any questions?'

One of the new franchisees said, 'What exactly is our business?'

Harold Szirtes stood up and said, 'A good question, a very good question. Our core business is the oldest profession in the world, but it has to be run discreetly; people do not like to see prostitution conducted openly, especially wives.'

THE HOUSE OF ATTILA

Harold let out a loud laugh at his own joke and the company duly responded.

He continued. 'Our customers appreciate discretion, successful businesses are customer-oriented and we aim to be the most successful in the business so we will be the most discreet. That means that each of you needs to open a low profile brothel. I know that all of you here owns failing hotels and the reason you approached the House of Attila was to find a solution for your failing hotel before you go out of business.

'The House of Attila can supply cooks, waitresses, cleaners and prostitutes from the masses of illegal immigrants trying to get away from oppression and conflict. The advantage to you is they only need board and lodgings. You don't pay them wages; you just let them keep any tips.

'The first saving you will make is to find excuses to get rid of your present paid staff and immediately replace them with unpaid staff supplied as you need them from the House of Attila.

'Some of these girls will be willing to break into the more lucrative business of prostitution for a little extra financial reward; some will need to be forced by brutality or induced drug addiction.

'If you have potential in your hotel to install nightclubs, beauty parlours, tanning and pampering suites, they are excellent ways of disguising the illegitimate side of your business. This is very important, the more legitimate business you run alongside your illegal business the more difficult it is to detect.' With that he beamed towards his questioner and said, 'I hope that answers your question.'

Another guest put his hand up. Herr Shoemaker immediately responded with the words, 'Yes, sir you have a question.'

The guest said, 'What about drugs?'

Harold Szirtes stood up and said, 'You don't want to

dabble in drugs until you are well established. Drug territories are already in place, if you start to mess with them you will need to be very well organised and prepared for a total and decisive battle that you must win quickly. In other words be careful not to start a fight unless you are absolutely sure you will win. Is that quite clear?'

Another guest put up his hand and said, 'What about protection rackets?'

Harold again stood up and said, 'Drug dealing networks and protection rackets usually go hand in hand. If you are not presently paying protection money it probably won't be a problem until you are well established. By that time you will have a full intelligence profile on your local area and will know all the players in the local scene including their strengths and weaknesses. Then with the help of the House of Attila we will eliminate the competition in a clean and decisive sweep.

'Your first job is to turn round your failing business and to build your local intelligence profile and contacts.'

Another guest nervously put his hand up and said, 'What can I do? I have lost my alcohol licence.'

Harold Szirtes stood up and said, 'That was very careless, was it not?' Without waiting for an answer he carried on. 'The first thing you need to learn is that you are working with a very professional organisation, and you need to be the same. The House of Attila is not like these shabby local gangsters. The House of Attila is a modern global player, where sex is glamorous, exciting and a huge business opportunity and you are in on the ground floor. Felix is in charge of intelligence, he will come to your hotel and look into your local situation and advise you how to renew your alcohol licence and also to begin the process of building your local intelligence profile.'

The questions continued, progressively getting more trivial. When the hour was up Herr Shoemaker intervened, saying, 'OK, we have done enough work for today and now it is time to relax.'

He made a gesture by raising his hand high in the air and snapping his fingers. A man came running over and he said to him, 'Bring on the band.' A few minutes later four men appeared carrying musical instruments. The men were smartly dressed in black trousers, white shirts and black bow-ties.

Herr Shoemaker intoduced them as a small but highly acclaimed brass band from the nearby town and the waitresses came round serving more of the Jadoginsko bottled beer.

The band played a variety of well known tunes in the background and the assembled company quickly chattered away.

13
Warlords

The Saturday morning started before breakfast with a horse riding lesson. The horses at the stables were mature, experienced horses and not particularly difficult to ride, but most of the franchisees were not experienced riders. Herr Shoemaker led the activities impeccably dressed in formal riding dress as only he could wear it. The twenty-one guests were taken to the stables to dress in riding clothing: hard hat, long riding boots, jacket, hunting tie. Once Herr Shoemaker was satisfied that they were properly dressed, he led them to the stables to be matched to suitable horses already bridled and saddled. They each led out their allocated horse to a large fenced field with flat new-mown grass now covered with a fresh fall of snow. One by one they were helped by stable-hands into the saddle and they began by walking.

Herr Shoemaker quickly upped the stakes by asking them to trot. As usual, Prince did his fast trot and the rider lost his balance and ended up in an undignified heaving heap of disjointed limbs, almost buried in the snow. The rider was helped back on to his horse. Herr Shoemaker reminded the group that they needed to move in time with the horse's rhythm. He said, 'Sounds simple, but most beginners tense out of anxiety, or concentration, or whatever, but the result is not good. Visualise a nice canter as you enter the corner before you do a short side in trot, then halfway along the short side, focus on a point around the field and then canter.'

Astonishingly, it worked! Even if it was only for a couple of strides, but that was huge progress. Herr Shoemaker practised them a few more times then, as there were twenty-one new franchisee riders, they took it in turns to have a one-to-one with the seven stable-hands and practised more of what they had learned.

This was not good for Prince. He was in a rebellious mood and he put his foot down very firmly and in this way said he'd done enough, and he wasn't going to do any more. Herr Shoemaker was good and right on the ball as usual and gave the rider some tips to help get Prince moving forward. He was trying to plant his feet and even reversed to avoid going forward. Prince was changing direction frequently and at one point Herr Shoemaker asked the rider to deliberately walk backwards to the point they were aiming for. The rider shouted, 'All this and trying to remember to relax and move with the horse's rhythm at the same time!'

Herr Shoemaker told the watching group not to focus on what the horses won't do, but to concentrate on what you want the horses to do.

Eventually the group took a break and the horses went back into the stables for a chill-out and to munch on their hay nets, and the riders thankfully retired to the House of Attila for a well earned breakfast.

The late breakfast was good and the conversation lively. When they finished eating, Herr Shoemaker stood on a small stage in front of a lectern fitted with a microphone. He said, 'Let us now start the serious business of the day.' The curtains on the windows were drawn and a slide show presentation was projected on to a screen beside the lectern; the main slide was a map of the Balkans.

Herr Shoemaker began. 'The Adriatic and Ionian seas define the Balkan Peninsula on the west, and the Aegean and the Black Sea on the east. To the north lie open plains crossed by the mountains. The line of the Danube is taken as the northern boundary of the region.

'In classical times the Balkans was at the heart of a single Greco-Roman civilisation. But later it became a troubled interface between Roman and Greek Christianity and between Christianity and Islam. It has been a seismic fault between Europe and Asia.'

Herr Shoemaker continued. 'After the collapse of the empire of the Huns, in the fifth century, the Slavs began to expand their territory. They moved west into Czechoslovakia and south towards the Adriatic and Aegean. Their separate regional and religious development as Slovenes, Croats, Serbs, Macedonians and Bulgarians makes the peninsula of the Balkans one of the most politically complex regions on the face of the earth.

'It is against this fascinating historic background that the House of Attila is beginning its conquest of the Balkans.'

Herr Shoemaker stopped speaking at that point and then announced, 'That is enough background to set the scene for our leader to address you. I now ask the head of the House of Attila to come forward.'

Harold Szirtes walked forward to the lectern. The introduction had given him confidence and he began by saying loudly, 'You are the first twenty-one franchisees of the House of Attila covering a population of fifty-five million people and you are selected from every corner of this wonderfully diverse region.

'You are now destined to become the underground rulers and warlords of the Balkans. Your clearly defined franchise areas each have equal starting potential with approximately equal numbers of people. Today you will become bonded in blood to respect and support each other in the war against democratic authorities and give your absolute allegiance to the House of Attila.

THE HOUSE OF ATTILA

'To be effective warlords you must learn to be ruthless. You will remember last night and Fredrick our boilerman. What did he do? He told a police officer about the House of Attila and the gathering and he offered to find out more information to pass on for financial return.

'You felt sorry for him when you saw what Karl did to him with his terrible whip, but what you need to be clear about is that Fredrick was prepared to sell us to the police.

'There is one rule you must remember, if you allow one rotten apple to stay in the barrel for more than a few moments it will ruin all the good apples.

'For your own survival you must be ruthless with any opposition but especially traitors within, as they know more about you.

'Occasionally a franchisee will get too big for his boots and will try to expand into another franchisee's territory. When that happens the whole organisation will rise up against that bad apple and eliminate his organisation completely. No individual member is bigger than the House of Attila.

'The House of Attila will always hunt down and eliminate opposition and especially delight in the elimination of a traitor.

'Gentlemen, you have a very important decision to make this morning. That is to join in the hunt to the death of the traitor Fredrick and afterwards take your rightful place as a successful franchisee of the House of Attila. You see, there is no option, we must be completely united in the battle to support the House of Attila in our collective interest. Or you can walk away now, after first considering the risks that walking away may entail.'

The room descended into a deathly silence, which Harold let prolong for a full minute. He then said, 'I take it no one wishes to leave.' He again let it hang in suspense for another full minute and the tension became electric, but no one moved.

Harold said, 'Congratulations, we are united as one in the House of Attila and the wolfhounds will only get one quarry today. Bring out the Bikavér and let us drink a toast to our lifelong partnership.'

Three men with trays of large wine glasses full of red wine appeared and dispensed the glasses to the assembled men. Harold, holding up his glass, announced in a loud voice. 'To the House of Attila.' The assembled company repeated the toast enthusiastically and threw back their heads, draining their glasses in one gulp.

Harold said, 'Unfortunately, I cannot join you this afternoon as I have a public engagement with local politicians in town. Karl will lead the manhunt in my place. Good hunting, gentlemen.'

With that last remark Harold Szirtes strode purposefully out of the hall, unable to suppress the smile forming across his lips as he thought of the perfect alibi he would have this afternoon by mixing very publicly with the local politicians at a charity event while the traitor Fredrick was killed.

14

The Manhunt

Karl Stonier moved into the centre of the room and said, 'Let's go to the stables and get your horses again.'

The twenty-one franchisees made their way out of the hall and walked towards the stables. They got dressed in their riding gear and led their already saddled and bridled horses out. Karl gave the instruction to mount and, with the assistance of the seven stable-hands, they all mounted.

Following Karl, they slowly walked the horses round the outside of the paddock and along a path through heavily wooded areas.

The trees were mostly mature deciduous of many varieties, now bare of their leaves, with a few evergreen species scattered throughout. It was now early afternoon and the weather was fine. After about half an hour Karl stopped the group as they approached a cottage, at the side of which were extensive kennels containing large wolfhound hunting dogs which were now barking loudly. He said, 'Dismount for a rest.'

The hound master came out and spoke to Karl. It was clear that they were old friends and they chatted for about fifteen minutes.

Karl knew what he was doing and that it was important to bond this first and key group of core franchisees. They were not experienced horsemen, so it was important to keep the chase easy so as not to have a serious accident, but sufficient that they should also experience the excitement of the chase. He wanted this day to be etched on their minds until their dying days.

After fifteen minutes rest Karl told them to remount and sent the master of the hounds to release the dogs.

Karl said, 'Fredrick will be given his chance to escape, and to give him a sporting chance we have come to the far side of the estate. He will be told to run in the opposite direction from where we are now, so if we are to catch him before he gets clear of the estate we will need to hurry.'

The master of the hounds rode up, leading the excited dogs as he blew his hunting horn. He took the lead and the other riders followed. He was well aware of their limited riding ability and kept the pace slow by riding the hounds in great diagonal sweeps, which seemed to suit them. Karl kept the main party of riders on a straight course, which allowed them to keep up with the hounds that were running about ten times the distance that they were covering.

The stable-hands were riding at the rear of the group, assisting any fallen riders and gathering the occasional runaway.

They rode along one boundary of the estate for about an hour and then the wolfhounds saw the running figure of Fredrick. He could hear them coming and his face was contorted with fear and the pain of trying to drive his tortured limbs beyond their capacity.

The chase did not last long; wolfhounds are the tallest breed of dog and when they see their quarry they are like lightning. Although it was bloody, Fredrick did not last very long when the pack started to fight for what they could get.

The master of the hounds let the wolfhounds satisfy their blood lust, and then he began to call them away, blowing his hunting horn. He was given assistance with physical encouragement from the stable-hands. As he got them under control he rode away, taking the hounds with him.

Karl shouted to the franchisees. 'Dismount and tie your horses to the trees.'

The stable-hands produced plastic bags and plastic snow shovels, which they had brought with them on a pack-horse. Karl said, 'Every one of you must participate in cleaning up the mess. Bag every piece of bone or flesh and every bit of blood-stained snow.'

Reluctantly the twenty-one franchisees began bagging the main body of Fredrick in a very large bin bag, then they double bagged it and treble bagged it and placed it on the back of the pack-horse, securely lashing it in place with ropes supplied by the stable-hands.

When they finished securing the main bag Karl shouted, 'Now search the entire area of the kill and bag any fragment of bone, flesh, clothing or blood-stained snow.'

With their gory but securely bagged cargo of human remains on the pack-horse, the hunting party slowly made its way back to the stables.

With Karl directing them, they unsaddled the horses, removed their reins and put the horses in their stalls for the stable-hands to finish.

Karl said, 'Lead the pack-horse round to the boiler room.' He went ahead of them, entering the boiler room first. He found Nico and said, 'Pile as many logs as you can into the fire and open the fire door as wide as it will go.' Nico did as he was instructed. 'Now go and lose yourself for four hours and be sure not to come near the boiler house for at least four hours. Do you understand?' Nico nodded, left the boiler house and went to the kitchen of the mansion house. He saw Valda and said, 'I have to stay out of the way for four hours, can you give me a job?'

Valda said, 'Yes, I was just looking for a good fairy to clean all these glasses and dishes.'

Karl opened the external door of the boiler house and said to the twenty-one franchisees standing outside. 'Bring in the pack-horse.'

The franchisees brought the pack-horse into the boiler house. Karl pointed to a set of stairs leading to a platform about halfway up the side of the boiler. He said, 'That is the incineration chamber. Carry the bags up and drop them into the fire through the access door.' While they were doing that, Karl went to a sink and opened a hot water tap and left it running, to run off hot water and pull in cold water to prevent the intense heat from boiling the system.

Working together, the twenty-one franchisees carried out Karl's instructions. Then they all gathered round the open fire door, looking into the inferno and feeling the intense heat being driven by the powerful draught caused by the huge volume of air rushing in through the wide open fire door.

When the logs burned down they quickly replenished them with fresh logs dropped down on to the fire from the incineration chamber access door, which avoided the scorching heat radiating from the normal fire door.

After a good hour Karl climbed up to the incineration chamber, opened the door and peered into the fire. He could only distinguish the bright red fire. He decided that everything organic had been consumed by the intense heat. He came down the steps and returned to the front of the boiler and said, 'We need to let the boiler cool down and as soon as we can bear it we must retrieve the bones from the ashes.'

When the heat was just bearable they raked the ash out of the fire bed and ash pit and retrieved all the bone fragments by filtering the ash through a mechanical sieve. After hosing them with cold water they put the bone fragments in a double polythene bag and Felix took them away to put them through the stone crusher at the estate quarry.

THE HOUSE OF ATTILA

Karl put two new logs in the fire bed, which immediately ignited from the heat radiating from the still red hot refractory bricks and closed the fire door.

He said, 'Now clean this boiler house like it has never been cleaned before. There must be no evidence left as to what has happened here today.'

When they finished he said, 'Now throw all the debris on to the fire.'

Three men with trays of large wine glasses appeared and dispensed them to the assembled men. Karl, holding up his glass, announced in a loud voice, 'I wish death to all those conspiring against the House of Attila.' The assembled company responded and drank down their drinks.

Karl then instructed, 'The time is now four o'clock, go to the stables, shower and change back into your own clothes. Then go to your rooms for a rest before assembling in the dining annexe at seven o'clock for dinner. Dress will be smart-casual and tonight will be a fun night although the theme will still be dominance.'

The franchisees filed out of the boiler house and Karl went to the sink and turned off the running hot water tap.

As the franchisees came out into the cold air, one of them said, laughing, 'Look at the chimney, the water sure is boiling.' They all looked up at the chimney and the great plume of steam discharging skywards from the pressure relief valve.

They made their way to the stables, showered, changed and went up to their rooms to ponder the events of the day.

15
Dominance

The franchisees were gathering just before seven o'clock when Harold Szirtes, Imri Szirtes and three well known local politicians, who often attended parties at the House of Attila, entered.

They had just arrived back from a charity event run by the extreme right-wing party, of which Harold Szirtes was a significant financial backer.

Harold was in an extremely good mood and he instructed Herr Shoemaker. 'Set four extra places at the dining table.' He found Felix and said quietly, 'Felix, make sure you get good photographs of the three politicians tonight.'

He then sought out Herr Shoemaker and said, 'Martin, is dinner ready yet? I am starving!'

Herr Shoemaker said, 'If you stay with your guests for a moment I will get the franchisees seated and ready to receive you.'

When the franchisees were seated in the dining annexe a trumpeter from the brass band hired for the evening blew a fanfare and Herr Shoemaker announced loudly, 'Receive our guests of honour.' He started a slow hand clap which the franchisees quickly took up.

Harold led the top table party right round all the tables on the three sides of the dining annexe before arriving at the top table. The hand clapping became faster and faster until they finally arrived at their places, much to the delight of the assembled company who ended the ceremonial with a huge cheer.

Herr Shoemaker came forward and said loudly, 'Gentlemen we have a special treat, tonight the chef has produced her special Hungarian menu for us. The Hungarian Delight. The wine tonight is Tokaji, formerly known as Tokay and perhps the greatest sweet wine on earth. The wine is made in the little town of Mad in north-east Hungary, enjoy but take care, too much makes you mad.' He got a big laugh with the final remark and a round of applause. The atmosphere was warming up.

The all-male waiters quickly served the wine followed by soup with crisply heated bread rolls. The other courses followed, from cold goose liver served with green pepper and tomato to roast leg of suckling pig with *saláta*.

After the meal Harold was impatient to get on with the main event of the evening and he summoned Herr Shoemaker and said, 'Come on, Martin, get on with it.'

Herr Shoemaker quickly ushered everyone into the second annexe where a bar had been set up. He said, 'This next session is naked female wrestling.'

A big cheer erupted from the company.

He continued. 'This is your chance to select a girl by bidding for her and to take her back to your own hotel with you to start working for you as a prostitute.' He paused to let that sink in, then said, 'After the wrestling, which will exhaust the girls, you can take them to your room to finish breaking them in.

'Remember, you must be dominant with her and leave her in no doubt about who is boss. Now while we get the girls prepared, go to the bar and have drinks. Remember, if you are going to work prostitutes you must be hard on them. Be back in the main hall in half an hour when the fun will begin.'

The twenty-one franchisees and the three politicians retired to the other annexe where they found a self service bar set up. They were now mixing freely in small groups. The fourteen existing franchisees found themselves reassuring the seven new ones saying things like, 'It's not nearly as extreme as you have seen this weekend. I have not had any problems with the girl I bought and so far I have not had to resort to using drugs on her. She soon got the message, wink, wink, you know what I mean.' The last type of comment resulted in lots of loud laughter, which relieved the underlying tension. The franchisees and the politicians took a few drinks. The thirty minutes were soon up and Karl came looking for them, shouting, 'Come on, come on, let's get back to the hall.'

Once they were all seated the lights round the side of the great hall were dimmed and only the spotlights illuminated the carpeted area.

Karl stepped on to the carpet and announced loudly, 'Gentlemen, it's now competition time. We have twenty-four girls, which is a coincidence considering that there are exactly twenty-four guests.' A great roar of approval went up followed by much laughter.

Karl continued shouting, 'The girls you will see shortly have been downright obstinate to our various existing franchisees; two in particular have been troublemakers and we have driven them more than seven hundred kilometres just for your entertainment and sport tonight.' Again there was a great roar of approval from the audience.

Karl continued. 'However, the main purpose is to break these girls in, so that they will go back with their franchise master as an obedient worker.' Now he really shouted out: 'This is the kind of support you get from the House of Attila.' Again a great roar of approval went up followed by much laughter.

THE HOUSE OF ATTILA

Karl continued. 'As I said, we have twenty-four girls, which makes six sets of four girls. One girl from each set will wrestle one girl from another set all at once on the mat, which means three pairs of girls will be wrestling on the mat at a time.

'The winner in each match will be the girl who manages to sexually abuse the other the most. Gentlemen, you will be the judges so you will need to concentrate.

'There will be four sessions of ten minutes each. With change over time added that should last about one hour. This will be followed by a rest break as I am sure you gentlemen will be exhausted by then.'

The expectation in the audience was visibly apparent and there was a feeling of crowd hysteria building.

He continued. 'After your refreshment break the girls will be matched again, the losers wrestling the losers and the winners wrestling the winners. This will again comprise of twelve matches over four sessions of three pairs at one time. Once again lasting a total time of about one hour.'

Karl walked to the side of the carpet and picked up his whip and said, 'The rules are simple. No biting, no scratching, no gouging and no quitting, and I will enforce this with my famous whip.

'By the time the wrestling is finished every girl will be completely exhausted. As the contest goes on, you can bid for the girl you would like to take to your room to finish off the process of breaking her in. Making a bid for a girl is simple. You will draw Felix's attention, he will come over to you and you will tell him your bid. He will mark the bid on the big board at the side of the hall. If the bid stands for two minutes without being bettered, the deal is made.'

Karl called out. 'Go and get the girls.'

While they were waiting, Karl brought out a pole fixed to a base plate; the pole stood vertically about one and a half metres high with a pointed spike sticking up from the end.

He went back to the side of the hall and carried a basket containing three cabbages on to the carpet.

The sound of the girls being herded along filtered into the great hall. Then suddenly into the hall shuffled twenty-four naked girls being shepherded by half a dozen men carrying menacing looking brush handles.

They were herded on to the carpet, blinking in the bright spotlights and each had their first names written on their backs in six different coloured indelible inks. The different colours designated the six wrestling teams.

Karl did not give the girls a chance to react to the situation. He shouted loudly, 'Watch carefully.' He took a cabbage and stuck it firmly on to the spike on the top of the vertical pole. He then walked along the line of trembling girls, looking directly into their faces and saying to them three times loudly, 'This cabbage represents your skin and flesh. This cabbage represents your skin and flesh. This cabbage represents your skin and flesh.'

He then took his whip and swung it in the same whipping motion that he had used on Fredrick the boiler man, only this time in a sideways backhand style.

The first lash of the nine heavy thongs tore about one third of the cabbage apart, leaving the rest hanging precariously on the spike. The second lash destroyed it completely, leaving the cabbage scattered in pieces across the carpet.

To reinforce the threat he repeated the demonstration with the other two cabbages and then threw the empty basket to the side of the hall.

He now clearly had the girls' undivided attention. Karl appeared to grow in stature and confidence, though he lacked neither. However, he was in his element and spoke loudly with menacing clarity.

'Right, girls! Into the annexe and sort out your teams – the first wrestling matches will begin in five minutes.'

Herr Shoemaker carried out a flip chart with a paper flip

pad attached. It was in the form of a table with vertical columns headed: Girl's name, Win or lose, Winning bid, and Winner of bidding.

The first six girls were pushed onto the mat.

They separated into pairs facing each other. Karl shouted, 'Ready, steady, go.' The six girls started to grapple, but it was not long before they were down on the plastic sheet covering the carpet. Often the wrestling pairs would collide with one another and become a confusion of naked bodies and limbs, much to the delight of the audience who shrieked and shouted.

Karl was kept busy trying to keep some semblance of order; he had designed this contest from his personal experience of forced rape. One girl would manage to get on top of the other, but in trying to reach back to abuse her victim she would become unbalanced and her opponent would throw her off. The wrestling matches tended to swing to and fro with one girl gaining the upper hand, then the same thing would happen to her and the other girl would be on top for a time.

Felix blew a whistle when ten minutes had elapsed and Karl got the girls to stop wrestling.

Herr Shoemaker asked the audience to decide who had won each match and recorded the results on his board.

At this early stage only two bids were made by two of the franchisees who had been to a previous gathering, and in each case the buyer bought a girl for one thousand Czech Crowns with no opposing bids. Herr Shoemaker recorded the buyer and the price paid on his board. Felix collected the payments.

The girls retired back to the annexe and two men came out with mops and buckets and quickly washed and dried the plastic sheet covering the carpet.

The franchisees and the three politicians were getting excited as they understood how the game worked and were already forming attachments to particular girls.

The next three matches went much the same way. However, at the end of these competitive bidding occurred with one girl being sold for 10,000 Czech Crowns.

At the end of the first four sessions Karl announced a half hour comfort break. The three politicians led the franchisees back to the annexe set up with the bar and indulged in a few drinks and much animated conversation.

When the half hour was up Herr Shoemaker quickly ushered them back to the great hall ready for the next twelve matches. These went much the same way as before except the bidding for the girls increased until the last girl went for an incredible 50,000 Czech Crowns.

At the end of the bidding all the girls were assembled still naked and clearly exhausted on the plastic-covered carpet.

Herr Shoemaker shouted out each girl's name, then the buyer's name and said, 'Come and take your prize away.' He repeated this for every girl and every buyer until there were none left.

Harold Szirtes, Imri Szirtes, Felix Hienmann, Karl Stonier and Martin Shoemaker made their way to the empty bar in the annexe and filled their glasses. Harold Szirtes said, 'The weekend has gone really well; these franchisees are very committed and it is important that we support them to improve their businesses.'

He continued speaking. 'Felix, you will give them your basic intelligence questionnaire to complete and return to you by post within one month.

'Karl, you will give them the Running a Prostitute guide. Martin, you will give them your Replace Paid Staff with Unpaid Staff Guide. Martin, you will also give them an invitation to return to a special business improvement gathering in three months' time. Make it clear to them that they will be able to purchase another girl to grow their business. Felix, remember to get good photographs of our politicians playing with the girls in their bedrooms.' The five of them remained in the bar with the brass band playing for a further hour.

None of the franchisees or the politicians made breakfast the following Sunday morning. The politicians staggered down between eleven and twelve and left immediately in their cars without eating. The twenty-one franchisees assembled in the great hall after breakfast at about 12.30, where Harold Szirtes addressed them for the last time before their departure with their newly purchased girls.

His inspirational talk was similar to his opening speech at the beginning of the weekend.

Harold picked up the sword from its stand and, holding it vertically in front of him, he declared loudly, 'The Sword of Attila the Hun. Ruler of the world. You will rule from a town sitting under a crown beyond the Pillars of Hercules. The House of Attila is rising again at this present time. This time we will rule the world and you will be part of our success and share in all its bounty.

'Gentlemen you have purchased a franchise from the House of Attila.

'You have committed yourselves together, bonded by the blood of the boiler man and traitor Fredrick. Remember, gentlemen, the biggest resource the House of Attila has is illegal immigrants. Their lives were in danger where they previously lived and the House of Attila finds them work and secure places to live. They can benefit your business by saving you wages.

'You are now destined to become warlords in your exclusive franchise area. You will respect the territories of other House of Attila franchisees and give your absolute allegiance to the House of Attila. Now go to your respective territories and with the support of the House of Attila begin to make a success of your business.'

16

Reunion with Prince

When Karl instructed: 'Nico, go and lose yourself for four hours and be sure not to return to the boiler house for at least four hours,' the threat was not lost on Nico and he had made his way over to the kitchen of the mansion house.

After helping Valda with the washing-up, a little while later he saw her carrying a large suitcase. He shouted to her, 'Are you leaving?' She looked up, laughed and said, 'No, I am not leaving.' She lowered her voice to almost a whisper. 'Imri has just given me an awful brow beating, complaining that I do not keep his room tidy enough. He really shouted at me that his room is full of junk. He told me that if I don't get it sorted he will get Karl to sell me off as a prostitute. I am so worried, I have heard stories about Karl that scare me to death. So I am trying to clear some of the stuff that has been lying in his room for ages. It is so hard to decide; some of it is brand new and has never been used. This case is full of football boots, football strips, track suits and football socks.'

Nico said, 'Let me see.' Valda opened the case and Nico picked out a training shoe. 'Size eight, that's my size.' He picked out several more, they were all size eight. He said, 'Valda, what are you going to do with them?'

She replied, 'I am going to put them in the big waste bin.'

Nico said, 'Can I have them and is there somewhere I can

hide them until I can take them to the boiler house as I have to stay away from there for four hours?'

Valda said, 'If you want them put them in this store room beside the waste bins and then you can take them away when you can.'

Nico said, 'Are you going to throw out any footballs?'

Valda looked surprised and said, 'Yes, how did you know that there were footballs on top of the wardrobes?'

Nico replied, 'I didn't know, just a hunch. If you don't mind, please put two or three footballs in the store and any carry bags that go with them.'

They put the suitcase in the store and returned to the kitchen. Nico noticed that the clock indicated five o'clock and he said, 'I need to stay here until eight o'clock.'

Valda said, 'There is plenty of soup and bread, help yourself, I need to go and clear more stuff out of Imri's room. I will put three balls and ball bags in the store.'

Nico helped himself to a plate of soup and some bread and cheese. He found a quiet annexe just off the kitchen, used as a vegetable store and preparation room. It had a table and four chairs and he sat on one to eat his meal and also to keep out of sight. When he finished the bowl of soup he went back to the kitchen and got a refill.

Although he could hear people coming and going to the kitchen, he stayed mostly where he was, only occasionally going to the kitchen to see the clock until the four hours were up.

Nico left his small vegetable annexe and began to make his way back to the boiler house. He saw Herr Shoemaker approaching as he passed the stables. Before he reached him, a stable-hand came running out of the stable door and shouted, 'Herr Shoemaker, you need to get rid of this crazy white horse. I can't do anything with him, he is as obstinate as a mule.'

When Nico heard this he knew that it could only be Prince

he was talking about. Herr Shoemaker said, 'OK, I will phone the slaughterhouse tomorrow, at least we will get something if only horse meat prices for him.'

Nico ran over and said, 'Herr Shoemaker, I noticed a couple of horse-drawn timber wagons in the big hay shed. If I could use this stubborn horse to pull one of the wagons back to the forest in the morning after setting up the boiler for the day, I could cut the logs, then use both horses to bring back a wagon full of logs each night and tend the boiler. You wouldn't need to send a lorry and you wouldn't need another boiler man.'

Nico held his breath but Herr Shoemaker's face broke into a huge smile and he said, 'I really like that idea, it's a lot of work for one person. Good that's what we will do.' He turned to the stable-hand and said, 'Do you know if the wagons are in good condition?'

The stable-hand said, 'Yes, they are in perfect condition; we used them both to pull Father Christmas and his presents through the town.'

Herr Shoemaker said, 'That's good. Nico, you can take one of the wagons tomorrow morning and I hope you can get the crazy horse to work for you.'

Nico said to the stable-hand, 'If you leave me to quietly settle the horse I think I can manage.' The stable-hand seemed pleased to get away and walked off towards some estate workers' cottages at the north end of the mansion house.

Nico went into the stable and saw Prince was out in the passageway; he walked quietly towards the horse, saying, 'Quiet, boy, everything is fine, everything is fine.' He took Prince's face in this hands and gave him a big hug, saying, 'Just settle down, everything is going to be fine.' Prince responded in his own way by nudging Nico with his nose, communicating the message, 'I am glad to see you too.' Nico led him to to his stall; he fetched some fresh water, oats and hay for his troughs and then found his grooming brush and started to rub him down.

Herr Shoemaker smiled as he quietly watched from the stable door, thinking to himself, 'There is something special about this boy.'

After he had finished with Prince, Nico went back to the store by the waste bins compound, retrieved the case of football gear and carried it back to the boiler house. He immediately noticed the high heat radiating from the still hot boiler. He quickly checked all the systems and realised that the boiler was all right but the refractory brick was holding the heat.

He hid the case of football gear in the large enclosed space at the base of the chimney. He went back to the storeroom and retrieved the three footballs complete with net bags and carried these to the hiding place in the base of the chimney.

He was pleasantly surprised when he explored Fredrick's old room. Valda had made a really good job of cleaning it out and putting clean bed clothes on the bed. She had also placed an alarm clock on the bedside table. He judged that it told roughly the right time.

Nico was ready for his bed; it had been a strange day and he dropped to his knees and said, 'Dear Father, I come before You in the name of Jesus to ask You to protect and to bless Maria, my sister. I thank You that I have been allowed to take Prince in hand. I thank You for Valda and her kindnesses. I ask You to protect me from the evil I feel in this place.'

'Oh! As an afterthought, bless Herr Shoemaker who seems to be helping me.'

He curled up and went immediately to sleep.

As usual Nico woke early. There was a bright full moon shining in the window. He looked at the alarm clock and saw that it was just five o'clock. He decided to go for a run and went through to the base of the chimney to get some gear from the suitcase. The temperature of the boiler was still a bit higher than normal, indicating the thickness of the refractory brick lining. He opened the suitcase and selected a track suit, a pair of shorts, a T-shirt, a pair of socks and a pair of training shoes. He took them to his room and dressed for his run.

He checked the boiler, loaded the fire bed with four logs and closed the fire doors after he saw the logs catching alight from the heat radiated by the refractory brick.

Nico came out of the warm boiler house into a cold and frosty morning. There was about twenty millimetres of snow lying on the ground. The sky was clear of clouds and he could see myriad stars and the full moon illuminated the road. He followed the road out to the forest, running at a medium comfortable pace. Although he had not been able to train for a few weeks he felt very comfortable.

When he arrived at the log cabin he immediately went round to the stable to see if Charlie was OK. He greeted Charlie with a few light pats then he gave him a good rub under his chin. He said, 'How are you doing, Charlie? Have you missed me? I see you still have food and water.'

He put a bridle on Charlie and took him out for a short walk in the snow. After the short walk Nico put the harness and chain on Charlie and fastened it to the sledge and they made their way to where they had last been cutting trees.

Nico quickly loaded four logs on to the sledge and they pulled them over the snow-covered track to the roadside pile of logs waiting transportation.

Nico said, 'Charlie, the snow makes it so easy that it would be a pity to pass this opportunity up.' Charlie looked sideways at Nico and snorted as if to say, 'Don't you know it's Sunday, it's my day of rest.' Nico laughed. 'Come on, you lazy lump, we will move the whole stack, in these conditions it will take us less than an hour.' Nico just wanted to use the opportunity for physical training, lifting each log weighing approximately fifty kilograms was good exercise in itself, but Nico used each log to strengthen his thighs, calves and feet muscles to the maximum.

They pulled the last four logs over to the pile at the roadside and Nico said, 'I told you it would not take long.' Charlie responded with an appropriate sceptical and withering look. They made their way back to the stable and Nico unharnessed Charlie and led him back to his stall. He got a barrow and a shovel and cleaned out Charlie's stall, giving him the odd shove as he worked round him.

He cleaned out the two food troughs and refilled them with fresh hay and oats. He then emptied the water bucket, cleaned it and filled it with fresh water.

He cleaned out the other stall ready for Prince, talking all the time to Charlie and telling him he was going to get a new friend.

He said goodbye to Charlie, saying, 'I will see you first thing in the morning and you be ready to pull a timber cart.'

He shut the stable door, checked out his log cabin and, satisfied that everything was OK, he began running back.

He arrived back at the House of Attila at nine o'clock in the morning. There was no sign of movement on the outside of the back of the house. He went to the boiler house and collected his working clothes. He made his way to the stables. He could see from the undisturbed snow that no one had entered the stables recently.

Stopping for a moment to pat and greet Prince, he made his way into the changing rooms used by the hunting party on Saturdays. He stripped off and showered, using the luxury soaps and shampoos. He washed out the shower cubicle, dried himself off and changed into his working clothes and boots.

He took his used training clothing and put it in a laundry bag and put the training shoes back in the suitcase in the cavity at the base of the chimney.

Nico walked over to the kitchen of the mansion house and found the kitchen and serving staff eating breakfast. Valda looked up with a big smile and said, 'Good morning, Nico, help yourself to some breakfast.'

Nico said, 'Thank you and good morning to you.' He filled a bowl with porridge and milk and found a corner of the big table and ate it.

He filled a plate with four slices of buttered toast and sat down to eat them. When he finished eating he poured a large mug of tea, added some milk and sat down to drink it. When he finished, he said, 'Thank you, girls, it is much appreciated.' He made his way back to the boiler house.

Nico noticed that the snow had stopped and the sun had come out. He decided to unload the logs from the lorry and stack them in the boiler house. As he was finishing the job, Herr Shoemaker came out of the house, walked over to Nico and said, 'Well done, Nico. You have been working hard this morning.'

Nico said, 'Yes I will stoke up the boiler and then take the white horse and cart to the forest log cabin and stable and then run back to tend the boiler tonight. The two horses will be at the forest ready for work tomorrow morning and I can run there as soon as it gets light.'

Herr Shoemaker said, 'Well, I am surprised by your energy, but it suits me very well to have such a good worker.'

Nico then stocked up the boiler with three logs and closed the fire door fully shut, checked that his room was tidy, noticing that the clock was indicating 1.30, then he went to the kitchen of the mansion house and spoke to the girls who gave him soup and bread, which he ate and then he went to the stables to get Prince.

The stable-hand who had complained about Prince was there. Nico told him, 'I am taking him to the forest to work, but I will need two empty stalls each night for the two horses I will be using to bring a cart full of logs back.'

The stable-hand said, 'That's fine, there are plenty of empty stalls, I hope you get on better with him than I did.'

Nico then put a bridle on Prince and led him out and round to the big hay shed.

The timber carts were designed for two horses to pull, however, when empty, one horse could easily manage to pull it on flat terrain; they were strongly constructed flat beds with log retaining sides running on four big timber wheels with wide heat-shrunk steel rims.

Nico carefully inspected several harnesses before finally selecting one. He fitted it on to Prince and then backed him slowly into the shafts, fastening them in place. He loaded the other harnesses, half a dozen coils of rope and some other equipment on to the cart.

Nico then led Prince, pulling the large, flat-bed cart over to the stables; he went in and said to the stable-hand, 'I need some horse feed for the horses in the forest.'

The stable-hand said, 'Yes, come and I will give you a hand.'

They soon loaded the feed. Nico led Prince over to the boiler house and he said to the horse, 'Just wait until I get my training gear and some spare clothing.'

Once he had everything loaded they started off with Nico walking beside Prince pulling the almost empty flat-bed cart along the road towards the forest log cabin. Walking slowly because of the snow, they reached the cabin in about one and a half hours. Nico said to Prince, 'I hope you realise that I am doing this to keep us together. Now that I have found you, all I have to do is find Maria and, God willing, we will.'

Nico settled Prince in the stable stall beside Charlie, taking care to introduce them to each other. He also made sure they were well provided with feed and water.

He then went to the log cabin and changed out of his working gear and into his training gear. He closed up the cabin and began to run back to the House of Attila. In the snowy conditions he took about forty minutes.

As he approached the mansion house he saw the bus leaving followed by a cavalcade of cars. As they drove past he noticed Imri Szirtes looking intently at him out of one of the cars.

The cavalcade had just come from the final session of the weekend where Harold Szirtes had given the franchisees their business building objectives for the next three months. The franchisees were leaving with the girls that they had purchased, taking them back to their respective hotels to put them to work.

17

The Challenge

By the Sunday morning the rumours were sweeping the House of Attila that there had been a real manhunt and that Fredrick the boiler man had paid dearly for his treachery.

When the weekend guests had left the gathering, Freda and her girls cleaned up all the rooms, including renewing all the bed linen ready for new guests. During her work supervising the girls Freda happened to look out of a bedroom window overlooking the front entrance to the mansion house. She suddenly stopped what she was about to do and went to the window. She watched first Ramana being pulled forcibly into the back seat of a car, the man inside the car obviously holding her tightly so that she could not move. Another man, holding what appeared to be a syringe, took hold of her arm and appeared to inject her. The man in the car held her for a minute or two and then Ramana seemed to go limp and the man laid her across the back seat of the car, tucking her arms and legs in before shutting both rear doors. Almost immediately Lillie was dragged out of the mansion house and again pulled into a second car, where the same treatment awaited her. The two cars drove off and joined the back of the cavalcade of cars coming from the rear of the mansion house. They disappeared along the drive towards the road.

Freda felt a cold constriction about her heart as she

watched the cars dwindle in the distance and she visualised the two powerless girls lying in the back of the cars driven by cruel and ruthless men.

When they were all finished cleaning up, the staff had dinner together. When the meal was over Freda stood up and thanked them all for their hard work and excellent service. She added, 'You may not get your reward in this age of men, but there is always hope of a better world to come.'

The bus arrived and Freda and the girls she had brought with her got on with their overnight bags. The bus drove off to waves, shouts and whistles from the girls who were the permanent staff at the House of Attila.

Arriving back at Harold Szirtes' hotel in town, Freda was so pleased to find everything going smoothly and in good order. When the last customers left and the kitchen was cleaned Freda said to Maria. 'Let's have a cup of tea to ourselves.'

When they had poured the tea and buttered some toast Freda said, 'Well done, Maria, you seem to have done a very good job with very few staff. Did everything really go all right?'

Maria replied, 'All the staff worked very hard and they deserve the credit, which reminds me, I was given this five thousand Czech Crowns tip by a customer on Saturday evening. He would not let me refuse and I did not know what to do with it, so I kept it until you came back.'

Freda said, 'The rules of the hotel are that staff can keep tips given by customers.'

Maria said, 'I would like it to be shared among all the girls in the hotel.'

She handed the money to Freda.

Freda replied, 'That is very generous of you, I will see that they all get an equal share including yourself.'

Maria cried out, 'And you!'

Freda said, 'No, I actually get a small salary, which proves that it is possible for some of us to rise up, even if it's only a little in this unfair man's world.' Her voice betrayed her bitterness at the end of the statement.

She broke into tears saying, 'Oh! Maria. I need to tell someone, terrible things went on at the House of Attila at the weekend. It seems that there was a man hunted to his death. I also saw Ramana and Lillie physically forced into two cars, drugged and driven away and I don't think I will ever see them again.'

There was not much that Maria could say but Freda seemed to get relief from being able to tell someone. They finished their tea and toast and retired to bed.

Things at the hotel fell quickly into their routine during the week; however, Harold Szirtes and Karl paid a visit on the Saturday evening. During their meal Harold sent for Maria to come to his table. When she approached he said, 'Sit down at the table until I tell you what I want you to do.' He continued. 'There is a winter-snow sculpting festival on in three weeks' time. There are also competitions for the preparation and cooking of traditional foods at the festival. The reason it includes the preparation and cooking, is to stop the professionals cheating by bringing ready prepared foods; they have to prepare the dishes from very basic traditional ingredients strictly supplied by the organisers. I want my hotel to win a prize for traditional foods.

'I want you to prepare to compete in this competition, I have here an envelope containing all the details and application forms for all the competitions.

'Enter the competition in the name of the Harold Szirtes Hotel. I will drive you to the event on the Saturday morning, the competition takes place through the afternoon and we will drive back with the prize in the evening to celebrate here in the hotel on the Saturday night.' He handed Maria a big envelope with a big smile on his face, saying, 'I have every confidence in you; now on you go and prepare to win.'

Maria retired to the kitchen very apprehensive about the prospects of being expected to win. What would his reaction be if she did not win? It was too scary to even think about.

18

The Football Team

Arriving at the House of Attila after running the four miles from the forest log cabin, Nico first checked out the boiler house and the boiler. The fire had lasted as he expected and he added two new logs to the fire and closed the fire door. He checked the water temperatures and they were fine. He climbed up to the water head tanks and checked that the water ballcocks were working properly.

Satisfied that the boiler was OK, he selected a change of underwear and socks and went over to the stables. There was no one in the changing rooms as all the guests had gone and it was late Sunday afternoon. He enjoyed a good hot shower, dressed in his fresh underwear, track suit and trainers.

He made his way over to the mansion house kitchens and was surprised no one was about. He presumed that they were resting after their hard weekend. He was starving and was more concerned with finding food than people. He looked in one of the big refrigerators and saw there were plenty of leftovers from the big social gathering. He selected some leftover chicken, four slices of bread and a mug of milk, which he quickly consumed.

Then he made several sandwiches, some filled with chicken and some filled with boiled ham. He took several tomatoes, an onion and several hard-boiled eggs. He carefully wrapped them in plastic bags and put them in a plastic carry bag.

He found a newspaper, made a mug of tea and spent about half an hour reading the paper.

He felt really good after his run and the physical work cutting and loading timber. Loading, unloading, carrying the logs was all good exercise for his upper body strength.

He went back to the boiler house and put the plastic carry bag with the sandwiches into the small fridge in his room.

He then went to the cavity under the chimney and got out one of the footballs. He had previously noticed that there was street lighting in the car park at the back of the mansion house and it came on every night as it began to get dark.

He took the football out to the now empty car park and began to dribble about with it on the area clear of snow where the visitors' cars had been parked.

He played on his own for about twenty minutes then two of the estate workers came out of their houses and asked if they could join in. Within a further five minutes three more estate workers came out and they decided to play three-a-side.

They played hard for about an hour then finally someone said next goal was the winner. They finished in high spirits and someone suggested going to the kitchen to get some tea and sandwiches.

Several of the cooking and cleaning staff were in the kitchen and they all sat round the big kitchen table with tea and toast and swapping banter.

The overshadowing topic was what had happened to Fredrick the boiler man. The general knowledge was that he had come to a sticky end, but the stable-hands were not keen to say what they knew.

The two stable-hands who had treated his wounds resulting from the cruel whipping, described the wounds in graphic detail, but when one of the girls asked if Karl had inflicted the beating, the two men suddenly clammed up. Despite further probing the men were scared that they had said too much already.

THE HOUSE OF ATTILA

Some of the male estate workers who had been serving meals and drinks were conscripted to help control the naked wrestlers when they became difficult. They were only too keen to describe the glimpses of the naked wrestling that they had seen and how they had to physically restrain some of the girls who were proving difficult behind the scenes. Their audience was only too willing to hear every exaggerated claim and cried for more and more detail.

They were all enjoying themselves so much that they were surprised to hear the big clock chime eleven o'clock. Laughing and joking, they all got up and washed their individual plates and mugs, reluctantly making their way to their homes and bedrooms for a good night's sleep.

Nico woke before his alarm clock in the morning. He got up and dressed in his running gear. He checked the boiler systems, raked out the fire bed and ash pit, loaded four logs into the fire and shut the fire door. He was confident with no guests in the mansion house that the four logs with the fire door shut would last until he returned.

Nico put his sandwiches in a small backpack and locked his room before stepping outside. It was a cold, frosty morning and Nico ran at a good moderate pace despite the slippy conditions.

Nico soon arrived at the log cabin, unlocked the door, went in and put on the kettle. He made a mug of tea and ate two of his sandwiches, a boiled egg and a tomato. After changing into his working clothes and boots, he went round the stables. As he approached the horses, he started speaking. 'Hello, you two, you seem to be quite comfortable in here. But you have to work for your keep.' He patted Prince first, giving him a hug. 'I see you have plenty of food and water left.' Nico then gave Charlie a pat and said, 'You first, Charlie.' He put the harness on, then the bridle, and hooked the chain to the sledge. Nico loaded his working tools on to the sledge, then fuel and finally his personal protective equipment. They made their way dragging the sledge to the next work area.

Nico worked steadily, felling, trimming and cutting timber. When he had accumulated twelve logs he loaded four on to the sledge and Charlie dragged the sledge out to the timber cart at the side of the road. He repeated the dragging until twelve logs were loaded on to the timber cart.

Nico took Charlie back to the stables. He went in to the cabin, made a mug of tea and ate more of his food.

Nico then repeated the same work process with Prince. When they finished, he tied Prince to the now loaded timber cart and went back to the cabin.

Nico was ready for the rest of his food, washed down with another mug of tea. He changed back into his running gear, put on the army great coat over it, locked the cabin and made his way round to the stable. He brought Charlie out, closed the stable door and led Charlie round to the timber wagon. Talking all the time, he backed Charlie into the shaft and harnessed him in, then he untied Prince and, talking to him, slowly backed him into position on the other side of the shaft and fastened the harness.

Satisfied everything was OK, he knocked out the shaft supporting timbers and the weight of the shaft slowly settled through the harnesses equally on to both horses. He put the shaft shoring timbers onto the cart.

Nico then went round to the front and slowly encouraged the two horses to walk forward. He buttoned up his great coat collar and began to sing a Serbian folk song – 'Saddling a Horse'. Both Charlie and Prince looked at each other as if to say 'Oh! Here we go again.' They soon settled into a comfortable pace.

The two horses seemed to be compatible, and easily pulled the loaded timber cart. They arrived at the boiler house about mid afternoon. Nico parked the horses and wedged the wheels with the four timber wedges that were hanging by light chains from the sides of the cart at each of the four wheels.

Speaking all the time to both horses, he wedged in the shoring props under main shaft until they bore the weight of the shaft.

He loosened the harness on Charlie and led him round to the drinking trough and tied him there. He then loosened the harness on Prince and walked him to the drinking trough. He allowed the horses to drink and then put them in their stalls and gave them sufficient food and water.

As he came out of the stables one of the stable-hands shouted to him, 'Do you feel like another game of football tonight?'

Nico shouted back, 'Yes, I will see you out the back about half past six.' He made his way back to the boiler house and unloaded the logs. He was pleased with his work, because by managing the fire well and the efficiency of the sledge he was building up a surplus of logs and had now started to build a big pile, which he kept covered with a big tarpaulin.

Nico made his way over to the kitchen and found Valda. He asked her, 'Valda, what's that nice smell?'

Valda laughed and said, 'Yes, I have special soup tonight, ham and pea soup. It is special because it is made with a whole ham shank. The master of the hounds was training two of his young hounds up on the ridge above the quarry. The hounds startled a young wild boar in the woods and the two hounds chased it to the very edge of the quarry. The boar was facing them off on the edge and lost its footing. When they made their way down the young boar was dead.

'The master of the hounds managed to get it over his horse and brought it to me and asked me to help him butcher it. He gave me a whole ham shank to make the soup with.

'Help yourself and there is newly baked bread in the bread bin.'

Nico went over to the large catering-sized soup container simmering on the hotplate.

The soup was everything that Valda had claimed and the new wholemeal bread was beautiful. After the first bowl Nico had to stop himself from going for more and eating too much as he wanted to play football. He made a big mug of tea and contented himself with that and sat back to let it all go down.

When the clock neared half past six, Nico said, 'Thanks, Valda, your soup and bread was really lovely.' He left the kitchen and made his way to the boiler house and changed into his football training kit. He checked the boiler and put two new logs on the fire and closed the fire door. He collected the football and went out to the rear car park. The five estate workers were already waiting for him and they soon had the three-a-side game going.

It wasn't until they finished playing that they noticed Herr Shoemaker and Imri watching them from a distance. Imri walked over to Nico and said, 'Where did you learn to play football like that and what age are you?'

Nico replied, 'At school, and I am fourteen.'

Imri said, 'I am fifteen and I play with my father's under sixteens team. We train Tuesday and Thursday evenings. I am centre forward and the way you can cross a ball from the wing would set up many goals for me. The wingers we have got just now are hopeless. Herr Shoemaker will pick up the two of us here at six o'clock tomorrow evening. Do not be late.' Imri turned and left without waiting for an answer.

The following day Nico worked all day, elated with anticipation about the football training, and was ready dressed in his training kit when Herr Shoemaker turned up driving a Mercedes.

Imri got into the front passenger seat so Nico got into the back seat. Herr Shoemaker drove off. They drove to the nearby town and parked at a couple of football pitches with a small complex of changing rooms with showers and toilets.

They went into the changing rooms and Herr Shoemaker simply introduced Nico by saying, 'This is Nico, he will be training with us until we see what he is like. Now get ready, we are going to do an hour's training, then one hour's football.'

Nico was already changed so he went outside. The pitches were between two main roads. Because they were in the city both roads had high street lights giving the football pitches plenty of light.

Although Nico was only fourteen years of age he found the training fairly easy. He did not want to stand out so he stayed in the middle of the pack. When they finished the training session two teams were picked. One by Imri and one by Herr Shoemaker. Imri had first pick and picked Nico. As the two teams assembled in their respective halves Imri said to Nico, 'You play on the left wing and try to get some good crosses in to me to score.'

Nico played well, getting several good crosses into Imri who managed to convert two of them into goals.

Generally the standard of play was less than Nico was used to with his school team because there was less tactical sense about the play. Most of the players tended to chase the ball and it was more of a dribbling game, going first one way and then the other.

After training Herr Shoemaker drove Imri and Nico back to the House of Attila. He parked the car at the front of the house and said, 'See you both on Thursday, same place, same time.'

He and Imri went in the front door and Nico went round to the back. He nipped into the kitchen. There was no one about as it was eleven o'clock and the girls had gone to bed. He made fresh sandwiches and wrapped them in plastic bags for his work tomorrow. Then he made two sandwiches which he ate hungrily. He then made his way to the boiler house and put two new logs in the fire, closed the fire door and went to bed.

Wednesday and Thursday went by quickly for Nico now that efficient work routines had been established and he had something to look forward to.

Herr Shoemaker picked the boys up and the training followed the same pattern.

When Herr Shoemaker parked the car after the training at the front of the House of Attila he said, 'We are playing away on Saturday; I will get the bus to stop at the front gate at eleven thirty in the morning on its way to town.'

Imri did not wait but rushed in the front door. Herr Shoemaker followed him but turned round and said, 'Nico, you will be substitute on Saturday.'

Nico's heart jumped for joy. He thought, 'Substitute, that's a chance for me.'

Nico was glad now that he had been building up a reserve of logs. On Friday he loaded thirty-six logs on to the cart and brought them back.

On the Friday evening he took out a pair of football boots he had salvaged from Imri's room clearance. They were brand new and obviously unused. Nico could see they were expensive boots, lightweight and made of the softest of leather. He put on a pair of football socks and pulled the boots on. He walked about then fastened the laces and went out for a run across grassy parkland, breaking into an occasional sprint. They were a good fit and he was delighted with them.

The Saturday morning passed quickly and the bus turned up as expected. They picked up the other players in town, then the bus made for their destination. They arrived at a football ground and they were shown into a dressing-room. Herr Shoemaker read out the team selection, naming Nico one of two substitutes. The team changed into their strips and boots. Herr Shoemaker gave Nico and the other substitute track suits to wear over their strips.

The referee came in and said in a loud voice, 'I am very strict on foul play and foul language, so if you get booked or sent off it's entirely your own fault. Now go out and play a good clean game.'

The game started and was played at a fast pace, going from one end to the other. Nico noted that it was a bit like the training games with most of the players chasing the ball. Both teams had several chances but neither team converted them into goals.

The game was still goalless at half-time when the teams gathered on the side lines at opposite sides of the park. Herr Shoemaker was furious and shouting at several players about lack of commitment. Imri threw a tantrum and shouted, 'How can you expect me to score with these two wingers, they are hopeless – I did not get a decent ball the whole of the first half.'

One of the wingers made a lunge at Imri shouting, 'You useless bastard, you couldn't kick a haystack if it was put right in front of you.' The other players pulled him off before he could hit Imri.

Imri shouted at Herr Shoemaker, 'Get him off.'

Herr Shoemaker was a bit taken aback and hesitated, but then he said to the offending player, 'You are out of order. Goran, go back to the dressing-room and get changed.' He turned to Nico and said, 'Nico, get stripped. You are on.'

Imri said, 'Nico, you had better be better than him, I didn't get a decent ball the whole of the first half.'

Herr Shoemaker turned to the team and said, 'This game is there for the taking, but you have to take it. I keep telling you, in this life it's survival of the fittest. No one remembers who came second. Now go and win this game.'

* * *

The game started and continued as it had in the first half with everyone chasing the ball. Nico lay wide on the left wing hoping that someone would notice and give him a ball. It was his goalkeeper who noticed first and gave him two good balls; on both occasions he managed to get behind the defence and cut a ball back to Imri. But Imri was struggling for fitness and fluffed the chance both times.

It was close to full time when the third ball came out to Nico from midfield; he sprinted past the fullback and cut in towards the goal but Imri had given up.

He cut across the penalty area, looking for someone from his own team but there was no one running. He turned back to avoid a tackle and then spun round, trying to get a shot away, when the big centre half hit him with a two-footed tackle. Nico just managed to jump off the ground before the impact or he probably would have suffered a broken leg.

The referee immediately blew for a penalty kick. Imri came puffing up and grabbed the ball. He placed the ball on the penalty spot and walked back. He started to run a curious weaving run, trying to deceive the goalkeeper. He got into a bit of a muddle and as a result struck the ball weakly. The keeper dived too far, but because the ball was travelling so slowly, he managed to recover enough while still lying on his side to kick the ball away with his foot. Nico was the fastest to react and quickly went for the ball, passing it neatly away from the keeper sprawled on the ground and into the far corner of the net.

The team dived on Nico, celebrating the goal, and when they finally restarted the game, the referee immediately blew for time.

In the dressing-room after the game Herr Shoemaker was beaming like a lighthouse. Imri took a lot of stick from the team and two of them kept acting out the penalty and save in slow motion much to the amusement of the other players.

Herr Shoemaker said quietly to Nico, 'Well done, you played really well today; you will play from the start of the game next Saturday.'

The next week went well for Nico. He had the logging and the boiler house running like clockwork and had a full week's reserve of logs piled up under the cover behind the boiler house. It was as if Charlie and Prince had known each other all their lives, and as often as he could Nico would let them frolic freely in the big paddock beside the stables.

Valda, who was the same age as Nico, had developed a very friendly relationship with him, and they really enjoyed each other's company.

The Saturday came round very quickly and the football team were playing at home. Herr Shoemaker drove Imri and Nico to the football ground, which was a field on the outskirts of town. It was said that Harold Szirtes had won the field in a poker game and had turned it into a football ground for his boy Imri.

In one corner of the field was a car park with a small complex of changing rooms each equipped with toilets and shower rooms.

The playing surface was well maintained and the snow had been removed by the gang of estate workers from the House of Attila. The field had been lined using black sand, which contrasted well with the remaining thin layer of snow.

Herr Shoemaker was as usual a bag of highly strung nerves. There was almost total silence and a tension as he read out the team.

Nico was named in the left wing position and he found his number eleven strip hanging on the clothes peg. He quickly changed into his football kit and listened to Herr Shoemaker's instructions.

As they made their way out to the football pitch Imri sidled up to him and said, 'Right, boiler man, remember your position, your whole job is to feed me with crosses.'

As before, the game started fast and furious with the players of both teams chasing the ball and the game going from one end to the other and from one side of the field to the other, leaving big gaps.

Nico patiently filled the gap on his side of the field, making himself available for passes. Slowly his team began to recognise his movement off the ball and started to play him into the game. Initially he played a pure passing game, trying to get his team to keep the ball and so denying the other team.

Herr Shoemaker walked round the line to where Nico was playing most of his football and shouted, 'Nico, it is ten minutes to half-time, I want you to try a couple of runs up the wing and get a cross in to Imri before half-time.'

Nico managed three good wing runs, finishing with three good balls across the goal. Imri managed to get on the end of two of them and score two goals. The referee blew for half-time.

Imri was full of it at half-time and was not listening to anyone. Herr Shoemaker said, 'Nico, more of the same in the second half; get up that wing right from the start.'

The second half started, Nico did as instructed and within five minutes of the start he put a perfect ball on to Imri's head for his hat trick.

The game slowly deteriorated and Imri had to be substituted because he had slowed up due to his lack of fitness. The other team slowly got the upper hand and pulled two goals back before the end of the game.

Herr Shoemaker was ecstatic with the win even though they had only just scraped home. Of course Imri took all the credit.

Imri got into the front of the car with Herr Shoemaker and Nico got into the back seat. Herr Shoemaker started the car and said, 'I need to make a short detour to see Harold at the hotel, the meeting won't take long.'

Imri said, 'It had better not, I am starving.'

Shoemaker pulled up at the imposing front door of a large hotel and quickly ran inside.

Imri started to sing. 'Imri scored a hat trick. Imri scored a hat trick.' Over and over again.

Nico casually glanced out of the car window and noticed the brass nameplate with the fancy inscription – The Harold Szirtes Hotel. Herr Shoemaker reappeared after about fifteen minutes and ran back to the car. Imri changed the words of his song to. 'Imri's starving. Imri's starving.' Herr Shoemaker started the car and began to drive away. Nico suddenly sat bolt upright, his whole being tense as though electrified. As they passed the road leading to the hotel car park, he had caught sight of a girl putting something into waste bins at the side of the hotel.

He knew that girl was Maria, he would know her anywhere. Nico wanted to shout, 'Stop the car.' But he caught himself in time. Imri was still chanting, but Nico did not hear him. His head was swimming with adrenalin and joy, but he clamped his mouth shut, folded his arms very tightly and took deep, slow breaths until he calmed down.

19
The Award

Back in the kitchen Maria finished supervising the cleaning up, thanked Lette and Mary and told them they could go to bed. Freda came in for her end of day cup of tea and a chat. Maria said, as she placed two cups of tea and a plate of toast on the table, 'I have something to tell you.' She looked at Freda and said, 'I was summoned to Harold Szirtes' table tonight.'

Freda exclaimed, 'Oh! No. That can be dangerous.'

Maria continued, 'He gave me this envelope of information and entry forms for the winter snow-sculpting festival. He wants me to enter in the name of the Harold Szirtes Hotel and win an award in the traditional cooking competition.'

Freda said, 'Open the envelope and let us see what it is about.'

Maria read through the fairly short information pack. When she finished, Freda said, 'Read out the list of ingredients they are going to supply and I will write them down.' Freda got a notepad and pen.

Maria read out the list. 'Potatoes, cabbages, turnips, carrots, parsnips, onions, leeks, rice, parsley, sweet paprika, red peppers, green peppers, beef mince, pork mince, liver, meat bones, beef stock, eggs, salt, black pepper, celeriac, olive oil, plain flour, oatmeal, lard, suet, sour cream, mint, thyme, basil, nutmeg, mace.'

Freda said, 'Is that everything?' Maria nodded.

'Your favourite dish is Mecsek Highwaymen's Dumpling Soup. Can you make it out of those ingredients?'

Maria said, 'I think I should have everything I need.'

'There isn't anything difficult in the preparation is there?' asked Freda.

Maria said, 'No, not really.'

Freda smiled and said, 'Good, that's the number one entry sorted. Tomorrow night we will plan the second entry. Now let's get to bed.'

The following night when all the work was done Freda and Maria met for their wind-down tea and toast. Freda got her list of supplied ingredients and said, 'Now we need a second entry just in case your first does not win first prize.'

Maria said: 'One dish that my mother and I had success with was Serbian stuffed peppers.'

Freda said, 'OK, what do you need for them?'

Maria said, 'Six to eight red peppers, depending on size. One cup of rice. Two to three potatoes depending on size. Two carrots. Two onions. One tablespoon of chopped parsley. Two tablespoons of plain flour ...' And so on ...

They discussed the preparations and ingredients in detail until they were both satisfied they had what they needed.

Freda said, 'Right, that's us; we know what you are doing now. Tomorrow night we will fill in the entry forms and get them posted.'

Maria smiled and said, 'Thank you, Freda, I was so worried about this.'

Freda said, 'No worries, you will now offer these two dishes as a chef's special on the menu in order to allow you to practise preparing the two of them together as many times as possible before the competition. Now let's get to bed.'

* * *

The following night Freda and Maria filled out the entry forms and addressed the envelope ready for posting in the morning.

The three weeks passed very quickly and the two dishes became the favourites among the dining clientele. Harold Szirtes gave Freda extra money to get Maria nice clothing and a full chef's catering outfit. He said, 'Half the battle is won in the presentation.'

With Karl driving and Harold Szirtes sitting beside him and Maria sitting in the back seat, they started off at six o'clock in the morning in order to get to the competitor registration at twelve o'clock.

They arrived at the ancient market town just on eleven o'clock and parked in a hotel car park. When they entered the hotel they were warmly greeted by the hotel owner who obviously knew Harold Szirtes and Karl. The hotel was ideally placed, facing on to the public park where the snow festival was taking place.

They all went into the manager's office. Karl said, 'Change into your chef's uniform.'

Maria said, 'Is there somewhere private?'

Karl laughed and said, 'Oh! My goodness we have a shy one here. I think I will need to educate you.'

Harold Szirtes intervened. 'Not now, control yourself; we have to register for the competition. Maria, just get ready for the competition.'

Maria changed as discreetly as possible with Karl leering at her.

When Maria was ready, with Harold Szirtes leading the way, they made their way into the park. It was an amazing sight with large mounds of clean fresh snow that had been brought in by dump trucks that very morning. They made their way over to a group of marquees in the centre of the

THE HOUSE OF ATTILA

public park and found one with a sign saying, 'Traditional Cooking Competitions'.

Maria registered at the entrance and she was given a numbered armband with the number five to wear; she was then taken to the competitor's area.

This was the first competition without her mother being present, and although she looked very professional in her chef's uniform, Maria felt very nervous. She took slow deep breaths to calm herself.

The competitors were given a full induction and an individual copy of the rules. They were fairly basic, stipulating a two hour time limit; only the ingredients provided to be used; preparation and cooking utensils to be taken from the large supply; work to be carried out exclusively at your own sink-worktop and cooker.

There was a giant clock set up in the highest part of the marquee and the competition was started on the stroke of 2 p.m. However, the time limit was very comfortable for Maria's two recipes.

Maria started by collecting the preparation and cooking utensils she needed for the Serbian stuffed peppers. Then she collected the utensils for the soup.

She then gathered all the ingredients for both dishes.

Now she felt in control for the first time.

She checked her utensils and ingredients and double-checked them again and her nerves began to settle.

Maria then began to prepare the Serbian stuffed peppers as these had a longer cooking time.

Time flew and Maria's two dishes came to perfection as the clock approached four o'clock.

The judges made their way along the competitors' workstations, spooning samples into paper cups and tasting them. They spoke together at one end of the row of competitors and then they all approached first one workstation, then another. Then they all came to Maria's workstation; they sampled and tasted and finally stood in a circle conferring deeply. Three of the judges came back to Maria's workstation and first sampled the Serbian stuffed peppers and then the soup. They then rejoined the circle of judges.

After several minutes one of the judges took hold of the microphone of the public address system and said, 'The third prize for traditional soup goes to competitor number two.' There was applause while the woman, a farmer, collected her medal and plaque. 'Second prize for traditional soup goes to competitor number thirteen.' A chef from the Prague Hotel, and again there was applause as the man collected his medal and plaque.

Maria was ridged with tension and the man seemed to take forever, but he finally said, 'And the overall winner for traditional soup is competitor number five from the Harold Szirtes Hotel.'

Maria's head was in a whirl and she checked her armband just to make sure of her number. She began to walk forward. The applause seemed to fill the marquee. The man was wearing a great chain of office; it was made of gold and the light seemed to sparkle off its many reflective surfaces. He placed a medal round Maria's neck and kissed her on each cheek. He then lifted a large, highly polished wooden shield with lots of little silver shields to take winners' names set into the wood. 'Bring it back to me at the end of the presentations and I will engrave it for you.'

One of the judges carried the big shield back to Maria's workstation for her.

The judge on the microphone continued. 'Now we come to the prizes for traditional meals. Third prize goes to competitor number one from the Sajam Hotel.' There was applause when the woman collected her medal and plaque.

THE HOUSE OF ATTILA

'Second prize goes to competitor number fourteen from the Emmaus Community.' There was much applause and cheering when the man collected his medal and plaque.

The judge on the microphone said, 'And the overall winner for traditional meals is again competitor number five from the Harold Szirtes Hotel.'

Maria was overcome with emotion so Harold Szirtes came over to her. He said, 'Are you all right, Maria?' He signalled to Karl to come over. Harold then went up to the judge and collected the medal and a huge cup. The judge said, 'You can take the medal but you have to leave the cup to be engraved.'

Maria had fainted so Karl picked her up and carried her out of the marquee and over to the hotel. He went in to the empty manager's office. She was still unconscious so he quickly laid her on the large desk. He stripped off the chef's uniform and looked at her with only her underwear. He quickly removed her underwear and dropped his trousers and underpants. Harold Szirtes came into the hotel at that moment. The manager's office door was partly open and he saw Karl with his trousers at his ankles leaning over the naked Maria, who was beginning to regain consciousness.

Harold shouted, 'Karl can you not stop thinking about your prick for one minute. We have things to do.' Karl was sexually aroused and his primitive instincts were predominant. He turned and faced Harold with a snarl. Harold, used to being top dog for so long, was unused to any form of challenge from his employees. The red mist came down. He swung the medal he was holding by its neck band and struck Karl right on the end of his erect dick with the heavy cast-metal medal.

Karl collapsed on the floor moaning with pain.

While this confrontation was going on Maria slipped down off the desk and began putting her underwear on. Harold Szirtes then turned to her and helped her find her normal street clothing and she dressed herself.

Karl was still lying on the floor holding his sore dick, which had shrivelled up and was almost invisible.

Harold Szirtes kicked him quite hard saying, 'Get up and pull up your trousers before anyone sees you.' Karl, with difficulty, managed to get up and pulled up his underpants and trousers just before the hotel manager came into his office.

Harold Szirtes said to the hotel manager, 'The excitement was just too much for Maria here and she fainted, we used your office to let her recover. We need to go back to the marquee now to collect our trophies. We will be back in a couple of hours. Karl, Maria, come with me.'

They walked back to the public park with the pain causing Karl to limp along with very small shuffling steps and Harold Szirtes really tearing a strip off him. 'I don't know what you are thinking of. We are in a strange place and you are trying to rape a girl in full view of anyone who passes by. I sometimes wonder where I get my people from.'

They entered the marquee again and Harold Szirtes found the main judge and said to him, 'Do you know that the trophies have to be engraved with the name Harold Szirtes Hotel?'

The judge said, 'Yes, that is the name entered on the application form and that's what we go by. It will take about two hours to get them to the engraver and back.'

Harold Szirtes went back to Karl and Maria and said, 'It's going to take about two hours to get the trophies. We might as well have a look around at the snow sculptures and then have a bite to eat.'

They walked around the amazing snow sculptures, absorbed and fascinated by the shimmering visions reflecting the changing colours of the lighting. They meandered round and round the wonderland until Harold Szirtes realised that he was getting very cold.

He said. 'Let's go and get something hot to eat.' They

found the marquee with the big café sign and an empty table. The waitress came almost immediately. Harold Szirtes ordered a large pizza, tea for Maria and a bottle of wine for himself and Karl.

The large pizza turned out to be too large for three but they ate most of it.

The bottle of wine improved Harold Szirtes' mood. He said, 'Well this has been a fantastic day for the Harold Szirtes Hotel. It's been worth all the travelling and hard work. I suppose having come all this way we should quickly look in the other marquees.'

They left the café marquee and started walking round the other marquees, which were filled with stalls selling a huge variety of craft and traditional food products.

Harold Szirtes spotted a stall named 'Stamp and Postcard Collections'. He was an avid postcard collector and had very early examples of the world's first Austrian postcards from around 1869. He walked over and started browsing. He looked through several albums then suddenly exclaimed out loud, 'It's the town under the crown.' He took the postcard out of the album and read the information printed on the back. It was a night view of Oban, Scotland featuring the illuminated coliseum known as McCaig's Folly on the hill above Oban. The coliseum on the hill above Oban looked strikingly like a crown sitting above the town.

Harold was now obsessed with the picture on the postcard. It was more crown like than anything he had imagined. He said to himself, 'This must be the town sitting under a crown beyond the Pillars of Hercules written of on the blade of the Sword of Attila.'

He continued: 'The Pillars of Hercules are the Straits of Gibraltar, it all fits perfectly, Scotland is beyond the Pillars of Hercules and Oban is the town sitting under the crown.'

He said to the stallholder, 'How much do you want for this poscard?'

The stallholder said with a smile, 'No I don't sell them singly, it's not worth my while, you will need to buy the whole album.'

Szirtes said, 'All right, all right, how much for the album?'

'Six hundred Czech Crowns,' the stallholder replied.

Harold took out his wallet and paid the stallholder. He placed the postcard safely in the album and carried it away from the stall. He spotted Maria who was waiting for him just outside the marquee and walked over to her. 'Where is Karl?' he demanded. She pointed over to another marquee with a sign 'Martial Arts and Combat Weapons'. He said, 'Go and tell him we are leaving.'

Maria ran over to the marquee and re-emerged with Karl. Harold said, 'Karl, you get the car and we will get the trophies.'

20

Reunion with Maria

Imri was chanting all the way during the twenty mile drive to the House of Attila but Nico did not hear him. He was elated almost like he was on a different planet. He kept seeing in his mind Maria's profile, but doubts crept in. He had only just got a brief glimpse. What if it was only someone who looked like Maria? His brain was racing. How could he find a way to see her? He must find a way to visit the back of the hotel.

When they arrived back at the mansion house, Herr Shoemaker parked the car at the front door. He said, 'Imri, if you want to come back to town with me, be back here in half an hour.' Imri complained, 'Half an hour is too soon.'

Herr Shoemaker said, 'If you are not here I will go without you.'

Herr Shoemaker and Imri disappeared in the front door.

Nico went round to the back of the house and over to the boiler house. He cleaned his football boots and put them away in the case under the chimney. He then checked the boilers and gave the fire bed a good raking with the long metal poker.

He loaded four logs into the fire bed and closed the fire door. He checked the water temperatures and climbed up to the water head tanks. The ballcocks were working perfectly and he took care to see that the insulated tank lids were properly in place.

Nico then went to the stables and went over to Prince. Stroking his shoulder he said, 'Prince, I think I saw Maria today.' Prince bent his neck right round and looked intently at Nico. Feeling he was being questioned, he continued, 'Well, I am sure it was her. It was just a glimpse but I would know Maria anywhere.' Prince let out a short whinny. Nico took this as support and replenished his food and water.

He quickly cleaned out their stalls then went into the shower room where he had a good long shower and dressed again.

He made his way round to the kitchen. The girls knew Imri and Herr Shoemaker had gone to town and were preparing a feast for themselves, knowing they could relax.

Nico was now accepted by them, almost as one of the girls, and was greeted warmly.

'How did you get on today?' Valda asked as she attended the big frying pan.

'Oh! We won three-one,' replied Nico.

'Who got the goals?' asked Valda.

'Imri got two and I got one.'

Valda brought a large plate of bacon over to the table. Milinka brought a large plate of eggs and Miljana brought over a large plate of sausages. Senca made a large pot of tea and brought it to the table then returned and fetched a large plate of buttered bread. The smell of the fried food made them all salivate. Valda said, 'Nico, do you know how to say grace?' Nico nodded. Valda said, 'Girls, come to the table; Nico is going to say grace.' They all sat at the table. Nico searched his mind and decided the grace they often used at school would be best.

'O, Lord, we thank you for our daily bread. May it strengthen and refresh our bodies. And we pray that you will nourish our souls with your grace through Jesus Christ, our Lord. Amen.'

They helped themselves in turn from the various plates,

enjoying the abundance of tasty food. Initially the conversation revolved round the sweetness and saltiness of the bacon and the size of the sausages.

Then, as they finished the food and started to drink their tea, they relaxed and began to share a little information about themselves.

Milinka and Miljana spoke together like a double-act, one supplying some of the words and the other supplying the rest. However, they were just understandable when they took their time. 'We come from, we don't know where; we were with nomads in the Mongolian desert. Then the horrible people traffickers captured us and sold us to Herr Shoemaker. We are sisters and we stick together, our names mean grace and charming, but we can't remember which one is which and they mean nearly the same, so we try to be a bit of each.' Then the two of them went into fits of laughter affecting everyone at the table until everyone was howling too.

The laughter finally subsided and Senca said, 'I can't give you so much fun. My name means shadow and, true to the meaning, I have been under a terrible shadow since my family were chased out of town by the brutes doing the ethnic cleansing. As I searched for food I got separated from my family and found myself a displaced person with no identity papers. I was beaten, raped and herded with others just like cattle into refugee camps. It was really terrible until Herr Shoemaker came to the camp and rescued me by bribing the security guards and bringing me to the House of Attila to be a servant.'

The mood round the table was now really depressed and the room remained quiet for fully two minutes as everyone digested what Senca had said.

Valda said quietly, 'My story is equally sad, but different. My family are very religious and believe in female circumcision. The meaning of my name is Renowned Ruler.

When I came of age my family tried to trick me into going to a health clinic for a medical check-up, but I knew from other girls what actually went on there. I know personally many of these girls and some are still suffering painful effects from the circumcision. I refused to go. There were terrible rows, but I stuck to my decision. My father publically disowned me. He contacted the people traffickers who came to the village and he sold me to them. Herr Shoemaker had already contacted the people traffickers for a young girl and they transported me immediately to the House of Attila. I cry almost every night thinking of my lost family.'

The atmosphere round the table was again very low and everyone remained silent for about a minute, then they all looked at Nico.

Nico said, 'Just prior to the siege of Sarajevo a group of soldiers who were infiltrating into the hills above Sarajevo, crept up on our neighbours and ourselves who were celebrating the New Year. They murdered our parents and carried off the children. I was one of the children and was transported to a cattle market where I was sold to Harold Szirtes and he brought me here.'

To cheer things up Senca led them in singing a few simple and well known songs.

The small group had become very close over the evening and ten o'clock came before they realised. They all mucked in and cleaned up everything, leaving the kitchen ready for the morning.

Nico checked the boilers and decided that with so few people staying in the mansion house the fire would last through to morning.

He got ready for bed, then, remembering the recent conversations, the Bible stories of the lost coin, the lost sheep and the lost son came to mind. He knelt down to pray. He gave thanks, first that he had seen Maria and asked that he might find a way to rescue her, and then he asked the Lord to

THE HOUSE OF ATTILA

bless each of the girls: Milinka, Miljana, Senca and Valda who had suffered so much. He gave thanks for the football team and asked that it might provide the opportunity to see Maria.

Although Nico worked hard all week the time seemed to go by slowly as his mind was constantly on Maria and working out how he could see her.

He had begun to hope that Herr Shoemaker would call into the hotel after the next home game and he could ask to use the toilet.

Unfortunately the team were playing away this weekend and the bus would not go near to the Harold Szirtes Hotel.

The football was a hard fought battle, but Imri did not help matters by getting sent off just before half-time for stamping on the face of an opposing player as the player lay on the ground. This caused a fight to erupt which only ended when Imri was sent off the field of play.

At the half-time interval Herr Shoemaker instructed the team to change its tactics and play for a draw. He rearranged the team in a four-four-one formation with Nico playing the lone forward.

It was a difficult role for Nico who was almost two years younger than the two centre backs. These were big physical players and were dirty with it.

They tried to intimidate Nico and make him retreat further down the park by punching him in the back when the referee wasn't looking.

With the extra man advantage, the opposing team was putting the Harold Szirtes Hotel team under severe pressure. However, their defence and their goalkeeper managed somehow to keep them from scoring.

As the time approached full-time one of Nico's team went down injured. As his injury was being attended to, Nico ran back to his own goalkeeper and said to him, 'You take the free kick. Watch me, I will make a run towards the left wing, drawing the two centre backs with me. You kick the ball long up the right wing.' The goalkeeper said, 'I will try anything, we have nothing to lose and if it's what you want, I will do it.'

The injured player indicated that he was ready to resume and Herr Shoemaker ran back off the pitch carrying his treatment bag.

Nico ran back up the field inducing the two big centre backs to come with him.

Just as the goalkeeper prepared to take the free kick, Nico started to run towards the left wing, shouting, 'Left wing, left wing.' The two centre backs immediately reacted to block Nico's progress towards the left wing. Just as the keeper started his run Nico suddenly reversed direction, catching the two centre backs wrong-footed and going in the wrong direction. He sprinted towards the right wing, running diagonally to stay on side. The ball came in behind him, bouncing once over his head and dropping just in front of him. He managed to take it cleanly on the run. He was through on the goalkeeper and two metres in front of the two central defenders. The keeper rushed out and Nico deftly stroked the ball past him into the goal just before one of the centre backs slid in, sending Nico about a metre into the air.

It took the team about ten minutes to calm down in the dressing-room. Going down to ten men against such a good team had been an impossible challenge. Everyone had expected a defeat. The victory was still unbelievable.

Eventually everyone calmed down and began to take off their boots and strips. Imri came into the dressing-room fully dressed and eating a meat pie. Herr Shoemaker's celebratory attitude suddenly changed. He stood up and moved right up to Imri and, looking down at him, he shouted, 'Imri, your behaviour today was completely unacceptable. You are dropped from the team for a full two weeks. If you want your place back you will need to prove your fitness first.'

Imri shouted back, 'You can't do that, my father pays for this team, if I don't play, no one plays.'

Herr Shoemaker said quietly, 'That is how it is, but if you do not train properly or obey team orders you will not play. I will tell your father about your behaviour today. I will tell your father that I am not going to waste my time on a lazy, undisciplined, alcoholic glutton. You will not play again until you are fit to do so. Do you understand me?'

Everyone in the dressing-room was silent, they knew Herr Shoemaker was a serious man and didn't waste words. They knew that if Imri did not play, his father would take the ball away or more exactly his lavish funding would dry up.

The bus journey back was a bit subdued considering they had won. Normally Imri would be up the back of the bus leading the celebrations. However, today he sat at the front beside Nico. Normally Nico sat by himself at the front of the bus, partly because he was nearly two years younger than the rest of the boys and partly because Imri made it clear that he was a displaced person and only in the team to serve him.

Imri said, 'Listen, Nico, after that blasting I got from Herr Shoemaker, I need to do something to get fit, I can't do it myself, I need a personal trainer.'

Nico didn't know what to say and just looked at him. Imri continued. 'Nico, I want you to be my personal trainer. Every night after work you will give me a training session. Do you understand?'

Nico replied, 'Fine! OK. We will start tonight.'

'Tonight,' Imri exploded, his face distorted with rage. Tonight is Saturday night; I go out with the boys on a Saturday night.' Nico looked at him straight in the eye and said, 'That's fine; you can go out after you have trained.'

Herr Shoemaker had been listening and intervened. 'Imri, if you are serious about getting in shape and changing your ways, starting tonight will convince me not to complain to your father. I don't mind waiting until you have finished before giving you a lift to town.'

Imri said, 'OK.' Then he went to the back of the bus.

Herr Shoemaker winked at Nico, also giving him a seldom seen smile.

The bus dropped Imri and Nico off at the gates to the House of Attila. Imri interfaced with the security system, identifying himself and verifying Nico as authorised to enter.

They walked along the drive in silence for about a minute, then Imri said, 'What time were you thinking about training tonight?'

Nico replied, 'It's seven o'clock now and I need about half an hour to check the boilers, would eight o'clock be OK for you?'

Imri said. 'How long do you think we will train for?'

Nico said. 'One hour.'

Imri replied, 'Oh! That's OK. Right, eight o'clock at the stables and don't be late.'

Nico said just before Imri went in the front door, 'Imri, don't eat anything before we train.'

The first thing Nico did was check Prince and Charlie as he had left them in the big paddock before he went to the football. They saw him coming and trotted over to the gate before he got to it. He greeted them both equally and then took them one at a time and installed them in their stalls. He checked and saw that they had plenty of food and water.

He then quickly checked the boilers and replenished the fire bed with fresh logs.

At exactly eight o'clock Nico met Imri in the big yard in front of the stables where the yard lights gave plenty of light. Nico said, 'First we need to warm up and do stretching exercises to prevent muscle strains in this cold weather. Then we will practise some heading and kicking techniques, then finally some speed exercises. We will finish in exactly one hour. For future sessions it would be good if we could find some heavy objects for weight exercises.'

Imri replied, 'I have a full set of weights.'

Nico paced the physical exercises to suit Imri's poor condition and the snow-covered ground conditions. Stretching his capability this early in the programme was not the priority.

Halfway through the one hour session Nico changed it to football technique. First Nico got Imri jumping up to head an imaginary ball until he was jumping high. Then continuing with jumping high, Nico taught him how to head the ball powerfully with the head held back and then using the neck muscles to strike with power.

Only when he was doing it well did Nico introduce a real ball, which he threw for Imri to head against the stable wall. Imri was delighted with the improvement in such a short time.

Nico said, 'Well done. We will practise this technique every time we train and in a few months you will be the best header of a ball in the whole league.

'Now let us practise kicking the ball with both feet. First let me show you how to kick a ball properly.' Nico took the ball and, standing about five metres away from the stable wall, he kicked the ball with his left foot against the wall. When the ball rebounded he kicked it first time with his right foot and then with his left and then again with his right. He continued doing it in a perfectly controlled way and then he began to explain the technique.

He said, 'Imri, watch my technique, it's all about getting your knee over the ball. See how my foot is stretched down like an extension of my lower leg. Notice how by getting my knee over the ball before I strike with the lower leg it keeps the ball down.' Nico continued another six kicks, saying, 'It's not about power, it's about control. Now you try it, but a bit closer to the wall.'

Imri tried it clumsily at first, and then began to get the hang of it.

Nico kept encouraging him, saying. 'Good, left now, take it first time, good; keep your knee over the ball. This is the basic skill exercise that you must practise all the time if you want to be a good footballer. Now you try it again but go nearer to the wall.'

When the hour was up Nico had to shout, 'Time up.'

Herr Shoemaker, who had arrived without the boys seeing him, shouted, 'Time up.' Then he said, 'Well that's a big improvement.'

Nico said to Herr Shoemaker, 'By the end of the week Imri will be kicking the ball with both feet from five metres.'

Imri was very pleased with his progress and spoiled it by forgetting to get his knee over the ball and it flew skyward right over the stable. Herr Shoemaker said, 'Imri, I am leaving in ten minutes whether you are with me or not.' Imri ran towards the mansion house, leaving Nico the job of finding the ball.

While Imri was away Herr Shoemaker said, 'Nico, I am so impressed with the progress you have made in one hour with Imri. No, I am more than impressed, I am absolutely amazed. You clearly know what you are doing, so I want you to take the training on Tuesdays and Thursdays. You don't have to worry, I will support you and although you are younger than the others, they already respect your ability.'

Nico said, 'I will need a wall at the training ground, the longer the better.'

Herr Shoemaker replied, 'You will have a wall within a week.'

Imri shouted, 'I am ready.' Herr Shoemaker made towards the car.

* * *

THE HOUSE OF ATTILA

Nico made his way round to the back of the stables and retrieved the football. After Herr Shoemaker and Imri left for town only the servants were left in the big mansion house. So Nico, Valda, Milinka, Miljana and Senca had a fry up and a relaxing night together in the kitchen swapping jokes, stories and songs together.

The following week went quickly and smoothly for Nico and Imri doing one-hour training sessions every evening except on the official training nights.

With Herr Shoemaker backing him strongly, the two training nights at the football pitch went well.

Nico started on the Tuesday evening by telling the team that they were not fit enough for the league and giving them a demanding workout. Several of the players were physically sick, not so much from the physical demands, but caused by just eating before coming to training. Nico used this to hammer home the fact that they must go to training and actual games hungry, with their digestive tract shut down if they wanted to perform well.

The Thursday training was less physical with more emphasis on ball work and team tactics.

Nico really laboured the fact that the whole team must work at keeping together. He said, 'You centre forwards must come back to the halfway line when our team is defending to give the others realistic passing options.

'You defenders must come up to the halfway line when our team is attacking. In this way you keep the pressure on the opposing team. The overall plan is to move up and down the park as a tight unit.'

He carried on emphasising his strategy. 'Defenders and midfield players must get up to quickly support forwards by regaining the ball if the move breaks down. They must take every opportunity to make runs at the opposition, which upsets their balanced marking plan.'

He explained, 'It is better to defend in the midfield rather than fall back too deep. When you fall back too deeply you put your own goalkeeper at risk.'

As they trained and practised set piece moves, Nico was pleased to notice that a long brick wall was being built along the far corner of the field.

Saturday's game was at home and Herr Shoemaker gave Imri and Nico a lift to the football field. The team played better, moving much more as a unit. Imri scored twice in the first half, one with his right foot and one with his head off a corner kick.

As usual Imri ran out of steam early in the second half and was substituted.

Nico was very pleased with the way the team were staying together and controlling the game mostly in the opposition's half.

Slowly the opposing team began to fatigue and the Harold Szirtes Hotel team scored again just before the final whistle. It was a spectacular goal by a midfield player running hard off the ball to meet a pass back from Nico and blasting it into the back of the net.

Herr Shoemaker was delighted and full of praise. 'See what you can do when you play as a unit. What a goal, Milek. Where did that one come from? What a team! Can we win the league? Yes, I think we can.'

Finally the celebrations calmed down and everyone got washed and changed. All the changing rooms were brushed out and then washed out with water and disinfectant by Nico and Herr Shoemaker. Finally Herr Shoemaker was satisfied and locked up the dressing-rooms. Imri was waiting at the car.

Herr Shoemaker got into the driving seat, Imri got into the front passenger seat and Nico got into the back. Nico was tensed up; he was silently praying that Herr Shoemaker

THE HOUSE OF ATTILA

would call into the Harold Szirtes Hotel. Sure enough Herr Shoemaker said, 'I need to go to the hotel to have a meeting with Harold, Karl and Felix; it should not take too long.'

Imri said, 'It had better not, I am starving.'

As they approached the hotel Nico said, 'I think I need the toilet.'

Herr Shoemaker said, 'Go round the back to the staff toilets.'

He saw a plume of condensing steam coming out of a ducting in a window and he guessed this must be the kitchen ventilation.

He climbed on to a bench seat positioned under the window and looked in. He could see Maria working at the large cooking range.

He tried knocking but she couldn't hear for the noise of the fan-driven ventilator. He jumped down, picked up a stone, then stepped back up on the bench and hit the metal ducting with the stone a few times. This time Maria looked up, saw him and came running out. They were in each other's arms hugging each other. After a few moments Nico broke the huddle and said, 'Are you all right? Are you safe?'

Maria replied, 'Yes I am fine; I am the cook at this hotel.'

Nico said, 'I am fine too; I am the boiler man at the House of Attila, Harold Szirtes' big estate about twenty kilometres from here. I must go now, we must not be seen together, and no one must know that I have found you. These are evil people we are working for. It may take some time but we will find a way out of this. God bless you, Maria.'

'And God bless you, too, Nico,' Maria said, with tears running down her cheeks.

Nico just got back into the car when Herr Shoemaker came out of the hotel. Imri had fallen asleep. He woke as Herr Shoemaker banged the car door shut and started the engine.

Imri said, 'I am very tired after scoring two goals; you don't know how much energy a forward uses. Do I have to train tonight after playing a game of football?'

Herr Shoemaker said, 'Correction, you only managed half a game, showing how unfit you are. You have a long way to go before you are really fit. However, you are right; it would be unreasonable to expect you to train after a game. Just make sure that you train with Nico every other night.'

Herr Shoemaker said with a smile, 'If you are so tired, do you want a lift back to town tonight? The meeting is postponed until tonight and I will have to go back in for eight o'clock.'

Imri stuttered. 'I … I … I … I promised to meet the boys tonight, I can't let them down, what time will you be leaving?'

Herr Shoemaker said sternly, 'Half past seven and don't be late.'

Nico could hardly contain his joy on the way back to the House of Attila after finding Maria. He was pleased that he didn't have to train Imri tonight. As soon as he got out of the car he ran round to the stables and went in to see the horses. There was no one else in the stables so he hugged Prince and whispered to him, 'Prince, I have found Maria, yes, I have found Maria.' He continued in a whisper, 'Yes, she is safe. Safe for the moment.' Then in a normal voice he said, 'Good boy, Prince, good boy, Prince.' He went over to Charlie, gave him a hug and said, 'Good boy, Charlie, good boy.'

He cleaned out their troughs and stalls, then replenished their troughs with fresh food and their water buckets with fresh water.

Nico then quickly attended to the boilers, showered and then went over to the kitchen for some food with Valda, Milinka, Miljan and Senca. While they were waiting for Herr Shoemaker and Imri to leave, they asked Nico about the game.

When they heard Imri and Herr Shoemaker leave they started the fry-up. This was the highlight of their week.

When they sat down to the feast they asked Nico to say grace. Nico immediately thought about mentioning his sister but resisted because he could not risk Maria's safety. Instead he thought about the fact that the girls were virtual prisoners in this big house twenty-four hours a day, seven days a week. He just started, 'Dear Lord, thank you for today and the friends and food we have, help us to hope for a new beginning. In Jesus' name, Amen.'

When he had finished, instead of getting stuck in immediately, they all hesitated for a moment as if deep in thought.

As they finished their meal the conversations centred on the general gossip about what was going on in the big house and surrounding estate. Senca then treated everyone to two beautiful folk songs and then led them all in a singsong.

Before Nico knew it the girls were washing up and saying it was time for bed.

Nico returned to his boiler house, put logs on the boilers and went to his room. He knelt down beside his bed and gave thanks for finding his sister Maria safe and well. He lay on his bed and thought about his good fortune and how he and Maria were protected even in this captivity. His mind wandered on to the Bible story of Joseph.

There seemed to be a parallel with Joseph's story and Maria's and his own situation. Joseph had great faith in God and his sense of right carried him through many difficult trials and injustices. Thinking these thoughts, Nico fell into a deep and peaceful sleep.

21

Prince is Sold

Following the meeting where he was instructed to go to Scotland, Herr Shoemaker sped back to the House of Attila in the taxi. He was glad to get away from Harold, Karl and Felix before any of the cruelty started. He knew they would get a bit drunk and then take a girl who was troublesome and take it in turn to rape her.

The taxi dropped him off at the House of Attila. He had a nice little self-contained bedsit at the mansion house; he kept it immaculate himself and would not let servants in to his rooms.

He switched on the air filter and ioniser, removed his clothes and put them in the laundry basket, took a shower, put on a dressing-gown and now he felt clean.

On the Wednesday afternoon as Nico began to unload the day's harvest of logs, Harold Szirtes approached him and said, 'Shoemaker tells me you are good with horses. I have entered you and the white horse you call Prince into a local competition. It's on a Saturday afternoon the fourth of April, so you will miss your football that day. I want to win this competition. It is scored on how the horse and harness is prepared for pulling logs. Shoemaker will supply everything you need, just tell him what you want and he will get it.'

THE HOUSE OF ATTILA

With that curt instruction Harold Szirtes strode away towards the mansion house.

Later that day Herr Shoemaker arrived and parked his car. Nico saw him and ran over, saying as he approached, 'Herr Shoemaker, Harold Szirtes came to see me today and told me he has entered Prince in a competition.'

Herr Shoemaker replied, 'Yes I know. He has just instructed me to get you anything you require to win this competition. One of his big local rivals has a horse entered, a thoroughbred horse, and they will be well prepared. Let's go into the stables and try to think what we need.'

They made their way to the stables and walked along to Prince's stall. Nico spoke to him. 'Good boy, good boy.' He also touched him gently as he moved along his side. When he reached his head Nico hugged and patted him. Nico said to Herr Shoemaker, 'Harold Szirtes said that the competition is scored on how the horse and harness are prepared for pulling logs. To stand a chance we need to get the best harness and traces. The best is an Amish collar with stainless steel hames and a deer hair pad. From the collar back the harness is Swedish, made by Tarnsjo, which allows Scandinavian shafts to be attached if necessary. Traces are attached direct to the pulling ring. The bit should be a Myler deep-ported driving bit. Equine chain tugs should be used between the tug hooks and pulling ring, replacing the Swedish tugs. We need nine millimetre climbing rope for the reins. I will make the traces myself from chain and draft springs. The swingle tree that I like is made with an integral draft spring and quick release "kick off dog".'

'Hold on. Hold on.' Herr Shoemaker shouted. 'I can't keep up with all that detail. Do you know where to get all this stuff?' Nico said, 'Yes if you drive and we start off really early in the morning we could be back in the evening of the same day. I have a good stock of logs at the back of the boiler house and could afford a day away from the forest.'

* * *

The following day they took the flatbed lorry and went to the big equine centre where Nico selected all the equipment he needed including a large list of grooming kit and horse care products.

It was Sunday before Nico had enough time to try out his new harnesses and traces.

Nico firmly believed that grooming should be a pleasure for the horse. Talking all the time to Prince, Nico spent a good hour starting at the top of Prince's neck and working his way to his rear, then switching sides and repeating. He started carefully with the rubber curry. Next, the dandy brush. Then the body brush.

Nico used the mane comb to gently comb the horse's mane. Then he used the dandy brush again to brush Prince's tail, wetting it with water then applying a tail conditioner to keep the tail from tangling. Nico ran his hand down Prince's legs in turn, gently squeezing his fetlocks. Then, using the hoof pick, he scraped the hoofs carefully away from himself, in order not to accidentally injure himself or Prince if the horse suddenly moved or pulled his foot away. As he did so he thought, 'It is so important to thoroughly clean out the hollow areas on both sides of the frog, and around the sole of the foot.' He finished him off by oiling his hoofs.

Then it dawned on him that all these good practices came from instructions that his father had patiently given him. For a moment Nico felt sadness welling up, but he quickly quelled it and resolved to keep doing these things his father had carefully taught him, knowing that his father would be proud of him.

Finally Nico took a rag to wipe over Prince's coat to bring out the shine. Nico then led Prince out of the stables and into the paddock where he had left the harness and traces.

Nico loosely tied Prince to the fence rails and said to him, 'Now, Prince, we will practise putting on the gear.'

Nico took the horse collar and carefully slid it upside down over Prince's head then he turned the collar until the widest part fitted over the thinnest part of his neck and settled it into place, saying, 'There you go, Prince, that was easy.'

Prince looked at Nico quizzically as if to say, 'Speak for yourself.' Nico laughed at him and said, 'OK! OK! We have still to fit the pad and this might be a bit more difficult since the collar is new.' Prince gave another peculiar look as if to say, 'I thought so.'

Nico very carefully stuffed the pad in under the collar from the front on one side and then the other side, finally pulling the collar forward and settling it all into place. He said to Prince, 'Come on, give your neck a shake you big lazy lump.' Nico then checked the fit of the collar with his flat hand just touching the horse's neck and collar comfortably.

He then said, 'Well that wasn't too difficult was it?' Prince snorted, lifting his head at the same time as if to say, 'Huh! Maybe not for you.'

Nico put on the back pad and fitted the britchen carefully, pulling Prince's tail out to make it comfortable. He then attached the offside meeter strap and tug. He then carefully checked all the offside straps then repeated the same for the nearside meeter strap and tug. When he was completely satisfied, he fastened the girth. He attached the nearside tug and fastened the belly band. He checked all the straps again. He finished the offside trace carrier and nearside trace carrier. He put on the bit carrier and fastened the pole strap.

He positioned the bit carrier and bit ready, fed the reins through the rings and attached on the nearside, then the offside. He hung the reins on the hames with the choker chain on the offside hame and the swingle tree on the nearside hame.

Then Nico said, 'Prince, you are ready to work.' Prince

reacted appropriately with a double snort and a toss of the head as if to say, 'In your dreams, Buddy.'

Nico stood back and looked long and hard at Prince. He looked really good in his new harness and traces, the jet black of the harness and traces contrasting starkly with the horse's pure white colour. Nico said, 'Who's a pretty boy then?' Prince looked up at the sky as if to disown the comment and stamped his hoof on the ground.

Nico practised this routine every Sunday in the weeks leading up to the competition, and Prince really enjoyed all the attention he was getting.

Nico also continued training Imri every night other than the normal team training nights and match days. Imri was quickly becoming fitter and much more skilled in heading and kicking the ball with both feet. The wall had been built at the football training ground and Nico incorporated the two-footed ball kicking exercises into the circuit training routine. The players started gently from three metres from the wall for a few weeks, until they could return the ball first time with alternate feet and consistently demonstrate good technique by getting their knee above the ball before accelerating their lower leg with foot extended to execute a perfectly controlled kick.

Imri, with his regular practice at Attila House, continued to be the two-footed standard for the rest to aspire to. Though when he became too big-headed about it, Nico brought him down to earth with a demonstration of really powerful controlled kicking from fully ten metres, taking the ball first time, with one foot and then the other. This was Nico's party piece and he believed that it was the core skill of a good football player, but like any good musician the skill needed to be practised constantly. At home games the wall exercises became part of the pre-match warm up, and the individual confidence of each player increased with this rapid improvement in skill.

THE HOUSE OF ATTILA

* * *

The day of the horse competition approached and on the Friday afternoon a horse transporter lorry driven by Felix Hienmann arrived and parked at the stables. Felix found Nico and said, 'I will drive the horse transporter because Herr Shoemaker will be taking the football team. I have left the back of the transporter unlocked. We will leave at eight o'clock sharp tomorrow morning when you must have everything ready and loaded to go.'

On the Friday evening Nico took Prince outside into the yard and tied him to a metal ring set into the wall. He connected a hose through a window to a cold water tap, as Prince gave him one of his quizzical looks. He first groomed him with a body brush, removing any loose hair and dirt, then hosed him all over to get his coat wetted. With Prince doing a lot of snorting, he applied shampoo carefully with a light scrubbing brush, then, using the hose, he rinsed all the shampoo from Prince's coat, finally removing excess water with a sweat scraper. Nico then used the dandy brush and a comb to carefully separate the hair on Prince's mane and tail. When he was satisfied, Nico braided Prince's tail and covered it with a tail bag. Then, using a soft sponge and the hose without shampoo, he gently washed Prince's face.

He said, 'Prince, you are nothing but a big softy, anyone listening would think I was being cruel to you.'

Nico finished the job by clipping the muzzle, fetlocks, the inside of the ears and the underside of Prince's face, and finally putting a blanket on to him, fastening it securely. 'Now, Prince, don't you get messed up before the show,' he concluded.

Nico put him in his stall and checked both Prince and Charlie's food and water, hosed the area where he had been working, cleaned and packed away his equipment.

He checked his boilers and, well pleased with everything,

he walked over to the mansion house kitchen to see if he could get a bite to eat, even though it was now late.

Fortunately Miljana was still up and the kitchen door was unlocked. Nico entered and said. 'Miljana, I wondered if there was any food left.'

She said, 'Yes, you are lucky, the others have gone to bed.' She made him a big cheese sandwich and a big mug of tea. Nico was hungry and polished them off quickly. Miljana was watching him intently as he ate, imagining his youthful but impressive physique below his clothing.

She said, 'I stayed up hoping you would come and help me put the laundry away. The freshly laundered bedding came today, will you help me put it away?'

Nico replied, 'Yes, of course I will, show me where it is.' She led him into a big store with shelves fitted on three sides right up to the ceiling. Sitting in the middle of the floor were three wicker laundry baskets.

Miljana opened one of the baskets and it was full of neatly pressed and folded bath towels. She opened another and it was full of neatly folded bed sheets and pillowcases. She opened the third and it was full of neatly folded duvet covers.

She said, 'We send these to the local laundry because they have giant steam-heated roller presses. As you can see they do a very good job. Much better than we could do by hand. The towels go on the bottom shelves, the duvet covers go on the middle shelves and the sheets and pillowcases on the top shelves.

'We shall start with the towels, I will take them out of the baskets and hand them to you. Place them carefully on the bottom shelves and try not to disturb the way they are folded.'

She bent over and picked up a small bundle of bath towels, saying, 'The secret is not to take too many at a time.' Nico quickly turned and placed the towels carefully on the bottom shelf.

THE HOUSE OF ATTILA

They soon dealt with the towels and started on the sheets and pillowcases. Miljana said, 'You need to stack them keeping the matching sheets and pillowcases together. I will pick them out in matching sets.' Miljana was only wearing a white cotton house coat with nothing underneath it and as Nico turned away she undid the top and bottom buttons.

As they continued to work she bent and stretched excessively, giving Nico an occasional glimpse of her breasts and thighs, with her brown skin starkly contrasting with her white house coat.

Nico was completely mesmerised by these brief glimpses and he desperately wanted to see more.

When they finished the basket of sheets and pillowcases, Miljana said. 'We are doing well, Nico, no one has ever stacked the laundry so quickly before.'

'I am taller than you, so let's reverse roles and I will put the duvet covers on the top shelves, you pick them out of the basket and pass them up to me.'

'Hold on a minute I will need a chair.' She went through to the kitchen and brought a chair back with her. As she set the chair below the shelves Nico noticed that only the one middle button on the house coat was fastened.

Miljana kicked off her shoes and said, 'Nico, stand beside the chair and steady it until I am settled on it, I don't have a good head for heights.' Holding Nico's shoulder with her right hand she placed her left foot on the chair. Nico froze as though an electric shock had gone through his nervous system. As she momentarily stood there preparing to push up Nico could see the hair between her legs.

She said, 'Stand firm and take my weight.' She pushed up and stood on the chair, saying, 'Good it's quite steady, now you can hand me up some duvet covers, but not too many.' Nico turned and took about eight duvet covers and handed them up to Miljana. She said, 'That's just a bit too many, I can barely manage them.' She lifted the bundle up, pulling her house coat up with it. Then she had the bundle on the shelf and her house coat fell back down. As she tidied the duvet covers on the shelf Nico was sweating and his breathing was laboured.

Nico kept the bundles much smaller and they soon emptied the basket; the last ones had to go on a higher shelf.

Nico handed up the last bundle and she turned to face the shelves and tried to put them on the top shelf by standing on her toes and stretching up as high as she could. Her house coat rode up her buttocks, giving Nico a perfect view of the gap between her legs.

Nico was seriously aroused and he felt a curious and powerful attraction to Miljana.

She exclaimed, 'Done it,' and fell backwards against Nico. He managed to hold her and prevent her falling off the chair. She unbuttoned the remaining button fastening the house coat and slipped her arms out of the sleeves. She turned to face Nico, letting the house coat slip to the floor and said, 'Nico, lift me down.' He lifted her down and she said, 'Nico, I don't think you know much about women. Come, I am going to teach you.'

Nico crept out of the mansion house about two o'clock in the morning and slept like a log.

Not surprisingly Nico slept a bit later in the morning. When he looked at the alarm clock it indicated a quarter to six.

They were due to leave at eight o'clock. He rolled out of bed and put on his clothing from the day before. He picked up fresh underwear and socks. Pulling a pair of trainers on to his bare feet, he rushed over to the stables.

He made sure Prince and Charlie had enough food and water, saying to Prince, 'You eat a good breakfast because it is going to be a long day.'

He packed a hay net with fresh hay, filled a nose bag with oats, filled a twenty litre drum with water and found an empty water bucket to take with them. Finally he oiled Prince's hoofs.

Nico then went to the shower room, showered and dressed.

He ran over to the kitchen where he found Valda making breakfast. He said, 'Valda, I am going with Felix Hienmann to show Prince today. Please make us two packed lunches to take with us.'

Valda gave Nico a big plate of tomato and cheese, with two slices of buttered bread and said, 'What show is this?'

Nico replied with his mouth full, 'It's a big equest...' and he had to hesitate until he had swallowed his food. 'It's a big equestrian show on one of the big country estates on the other side of town. Harold Szirtes has entered Prince and he wants to win the working horses competition and we are against one of his bitter rivals who has entered a thoroughbred.'

Valda said, 'What do you need to do to win?'

Nico replied, 'It's really about how many points you get based on the look of the horse, how well you harness your horse, how good the harness looks on the horse and how fast you drag the logs to the finish line.'

Nico finished his breakfast and Valda handed him two packed lunches and two large bottles of diluted orange juice. She said, 'The very best of luck,' and kissed him full on the lips.

Nico retreated from the kitchen blushing; he was becoming disorientated with all this affection. He quickly gathered his thoughts and said out loud, 'Let's think carefully. I need to make sure I have everything I need for the day. Make sure all the tackle is clean and all the items are loaded. I will do that first. Make sure I have all the horse care and grooming kit. I will do that second. Finally I need to take the smart show clothes. I will do that third. Oh! And yes. I need to take the entry acceptance letter and the numbered labels.'

Nico went to the stables; he checked the rear door of the horse transporter and found it to be unlocked. He said to himself, 'Good, it is as he said; I can load the stuff before Felix Hienmann comes out.'

He put the packed lunches and bottles of orange juice in one of the many storage panels built into the sides of the transporter. Then he carefully loaded all the other items. Once everything was neatly stored he checked it all again.

He then went into the stable and led Prince out. He said, 'It is still early; you have time for a walk in the paddock.' Nico led Prince round the paddock, stopping to let him urinate and defecate. Nico said, 'That's good, now we are ready to go.'

Nico led Prince up the ramp and into the horse transporter. As he finished closing and fastening the ramp, Felix Hienmann appeared. He said, 'Good boy, Nico, I see you have been up early. Are we all ready to go?'

Nico said, 'Yes.'

'OK then let's get started,' Felix Hienmann replied.

They arrived at the equestrian centre about eleven o'clock and Nico's competition was not due to start until two o'clock, giving Nico three hours spare. Nico said to Felix, 'We need to register with the entry clerk.'

Felix said, 'Yes you do that, I will guard the horse transporter until you come back.'

Nico followed a sign saying 'COMPETITORS' with an arrow pointing to a marquee. He approached a table and said to the woman sitting there, 'I am entered in the Working Horses Competition.'

The woman smiled and said, 'What is your entry name?'

Nico said 'Prince'.

The woman smiled again and said, 'No, not the horse's name, the entry name.'

Nico replied, 'It may be Harold Szirtes.'

THE HOUSE OF ATTILA

'Yes,' the woman said, 'I have Harold Szirtes here.' She handed Nico an entry pack, which consisted of instructions and number labels to attach to the horse and the handler.

Nico went back to the transporter and reported to Felix, who said. 'Good, you read the instructions and prepare the horse, while I go and have a look round the show.'

Nico lowered the ramp of the horse transporter and went inside. He said, 'Prince, I am going to give you a ride after your journey.' He had brought a saddle and bridle with him and he fitted these to Prince. The horse transporter was a full sized lorry, which allowed Nico to turn Prince to face the ramp and then lead him down into the field. The lorry was parked on one side of the big field close to the road and there was plenty of free space to ride at one side of the field away from the marquees and main events enclosure.

Nico mounted Prince and walked him towards the other corner of the square field. When they reached the corner Nico turned him and asked him to increase to a relaxed trot. When they reached the horse transporter they turned and trotted back to the other corner. They repeated this for about twenty minutes. Then Nico dismounted and tied Prince loosely to the side of the transporter. He removed the saddle and bridle, cleaned them and stored them away in the transporter.

Nico got out the horse care and grooming kits and started to very carefully groom Prince down with the curry comb, dandy brush and soft brush. He then very carefully combed out the mane and tail. At this point Nico became aware of a man standing watching him. Nico stood up and looked at the man.

The man stepped forward, holding out his hand. Nico bent down and washed his hands in the bucket of water, then, drying them on his tracksuit bottoms, he held out his hand to the man.

The man said, 'I was admiring your horse as I watched you

trot up and down; my name is Dmitar Hrvat, Breeding Manager, Al Quoz Stables in Dubai.' Here is my business card. He handed Nico a business card. 'I would like to buy your stallion subject to veterinary checks. He would have a good life in the most luxurious stables you have ever seen with a harem of pure white Arab mares. In the entire world I have not seen a better stallion for my breeding purposes.

'I have also been watching you work with the horse and I can see you are in perfect affinity with him. I can offer you a job looking after the horse and the stable of mares; these are not just any mares they are pure white Arabs and the sheik values them more than his wives.'

Nico said, 'I am sorry, the horse is not mine to sell. You will need to speak to Harold Szirtes, he will be here later to see the competition.'

The man said, 'I will come back after the competition and see Harold Szirtes, but you think about my job offer.' The man walked away.

Nico turned again to Prince and said, 'Where were we?' Nico quickly picked out Prince's hoofs just to make sure there were no stones stuck in them. As he did each one he oiled them again. He then took out some fly repellent and carefully applied it all over Prince, taking care not to get it near his eyes or mouth. 'Well, Prince, that's the best you will ever be,' Nico said. 'Here, lower your head for me to put your nose bag on. Now, it's time for me to get smartened up.' Nico got his bag of clothes and made his way over to the competitor's area to wash and change into his dress clothes and riding boots.

He made his way back to the horse transporter and said to Prince, 'Well how do I look?' Prince looked round at him then just carried on chewing. Nico said, 'Well so much for all my efforts.'

A few minutes later Felix Hienmann and Harold Szirtes arrived and Harold said, 'Are you ready?'

THE HOUSE OF ATTILA

Nico said, 'Yes.'

'Then let's get the harness and gear over to the competition ring.' Nico had packed the equipment in their individual canvas bags, which made it easy to hang them over the horse's back for transporting.

With Felix Hienmann helping, to impress Harold Szirtes, Nico loaded the bags on to Prince. He took off the horse's nose bag and gave his face a final wash with a big wet sponge and said, 'Now, Prince, it's up to you.'

They made their way over to the competitors' enclosure. As Nico led Prince in, Harold Szirtes said with an implied threat, 'Remember, Nico, I want to win this trophy.' Not waiting for an answer, he turned and walked away with Felix Hienmann towards the spectator stands.

Nico said, 'Good boy, Prince, it's just the two of us, let's do our best.'

A steward came towards Nico and said, 'Good you are nice and early, do you have your entry acceptance form and your numbered labels?'

Nico handed her the envelope containing the required items. The steward escorted them into the competition arena and led them to the far side against the fence. She said, 'I am placing you at the far side because you are first to arrive and you will not be disturbed by the others taking their places in the line. I have been doing this job for years and you will be less disturbed there. You know what they say, "The early bird catches the worm." Ho! Ho! Ho!' Prince cocked his head up and away from her as if to say, 'We have a right one here.'

Nico burst out laughing at Prince's antics. Fortunately the steward thought Nico was laughing at her joke. When they reached the far position along the fence she said, 'Tie the horse to the fence here. Unload the harnesses in the order of fitting. You know that this competition is won on the speed of preparing the horse for work, the overall look of the horse and the correctness of the harnesses. Pulling the log or logs is really just for display and only counts for a few points. You can use the wheeled arch with the two shafts supplied.' She pointed to the eight rows of wheeled arches with two long logs placed at each competitor's starting position. 'Or you can use your own swingle tree with the chains that I see you have with you. I wish you the best of luck,' and she headed off to deal with another competitor who had arrived.

Nico said to Prince, 'Well it looks like we have seven teams against us.' Nico looked at the two logs; he knew how to choker them together with the single chain. He kicked the ground several times. There had been a hard overnight frost and the ground was frozen solid, which meant the end of the logs would not dig in. Nico thought, 'Just perfect for dragging logs with the swingle tree. He estimated that it would take at least a minute longer to attach the wheeled arches with their two shafts to the harness. Using the swingle tree would give them a time advantage over teams using the wheeled arches. The other competitors were beginning to arrive and the steward was now running back and forward, taking them to their starting positions. She seemed to be the only one organising the competitors.

Nico took the numbered tabard, a sleeveless outer garment with open side seams bearing a big number one on its front and back, and slipped it over his head, pulling it down at the front and back. He said to Prince, 'They certainly want everyone to know that we are team number one.'

Nico looked along the row of seven other competitors. They were a mixed range of horses, most were typical farm horses but one was a stunning black stallion.

Nico said to Prince, 'We will concentrate on our performance and ignore the rest; we are just going to treat this like back at the estate.'

Eventually the loudspeakers announced the working horse competition and an official explained that at the starting gun each competitor would harness their horse and drag two logs to the finish line on the other side of the competition arena.

The announcer finished by saying, 'The judges will award points for looks, speed and style.'

The starter announced, 'On your marks, ready.' The starting gun went off.

Nico took the horse collar and carefully slid it upside down over Prince's head, as they had practised. One by one he began to assemble the complex harness system. Nico could hear shouting and some swearing from some of the other competitors but he did not look up. Once he was satisfied everything was in place, he untied Prince and led him just past the far end of the logs and placed the swingle tree ready. He said firmly, 'Stand.' Prince stood still and waited. Nico, using timber tongs to roll the logs to get the choker chain under, chokered up the chain with the hook pointing backwards towards the two logs. He attached the choker chain to the swingle tree and was ready to go.

As he moved off, two teams were ahead of him, but he did not panic; he just kept to his task. He kept Prince trotting to the finish line, thinking, at least I am third, but when he got there, the two other teams were turning and going back, and then it dawned on him that they had only dragged one log and were going back for the other one. He exclaimed, 'Well done, Prince, we are first.' Then the other five teams who had chosen to use the wheeled arches rushed up to the finishing line led by the beautiful black horse.

Nico patted Prince hard and said, 'Good boy, good boy, we've won the race.'

The horses and their handlers stood waiting for the judges to award their overall scores.

Nico looked over to the big black horse that had come in second. He certainly was a magnificent beast. It was going to be a close call. His handler was wearing number eight.

From the loudspeakers came the announcement reminding everyone that the points were awarded for looks, speed and style. The loudspeakers barked, 'In third place with seven points is team number four.'

'In second place with eight points is team number eight.'

'In first place with nine points is team number one.'

As each announcement was made, the girl steward came over to the respective horse and tied a rosette with Third, Second and First embroidered on it, and fastened it to the bridle of each horse in the correct order.

When she finally tied the First rosette on to Prince, she said to Nico, 'Follow me with the horse to receive the trophy.' Harold Szirtes came out of the spectators' stand and ran over, taking the reins from Nico, saying, 'You just walk beside the horse and I will pick up the trophy.'

The announcer said, 'First prize for the Working Horses Competition goes to Harold Szirtes,' and he handed the trophy to Harold.

Harold held the trophy high above his head, dancing around and showing it off to the crowded stand, finally posing with it in front of Prince for the local press photographer.

When all the fuss died down Harold made his way back to the spectator stand with the trophy and Nico led Prince back to the horse transporter. He tied him to the rear of the vehicle and stripped off all the harnesses, gave him a drink of water from the bucket, which Prince finished, and then fitted the still full nose bag over his muzzle.

Nico went into the rear of the horse transporter and changed from his dress clothes and boots back into track suit and trainers; he carefully packed up his good clothes and stored them in one of the side panel compartments.

He packed away all the harnesses and horse care equipment and materials.

The sun was shining and it was a nice spring day. Nico retrieved the lunch bag and orange juice, he then turned the empty water bucket upside down and sat on it and began eating his belated lunch.

He said, 'Well, Prince, even though I missed the football we did the job.'

Nico sat in the warm sun for half an hour before he saw Harold Szirtes, Felix Hienmann and Dmitar Hrvat coming. As they approached, Felix said, 'Nico, take a walk while we discuss business.'

Nico walked over to the show area, occasionally looking back with a worried expression. He could see them carefully examining Prince. After some time Harold Szirtes and Dmitar Hrvat started to walk back towards the main spectator stand and Felix Hienmann remained at the horse transporter. Nico made his way back to the horse transporter with a heavy heart. As he approached Felix shouted, 'Get the horse loaded and we will get on our way.'

Once Prince was loaded and he had checked that all the equipment was safely stowed, Nico closed the ramp and secured it in place. He climbed into the passenger seat; Felix started the engine and drove off. Nico said, 'Did you come to any conclusion about Prince?'

Felix snapped, 'In your position the less you know the better.'

That was the last of the conversation until they arrived back at the House of Attila and they parked the horse transporter. Felix said, 'Right, unload everything and clean the transporter before you do anything else.' With that he walked off and left Nico to get on with it.

The transporter remained parked at the stables all week. Nico went to football the following Saturday as usual. He even managed to sneak into the Harold Szirtes Hotel for a few minutes to see Maria and tell her about Prince winning the working horse trophy.

When he returned to the House of Attila he checked the

boilers and loaded them up with enough logs to last through until morning, because he half hoped that he could linger the night away with Miljana. He closed the fire door fully and went round to the stables to see Prince and Charlie.

As he approached the stables he saw that the horse transporter was gone. An icy band seemed to tighten round his stomach. He started to run, and ran into the stables, but Prince's stall was empty. Nico walked into the stall slowly like an old man. He felt physically sick; he stood holding on to the hayrick with his head bowed. There was nothing he could do; the feeling of sickness gave way to a corrosive sense of powerlessness. He thought, 'How can this happen to me? I have found Prince, then Maria and now I have lost Prince again.' As he grieved this loss one of his father's stories came to mind. He remembered quite vividly his father telling stories when he was a small boy. The story of Jonah came to mind. His father always said, 'When Jonah had lost all hope he turned his thoughts to the Lord.' Nico sank to his knees in the empty stable and he told God of all his grief.

He saw to Charlie's needs, then he ran back to the boiler house. He checked everything again then began to run out to the forest cabin. He hadn't eaten but he had decided to fast until morning. He went to the empty stable and lay on the straw, which smelled of Prince. He prayed and slept fitfully on the straw all night.

Nico wakened and was aware that he was very hungry. It was getting light; he got up from the straw, grieving over and he ran back to the House of Attila.

As he approached the House of Attila he saw Valda putting waste into the waste bins. He ran up to her, saying, 'Hi Valda, is there any breakfast ready this morning?'

She looked up and said, 'Have you been sleeping in a haystack all night?'

Nico replied, 'Yes, something like that.'

She said, 'Come on then, I have got some breakfast ready.'

Nico felt a lot better when he had some food in him and he washed it down with a big mug of tea. Valda was watching him and said, 'You are very hungry this morning.'

Nico said, 'Yes I was fasting last night as I spent the night with God.'

Valda said, 'I saw you run away after you discovered that they had taken Prince away.' She leaned over his shoulder and pulled his head round and kissed him. Then she said, 'I am glad you are back.'

22

Strategic Mistake

Maria watched Nico run down the road at the side of the hotel. She quickly wiped her tears on the bottom of her apron and returned to the kitchen.

It was Saturday evening and the hotel restaurant was fully booked. Maria, Lette and Mary were working very well as a team and the hotel was building a growing reputation for good food.

Freda came into the kitchen and said, 'Harold Szirtes, Martin Shoemaker, Karl Stonier and Felix Hienmann are having a meeting in the small private dining-room tonight. They have ordered your prize-winning dishes. The meeting starts at half past seven and the meal is ordered for nine o'clock.'

Maria put her hand on her forehead and gasped, 'Oh! No!'

Freda quickly put her arms around her and said, 'What's wrong. Maria?'

Lette and Mary gathered round.

'I don't want to see Karl,' Maria cried out with feeling.

Freda said. 'Why, what is wrong?'

Maria started to cry and said, between her wailing, 'Karl tried to rape me.'

Lette and Mary cried out in unison, 'He didn't, did he?'

Maria wailed, 'No, he didn't, but he was trying hard.'

Freda said, 'Calm down and have a cup of tea. Mary, fetch Maria a cup of strong sweet tea.'

Freda sat Maria down at the table and Mary brought her the tea. Lette and Mary sat down at the table, not wanting to miss anything.

Maria said, 'I am OK; I will tell you what happened.' Lette and Mary pulled their chairs in even closer. Maria began, 'You know that I went to the competition with Harold Szirtes and Karl. Well when they announced that I had won for the second time, I fainted and was completely unconscious. Karl must have carried me to the nearby hotel and put me on top of an office desk.

'When I woke up Karl was leaning over me and trying to insert his cock into me.'

Mary shouted, 'Was he naked?'

Maria said, 'No, he had his shirt and jacket on.'

Mary said, 'Where were his trousers?'

Maria said, 'Around his ankles.'

Mary said, 'Did you have your knickers on?'

Maria said, 'No, he had stripped me completely naked when I was unconscious.' Maria began to cry again.

Freda said, 'There now, just take it easy.'

Mary shouted, 'No, don't stop now, I need to know the end of the story.'

Maria pulled herself together and continued. 'Although he was so strong, I managed to keep twisting at the last moment and he couldn't get in. Then just in time, Harold Szirtes walked in the door and interrupted him.

'Karl turned and faced Harold Szirtes, snarling like a dog.' Maria cried out emotionally as she recalled the trauma.

'Harold Szirtes was carrying the medal that we had won; he was holding it by its neck band and he swung the heavy metal medal and hit Karl right on the end of his cock. Karl collapsed on the floor moaning loudly, obviously in great pain.'

Mary clapped her hands excitedly, shouting, 'Good for him.'

Maria continued. 'I took the opportunity while they were fighting to quickly get dressed.'

Mary said excitedly, 'What size was his cock?'

Freda said, 'Right that's enough. This is serious; we need to think this out. Maria, you cannot stay in the dormitory with the other girls any more. Karl, Felix and Harold Szirtes often raid the dormitories when they want a girl and Karl will have you in his sights after what has happened. There is only one answer. You will have to move in to my room with me.

'They already think I am a lesbian and if they think we are lovers they will probably leave you alone. However, you will need to share my bed, it's a double, there's not enough room for two singles.'

Mary and Lette let out a squeal of mock delight.

Freda said, 'Harold Szirtes and his party have not arrived yet. Maria, go up to your dormitory and take all your belongings down to my bedroom, I will go and clear out the small wardrobe for you to use. Mary, you go with her and help her. Listen to me before you go. Lette and Mary you must make sure Maria is not alone any time Karl is in the hotel. Do you understand how important that is?' They both nodded solemnly.

Maria and Mary soon collected what small belongings Maria had and brought them down to Freda's room.

Freda said. 'Mary you go back to the kitchen and start preparing for tonight's meals.' She showed Maria the wardrobe and together they sorted and put her clothing and toiletries away.

Freda showed Maria the room with its *en suite* bathroom and kitchen, taking time to show her how the shower worked. Maria said, 'It's a really nice flat, Freda. Thank you for sharing it with me.'

Freda said, 'What I like most about it is the strong door

and locks. This is where Harold Szirtes used to store his drugs when he first started up. Its door was recovered from a police cell when the old police station was being refurbished.'

Freda gave Maria a spare key on a neckband and told her to keep it round her neck at all times.

Freda and Maria went back to their duties.

Herr Shoemaker arrived first and prepared the meeting room. Harold Szirtes and Felix arrived shortly afterwards. Freda was waiting for Karl when he arrived and she gestured him to join her in a side room.

She shut the door behind her and turned and looked right into his face and said, 'Karl, the girl Maria and I sleep together.' She let the information sink in. She could see from slight facial gestures that Karl's mind was racing. She held her gaze, forcing Karl to break eye contact and said, 'I have been told about your confrontation with Harold Szirtes and your painful experience.'

She again paused for a moment while Karl began to squirm.

Freda left it at that and opened the door and walked out.

Karl hesitated for a few moments before making his way to the private dining-room. He entered quietly. He avoided eye contact with the other three and sat down to see what would materialise.

Harold picked up a postcard of Oban, one of several that he now passed round the table. He held up the night view of Oban harbour taken from a boat out at sea.

The whole seafront was illuminated, but what was specially striking was the illuminated architectural feature sitting high on the hill above the town.

Harold said, 'The coliseum on the hill above Oban is like a beautiful crown sitting above the town. I have never seen anything like this in the entire world. This must be the town sitting under a crown beyond the Pillars of Hercules, written of on the Sword of Attila. The Pillars of Hercules are the Straits of Gibraltar, it all fits perfectly: Scotland is beyond the Straits of Gibraltar and Oban is the town sitting under the crown.'

Harold was quiet for a minute before he said, 'I have decided, Martin, you will go to Scotland and find this place Oban and report back to me. If it is as I believe it to be, it will be our staging place into Britain and then America.'

Herr Shoemaker said, 'But what about the football team?'

Karl, seeing his opportunity, interjected, 'I will go to Scotland.'

Harold Szirtes reacted angrily, 'No you won't. I have not forgotten your indiscretion and insubordination at the snow sculpture competitions.'

Karl shrivelled up, his paranoia magnified and his imagination now rampant.

Harold Szirtes continued, annoyed that his presentation had been disrupted. He produced the sword from under the table and read out the words engraved on one side of its blade.

'Sword of Attila – Ruler of the World.'

He turned it over and read the words on the other side of its blade.

'You will rule from a town sitting under a crown …'

He then stood up, held his drink high and said, 'Gentlemen, I give you a toast. First, we will conquer the Balkans and then the world.' Everyone stood up and in unison said, 'First we will conquer the Balkans and then the world.'

Harold then announced, 'The meeting is closed.'

Herr Shoemaker left the meeting to tell Freda that the meeting was ended and dinner could be served.

After dinner the party stayed drinking for some time. Herr Shoemaker said, 'Harold when do you want me to go to Scotland?'

'Immediately, Martin,' Harold Szirtes replied. 'We have not got time to waste if we are to fulfil our destiny and rule the world.' He broke into insane laughter.

Herr Shoemaker said, 'Who will run the House of Attila while I am away?'

Harold said, 'There are no special guests at the house for several weeks and the servant girls can keep it ticking over until you get back. Instruct the girls before you go.'

Herr Shoemaker replied, 'Then I will say goodnight and get started.' Herr Shoemaker left the dining-room with Harold Szirtes saying, 'That's what I like about Shoemaker; he gets on with the job.'

When Herr Shoemaker left in a taxi, Karl said with an expressive leer, 'Good, now he's away we can get on with some fun. I have a cleaning girl, Nataša, here in the hotel, who has been insubordinate and she needs a harsh lesson.' Harold, who was now a little drunk, said, trying unsuccessfully to replicate Karl's leer, 'Leave it for one hour until we get rid of all the dining-room guests, then bring her down to the cellar.'

Harold went through to Freda and said, 'Tell the dining-room customers we have a water leak and have to shut the water off. Give them vouchers for a free meal at a later date. Close the dining-room and bar inside one hour.'

Freda said, 'I didn't know there was a leak.'

Harold snapped back, 'There isn't, just do what you are told and get on with it. Oh! Yes. I need the keys to the cellar, we will be sampling wines all night and we do not want to be disturbed, do you understand?' Freda went to the pantry and came back with a key and gave it to him. He said, 'Don't wait up, we will be down there for a long, long time.' He walked toward the cellar laughing loudly. Freda watched him go with a frown on her face and a fear in her stomach.

Harold went out of a side door into the delivery yard. There was a long sloping ramp down the side of the building leading to a cellar extending under the full area of the hotel.

The ramp was designed to roll barrels down and up from the cellar, but Harold, Karl and Felix found it useful for other purposes.

He went down the ramp, opened the heavy door and put the lights on.

About half an hour later Karl and Felix arrived manhandling one of the servant girls named Nataša. They dragged her into the cellar. Harold locked the door, switched on a radio and turned up the volume.

23

Nataša Disappears

When the dining-room and kitchen were cleared and cleaned and the girls had retired upstairs, Freda and Maria sat down with a cup of tea and some toast.

Maria said, 'I saw my brother Nico today. He is working at Harold Szirtes' big country estate, he has found Prince, my horse there, and he won the working horse competition with him.'

Freda and Maria had become close friends. Freda felt very protective towards Maria, but she knew how hopeless it was for displaced persons with no identity controlled by these ruthless men. She said, 'Maria, I am glad that you have seen your brother and he is well. But please do not raise your expectations. These men who control us are absolute bastards. You do not know how evil they are. Be so very careful. Do not be alone when Karl is in the hotel.'

They finished their toast and tea in a depressed silence. Finally Freda said, 'Come now, let's go to bed, tomorrow is a new day.'

Maria was very apprehensive, but followed Freda along to her room at the rear of the hotel. Freda opened the door and they both went in and Freda said pointing with her finger, 'That's the bed, you can take that side and I will take this side.'

Maria said, 'You don't have a spare nightdress do you.'

Freda laughed and replied, 'Sorry, I don't have such a thing, I don't like to be constrained when I am sleeping and I sleep in the nude.'

Maria said, 'Oh!' Followed by a silence, then she quickly slipped out of her kitchen work clothes and her bra and slipped under the duvet keeping her knickers on.

Freda realised her fear and sat on the bed. She said, 'Maria you don't need to be afraid of me. I love you like a mother loves a daughter, not in some sexual way. You need to appreciate that I am giving up what little comfort and privacy I have to protect you as best I can from Karl. Do you understand what I am saying?'

Maria said, 'Yes I appreciate all that, but I did have worries, I wasn't sure about you, the girls do say things behind your back.'

Freda said, 'Yes, I know but in a strange way that reputation has protected me for several years. Harold, Karl and Felix don't even consider me when they are looking for a girl to rape. However, if you want to share my bed and this small flat you will need to make some allowances and put up with my personal habits. This little flat and this bed is the only privacy I have and my spare time is very limited. But rest assured I will not come on to you in that way, you are my unofficial adopted daughter.'

Before she knew it Maria was asleep, exhausted from the hard and long day.

Maria awoke early and slipped out of bed without disturbing Freda. She went into the bathroom, showered and returned to the bedroom with the towel wrapped around her. It was still dark, but she managed to find new clothing and retreated into the bathroom to dress. Freda was still sleeping when Maria quietly slipped out of the bedroom, locking the door behind her and making her way to the kitchen.

Sunday was a new day and brought a new surprise with it.

THE HOUSE OF ATTILA

Dmitar Hrvat, Breeding Manager of the Al Quoz Stables in Dubai, arrived with his family, celebrating his grandmother's eightieth birthday, and ordered Mecsek Highwaymen's Dumpling Soup, followed by Serbian stuffed peppers. The waitresses were excited because they now knew that it was he who had been the big tipper of a few months earlier.

Word was passed back to the kitchen and everyone worked with a new sense of heightened expectation.

Sure enough, at the end of the meal he asked to see Maria, the chef. Freda said to Maria, 'Oh! He even remembers your name. Ooh la la.'

When Maria arrived at the table, he stood up and said, 'Please let me introduce you to my grandmother and my sisters. Now please sit with us and have coffee.' He pulled up another chair. Maria bent down and kissed the elegant lady. She said, 'You remind me of one of my own grandmothers. I wish you a very happy birthday.'

The lady said, 'Thank you, I wish you a happy future.'

Maria said, 'Excuse me a moment, I have something in the kitchen to do then I will come and have coffee.' Maria rushed back into the kitchen and found the key to the pantry where she kept special and valuable baking and cooking items. She opened a drawer and took out a birthday cake she had been working on just as a standby for such an occasion as this. The cake was just a plain iced cake with Happy Birthday scrolled on top. Maria found a packet of cake candles and candle holders and she quickly pushed in eight candle holders neatly around the edge and inserted the candles.

She carried the cake on a big flat plate and locked the pantry door. She approached the dining-room and asked one of the waitresses to get a box of matches. They lit the candles before entering the dining-room and Maria carried the cake into the room, singing, 'Happy birthday to you, Happy birthday to you.' The rest of the diners and the waitresses quickly picked up on the song, finishing with a huge cheer. She placed the cake in front of the birthday girl and everyone shouted, 'Blow out the candles.'

Once the excitement had died down, Maria sat down with the family and coffee was served with slices of birthday cake.

Dmitar said, 'You have a good singing voice, Maria; please sing my grandmother a song for her birthday.'

Maria said, 'Because you remind me of my own grandmother who taught me this song, I will sing you her song for your birthday.'

>'Over the river and through the woods
>To grandmother's house we go.
>The horse knows the way
>To carry the sleigh
>Through the white and drifted snow, O!
>
>'Over the river and through the woods
>Oh, how the wind does blow.
>It stings the nose
>And bites the toes
>As over the ground we go.
>
>'Over the river and through the woods
>Trot fast my dapple gray.
>Spring over the ground
>Like a hunting hound
>On this Thanksgiving Day, Hey!
>
>'Over the river and through the woods
>Now grandmother's face I spy.
>Hurrah for the fun,
>Is the pudding done?
>Hurrah for the pumpkin pie.'

THE HOUSE OF ATTILA

As everyone laughed and applauded Maria took the opportunity to retreat back to her kitchen to get on with her work.

Freda came into the kitchen about half an hour later saying, 'Come, Maria, and say goodbye to the birthday party.' As they made their way back to the dining-room Freda whispered, 'He has left a tip of one thousand Czech Crowns.'

As they wished all the guests goodbye, Dmitar came over and thanked Maria for making his grandmother's birthday so special. 'I have had a very successful visit in business terms, but my grandmother's happiness means more to me than anything else, thank you so much. On my next trip over I would like to take you out.'

Maria did not know what to say, so she remained silent.

They all waved goodbye as the family drove away.

Later, at the end of the Sunday night, when everything was tidied and cleaned up and the girls had retired, Freda and Maria sat down in the kitchen with their tea and coffee.

Freda said, 'The bad news is about Nataša: two of the girls say that last night Karl and Felix asked Nataša to go outside into the yard and they secretly watched them as they forced her down into the wine cellar in the basement.

'They have not seen Nataša since, but this afternoon they saw Karl and Felix reverse a white van close to the top of the ramp leading to the wine cellar. They then both carefully stole into the hotel as if trying to take care no one could see them. They reappeared carrying towels, mop, bucket and assorted cleaning materials. They went into the wine cellar for a long time before dragging out a loosely rolled up carpet, which seemed to contain something heavy inside.

'With some great difficulty they managed to lift and push the carpet into the van, shut and lock the doors. After a few minutes, to recover their breathing, they then went back to the wine cellar. They were inside for a while before bringing out the mop, bucket and a number of filled polythene bags, which they put into the van after unlocking and opening the doors. They kept looking about as if to see if anyone was watching, and finally they got into the van and drove off.

Freda said, 'Now that the girls have told me this I remember that Harold Szirtes came and asked me for the key of the wine cellar last night and I gave it to him. The key has not been returned.'

Freda said, 'I fear the worst for Nataša.' She was silent for a minute, then she said, 'O, Lord. Who but You is there to remember the dispossessed? Who but You is there to speak a memorial for the oppressed and the powerless? Only You will remember them and keep them in your care.'

They lapsed into a long silence.

Eventually Freda snapped out of her depression and said, 'Saint Francis of Assisi said, "Lord grant me the serenity to accept the things I cannot change, the courage to change the things I can, and the wisdom to know the difference."'

Freda said with a bitter tone to her voice, 'Terrible as it is, this is one of these times.' She suddenly sat up, forced herself to brighten up and said, 'Maria, let me give you the best advice I know. If bad things happen to you, focus on the good things. Even though we are helpless and afflicted, we are still surrounded by good things. Let's count our blessings today.

'First of all a one thousand Czech Crown tip to be shared by all the staff; this amount is unheard of, what a blessing, and it was your doing. It seems that this strange man has taken a fancy to you and who knows where that will lead?'

They both ended up laughing almost hysterically as though relieving a great strain before making their way to their bed.

Meanwhile, back at the country estate, Nico had found a spare filly at the stables and soon had her working as a team with Charlie.

THE HOUSE OF ATTILA

He spent a good part of the Sunday training them to work together and walked them out to the forest pulling the wood cart.

When he came back to the boiler house later that evening he was surprised to find the boiler structure way over temperature. This puzzled him and he could only conclude that someone had loaded the fire with logs and left the fire door fully open for some time.

Nico was so busy that the days and weeks flew by. The football team was now much improved and the players were highly motivated, brimming with confidence. They had won every game since the start of the second half of the season. The Harold Szirtes Under Sixteen Boys was now in contention with two other teams for the league title and Harold Szirtes was beginning to attend the games, hoping to lift the league trophy.

The team won the last game of the season, which left them tied on points with their rivals, Partizan Under Sixteen Boys. There was no precedent in the league for this situation, so it was agreed to have one more game two weeks later as a play-off between the two teams to determine the league winner.

24

Shoemaker Reports Back

Herr Shoemaker returned home on the Monday morning before the Saturday of the play-off. A meeting to hear about Herr Shoemaker's overseas trip was called at the Harold Szirtes Hotel for the Monday evening.

Freda was informed. 'Harold Szirtes, Martin Shoemaker, Karl Stonier and Felix Hienmann will be having a meeting in the small dining-room on Monday evening. The photographic slide projector and screen must be set up ready for Martin to show his photographs. The meeting is strictly private and must not be disturbed in any way. There will be no meal as we will all be leaving immediately after the meeting.'

On the Monday evening Freda had warned Maria to keep out of sight and stay in the bedroom until she knew the men had left. Harold Szirtes' party arrived together in a car. They briskly walked in and went straight to the private dining-room.

Harold Szirtes opened the meeting by saying, 'Gentlemen, we welcome back Martin Shoemaker from his expedition beyond the Pillars of Hercules and look forward to hearing his report. Without further ado, I give you Martin Shoemaker.'

Herr Shoemaker had already plugged in his photographic slide projector and set up the screen.

He started with the postcard view of McCaig's Folly illumi-

THE HOUSE OF ATTILA

nated at night that had first excited Harold Szirtes. He said, 'I rowed out to sea in a rowing boat in the middle of the night to get this photograph for you, Harold.'

Harold said laughing, 'I suppose you think that I am lucky you didn't drown.' Karl and Felix responded with hysterical laughter.

When the laughter eventually subsided Herr Shoemaker began his commentary of the full slide show, little realising how many emotive buttons it pressed for Harold Szirtes.

Herr Shoemaker spoke confidently and distinctly with all his artistic flair.

'Within Oban, the most outstanding feature is McCaig's Tower, more usually and descriptively called McCaig's Folly. This is a Colosseum lookalike that stands above the town. The tower was built by a local banker called McCaig in 1897. The aim was to provide work for local stonemasons during a financial depression and provide a lasting monument to his family.

'Visitors to the tower are surprised by an uncanny personal feel about it. The interior comprises a grassy hilltop, with the wall of the tower encircling it like a crown on an uneven human head.

'Oban has developed into Scotland's most popular west-coast holiday town. Beyond Oban lie the islands of the Inner Hebrides: Kerrera, which protects the town from Atlantic storms; the low, green island of Lismore; majestic Mull; and the granite mountains of the Morvern peninsula. Beyond them, the sacred island of Iona, then Coll, Colonsay and Tiree.'

Shoemaker continued, 'Looking out to these islands, they reminded me of the legend of the lost continent of Atlantis.'

At this description Harold Szirtes sat bolt upright, his attention completely focused.

Shoemaker continued. 'There had been a powerful empire located to the west of the "Pillars of Hercules" on an island in the Atlantic Ocean. According to the legend the nation there had been established by Poseidon, the God of the Sea.

'Poseidon fathered five sets of twins on the island. The first-born, Atlas, had the continent and the surrounding ocean named for him. Poseidon divided the land into ten sections, each to be ruled by a son, or his heirs. After the people of Atlantis became corrupt and greedy, the gods decided to destroy them. A violent earthquake shook the land, giant waves rolled over the shores, and the island sank into the sea, never to be seen again.'

Shoemaker looked at Harold and saw that his mind was far away so he paused for a few moments then continued.

'Oban today has a resident population of eight thousand five hundred and is the unofficial capital of the West Highlands. It is known as the Gateway to the Isles. The panoramic views of the mountains, lochs and islands, which have captivated artists, authors, composers and poets for centuries are as striking now as they were when Dunollie Castle, a ruined keep, which has stood sentinel over the narrow entrance to the sheltered bay for around six hundred years, was the northern outpost of the Dalriadic Scots.'

Harold Szirtes interrupted, saying, 'Gateway to the Isles.'

Shoemaker hesitated to see if there was more coming, and then continued.

'It is no surprise to find Oban in the twenty-first century remains a magnet for travellers from all over the world. The town's present day popularity owes much to pilgrim travellers touring Staffa, the inspiration for Mendelssohn's Hebridean Overture, and Iona, the home of Scottish Christianity since St Columba stepped ashore in AD 563.

'Indeed once Oban had the royal seal of approval from Queen Victoria, who called it "one of the finest spots we have seen", the town's destiny as an endearingly enchanting holiday destination was as firmly set as the lava columns of Fingal's Cave in Staffa.'

Herr Shoemaker hesitated to let his poetic description sink in. He then continued in a much more businesslike manner. 'From our point of view Oban is the perfect site. Its harbour fronts onto a remote and wild coastline of hundreds of miles, which is ideal for smuggling by sea. There is presently a hotel for sale on the harbour front and I have indicated my interest to the sellers who are keen to close the deal as the hotel has been on the market for some time.

'Gentlemen, my trip has been highly fruitful and I commend to you the town of Oban.'

Harold Szirtes was beside himself with excitement. He stood up and said, 'Thank you, Martin. Gentlemen, this is not some accident, I have been guided mysteriously to this decision. Who could have predicted how I came to discover this crown over the town? Who would believe that by accidentally entering a cooking competition I would be brought together with a complete stranger? A complete stranger who showed me a postcard of the crown above the town that I was looking for? How is it possible that we have been guided to such an ancient place so perfectly equipped for our purposes?'

Harold suddenly changed his manner.

'Martin, you will communicate a provisional ten per cent above the asking price offer for the hotel subject to confirmation by our lawyers. However, as lawyers will be involved and you know how slow they are, it will take a few weeks if not months to complete the deal and meanwhile we have another gathering of franchisees to arrange.

'I have another idea. First, make the offer for the hotel through our lawyer. Then concentrate on our football team and make sure we win the league decider this Saturday. After that, you and Felix Hienmann will arrange another gathering of franchisees.

'When the hotel is completely ours, you will return to Oban with some girls and establish our foothold in this hotel.'

Harold Szirtes announced, 'Meeting closed. Now, gentlemen, we have an appointment with one of our politician friends in Belgrade tonight.'

Herr Shoemaker carried out the instructions regarding the offer for the hotel by speaking to Harold Szirtes' lawyers on the Tuesday.

25

Football Play-offs

On the Tuesday Herr Shoemaker drove out to the forest to see Nico. He walked over to where Nico was felling the trees, watching him work as he approached. He appreciated how Nico had a graceful efficiency in the way he moved.

As he got close Nico caught sight of him and switched off the chain-saw. Herr Shoemaker said, 'Take a break, let's have a coffee and you can tell me about the football team.'

They made their way back to the cabin and Nico made two cups of coffee.

They sat facing each other across the small kitchen table. Herr Shoemaker said, 'Well, Nico, it seems you have made a success of running the football team in my absence. How do you think it will go on Saturday?'

Nico said, 'It will not be an easy game; on paper we don't really have a chance. Partizan Under Sixteen Boys are a feeder club for Partizan Belgrade and have some of the best under sixteen-year-old players in Serbia. We were lucky earlier in the season when we played them before they had sorted out their regular players.'

Herr Shoemaker looked at him and said, 'Do you have a plan?'

Nico said, 'Yes.' He continued. 'I think the best chance we have is to play five-four-one and try to hold out as long as we can. If we can keep them from scoring for the whole of the game, they may panic in the latter stages, letting their defenders recklessly play too far forward and leaving gaps in their defence.

'At the very end of the match if we suddenly switch to three-five-two, and if we can surprise them with one quick break-away, with their players out of position, we may just be lucky. It will be touch and go but it is all we can do.' Nico's father came into his mind and he added, 'Anything is possible.'

Herr Shoemaker said as he got up, 'We will instruct the team about your plan tonight. As they walked back towards the road, Herr Shoemaker said, 'Nico, you have done well and I really appreciate it. I will see you tonight when I pick you and Imri up to go to training.'

Nico worked on until he had the cart filled with logs. He harnessed the two horses to the cart, quickly locked up the cabin and stable and began the journey back to the House of Attila.

On the Friday afternoon Imri came over to Nico as he was unloading the logs from the cart and said, 'Nico, I can't do any training with you as usual tonight as I am going to a night out in town.'

Nico replied, 'Do you think that is a good idea with the big game tomorrow?'

Imri replied with a laugh, 'It is probably the best way to relax before a big game.' With a laugh he about turned and jogged away.

Nico awoke early as usual on the Saturday morning and went about his chores in a leisurely way. Saturdays had become an easy routine: he sorted his boilers first, then attended to the horses, then he showered, changed into his track suit and trainers, packed his football kit in a sports bag and went over to the kitchen of the mansion house to get breakfast with the girls.

Valda, Milinka, Miljana and Senca were already making breakfast when he came in. Senca said jokingly, 'You won't be wanting any breakfast before the big game.'

Nico fell for it and said, 'Yes, yes, I can eat just now, it's only nine o'clock and the game is six hours away.'

Senca said, 'No, I don't think it is good to eat before a big game.' Nico's serious and disappointed look caused the girls to fall about with laughter. When she recovered, Valda filled a big bowl of porridge and laid it on the table and said, 'Eat that while I make you four slices of thick toast.' Nico beamed widely, realising now that they had only been winding him up.

The five of them finished their breakfasts and Valda said, 'Keep your mugs and I will make another pot of tea.' The other girls quickly washed, dried the dishes and put them away. They then all sat round the table for what was a special treat, a second mug of tea.

Milinka said, 'Nico, do you think you will win today?'

Nico replied, 'Partizan Under Sixteen Boys are better players and it will be very difficult, but I still hope we can surprise them.'

Miljana said, 'I wish we could come and watch you play.'

Valda said, 'That's not possible, but still we wish you well for the game, Nico.'

Miljana said, 'I will keep my fingers crossed for you.'

Milinka said with some feeling, 'It would be better if you kept your legs crossed.'

There was a stunned silence as Herr Shoemaker walked in saying, 'Good morning, good morning, how are we all this morning?' He continued. 'Nico, where is Imri? We need to get going; it is a two hour bus trip.'

Senca said, 'We haven't seen Imri this morning, I will go and check his room.'

Harold Szirtes came into the kitchen and said, 'Make me some breakfast. Martin, we will all go on the team bus, I will come with you on the bus. We all need to be strong together today.'

Senca came back saying, 'I can't wake him; Imri is out for the count.'

Harold Szirtes jumped up from the table, shouting, 'I will soon wake the lazy bastard.' Herr Shoemaker followed Harold. Senca mouthed silently to the others, 'Imri's still drunk.'

Harold Szirtes and Herr Shoemaker came back into the kitchen pushing Imri wearing only underpants before them. Harold shouted at him, 'You are a drunken bum, a disgrace to the family name. Give him coffee, strong coffee to try to sober him up.'

Valda gave Harold Szirtes a big plate of porridge and toast and said to Herr Shoemaker, 'Would you like to have some breakfast?'

Herr Shoemaker replied, 'No thank you, I have already eaten.'

Senca gave Imri a mug of black coffee. Imri said, 'I feel sick; I think I am going to be sick.'

Senca said, 'You would be better to come into the sluice room.' Imri allowed Senca to lead him into the sluice room and she left him there.

Imri was leaning over one of the sinks in the sluice room making a lot of noise, but between retching and trying to speak it was difficult to make out what he was saying.

Harold Szirtes finished his breakfast and got up and went to the sluice room.

Imri was slumped over the sink with the cold tap running to wash away the vomit. Harold grabbed Imri by the hair and held his head face-up under the running cold water. Imri was almost choking on the stream of running water, and he was also trying to shout at the same time. Harold Szirtes shouted, 'Get the coffee pot.' Senca ran and brought the coffee pot through. Harold said, 'Put some cold water in it to make sure

THE HOUSE OF ATTILA

it is not too hot.' Senca did so. Harold pulled Imri up by the hair into a standing position with his face uppermost. He said, 'Now pour the whole coffee pot into his mouth.' Senca tried but Imri would not open his mouth. Karl had appeared and he pushed Senca out of the way and took the coffee pot from her.

Karl forced the spout of the coffee jug into Imri's mouth and poured some coffee in. Imri immediately choked and forcibly spewed coffee and vomit, forcing everyone to jump back.

He fell to the floor heaving for breath and still trying to spew, however, he seemed to have emptied his stomach. His convulsions slowly abated and his moaning died to a whimper as he lay in the pool of vomit.

Harold uncoiled a water hose and turned on the tap and began to hose Imri down, resulting in a lot of squealing. He directed the water jet away and said, 'We haven't all day. Come on now. Chop, chop. Strip those soiled underpants off him, come on.' Karl quickly grabbed the waist band of the underpants and yanked them off the sprawled out Imri. Harold redirected the water jet back on to him.

Imri immediately reacted by crawling into the corner. Then when he realised he couldn't escape he tried to stand, crying out, 'Dad, stop it, please stop it.' When he was on his feet Harold directed the water away and Imri started to cry.

Harold shouted at Senca, 'Hurry up, find clean clothes for him, hurry up, hurry up, we are now running late.'

Valda ran upstairs to Imri's room and got suitable sports clothes and trainers including a pair of football boots and brought them back to the kitchen, where she and Senca helped the still inebriated Imri into his clothing.

They helped him out to the car and into the back seat. Harold Szirtes and Karl got into the front seats and Nico and Herr Shoemaker got into the back seats with Imri.

They drove to the football ground where the other team

members were waiting at a parked bus. They got everyone on to the bus with Imri just managing to climb on and sink into a seat.

The bus drove off and after a few minutes Herr Shoemaker came down and sat beside Nico. He said, 'Nico, Harold Szirtes says that Imri must play.'

Nico said, 'That is not possible, have you seen the state of him?'

Herr Shoemaker said, 'Nico, I have no option, what Harold Szirtes says goes. You know that.'

Nico said, 'I know.'

After a long silence Nico added, 'If that is how it has to be, play Imri as the lone forward and tell the team they must stick to the game plan no matter how hard and futile it seems.

'I don't think Imri can last more than about fifteen minutes. List Diminshie as a substitute and when Imri finally expires put him on. It is possible that Diminshie's speed will catch them out.'

Imri slept the whole two hours of the bus journey. When the bus arrived at the football ground the team and their helpers were shown into the dressing-room.

Herr Shoemaker read out the team. There were a few resentful comments about Imrie's condition, but everyone was afraid of Harold Szirtes and his evil minder Karl.

As the team prepared, Herr Shoemaker gave them the game plan once again. They went out to the park with their track suits on to warm up. Harold Szirtes had bought new strips for the game. However, Imri remained in the dressing-room.

They came back into the dressing-room after about half an hour. Herr Shoemaker had hung the new strips up with the correct team numbers above each player's changing place. On seeing the new strips the boys' spirits lifted.

As they changed into the new strips Nico said, 'We know

THE HOUSE OF ATTILA

the opposition strength is in their two fantastic wingers. Our whole game plan is based on an unconventional formation. We are going to play five across the back to stop these two wingers. That effectively gives us two full backs and a centre half with two very mobile sweepers. Our four midfield players are there to command the midfield. Imri will play the lonely forward role to be a threat to their defence.'

A voice shouted out, 'Once they smell his breath he will be even more lonely.' The team fell about laughing while Karl suddenly sprung up and stared at each player trying to detect any sign of guilt.

When the hilarity subsided Nico carried on. 'If they can't get their wingers going and they don't score a goal, we have a chance. If we hold out long enough, they will throw caution to the wind and we may just get a quick break away, late in the game. We must be patient right to the end. Are we all agreed?' The whole dressing-room erupted with a huge shout, enough to scare the opposition. 'We are.'

Right from the start the Harold Szirtes Under Sixteen Boys were pushed back. Imri who was still half drunk, kept shouting loudly for the ball and as he staggered about he kept accidently bumping into the giant centre half.

The centre half thought Imri was trying to intimidate him and hit him with an almighty punch that he wound up from about a metre away.

Imri fell to the ground like a pole-axed bull gasping for breath. The assault occurred right in front of the linesman who immediately flagged to the referee.

The referee ran over to the linesman and listened to what he said. He immediately blew his whistle and gestured to the centre half.

He took out his book and pencil and wrote the player's number, name and time of the incident with the word 'punch'. The referee pointed to the dressing-room and said

'Off!' in an exaggerated way so that it was clear to everyone what his decision was.

The centre half and the entire Partizan Belgrade Under Sixteen Boys team engulfed the referee, protesting his decision.

Imri continued to lie on the ground gasping for breath. Herr Shoemaker ran up to him with his trainer's bag, but no amount of treatment seemed to revive Imri. After about a minute the referee insisted that he leave the field of play.

Two of the players helped him to his feet and assisted him to walk slowly off the pitch.

Herr Shoemaker shouted, 'Diminshie, get ready to play.'

Imri was allowed into the locked dressing-room and the door was relocked behind him. He immediately lay down on the bench and went to sleep.

At the first stoppage in play, Diminshie was allowed to go on.

Even though the Partizan Belgrade Under Sixteen Boys were down to ten men the rest of the first half was evenly balanced.

When the referee blew for half-time each team went to opposite sides of the pitch to listen to their coaches and take in a little water.

Herr Shoemaker said, 'Well done, boys. Nothing each is a good result for half-time and they are down to ten men. I think we can win this one, Nico, what do you think?'

Nico said, 'Even with ten men they are still dangerous, their two wingers are waiting to turn the game at the first opportunity. We must stick to the same game plan right to the end. They will not want to go to extra time having played most of the game with ten men. If we can keep them out for most of this next half they will become desperate and reckless and we may just get the break we need. If it goes into extra time with the extra man the game should swing our way. Stick to the game plan. Are we agreed?' The team again responded with an almighty shout. 'We are agreed!' They ran on to the pitch and took up their positions ready for the contest. The other team drifted on to the pitch in ones and two's.

The beginning of the second half continued as the end of the first half.

As the game progressed it was clear that the Harold Szirtes Hotel Under Sixteen Boys team were getting more possession.

With about five minutes to go suddenly Nico found himself clear on the wing; he looked up as he began his run and saw Diminshie start a blistering run from deep in midfield.

Nico released the ball in front of his projected run when Diminshie was still onside. He brought it under control without breaking stride and was through into the penalty area and the keeper ran out towards him. Diminshie sidestepped and the keeper grabbed his arm and pulled him down.

The referee immediately blew and pointed to the penalty spot. Diminshie retrieved the ball and held it out to Nico and said, 'Here, you take it.'

Nico took the ball and placed it on the penalty spot. He immediately turned his back on the keeper who was trying to wind him up.

Nico deliberately walked back slowly, thinking, 'This is what all these hours of practice were for. Know your target spot before you turn round and face the goal. Just concentrate on getting your knee over the ball.' Nico almost reached the eighteen metre line; he turned and looked intently at the ball. The referee blew his whistle. Nico raised himself on to his toes and started his run, focusing his eyes on the ball. He planted his left foot firmly at the side of the ball, then, concentrating on getting his right knee over the ball, he accelerated his lower leg, striking the ball sweetly with his extended foot, following through cleanly.

The keeper guessed correctly but before he could get down the ball rifled under his outstretched hand and into the corner of the net.

These moments were like slow motion to Nico who saw every detail until the mass of bodies descended upon him.

The team were ecstatic, but like many football games in history, the team that scores is often most at risk immediately after scoring. The celebrations and relief tends to momentarily break the concentration of the scoring team and it often has the opposite effect on the trailing team.

Sure enough, before the Harold Szirtes Under Sixteens finished celebrating, Partizan took the restart and immediately sent a long ball down the left wing. The winger quickly brought it under control and made for the line. The whole defence was caught out of position and the winger sent a beautiful cross over, which was met by their striker and the ball crashed into the back of the net. The referee blew his whistle and took out his notebook and recorded the goal.

The Harold Szirtes goalkeeper was still lying on the ground. The referee signalled the trainer to come on. Herr Shoemaker ran to attend the goalkeeper, clutching his treatment bag. The goalkeeper had collided with the goalpost in his effort to save the goal and had a nasty gash on his temple.

The referee said, 'This is a head injury and the player cannot carry on in case of concussion.'

Herr Shoemaker said, 'We don't have a substitute goalkeeper.' The referee replied, 'I can't help that, but you need to put someone in goal.' Herr Shoemaker quickly ran over to the substitutes and said, 'Can I have a volunteer to go in goal?'

Zach said, 'I will.'

They quickly got the goalkeeper's jersey and gloves off the injured keeper and gave them to Zach. He gave his name to the referee and ran to his position in the goalmouth.

Shortly after the goalkeeper's substitution the referee blew for the end of normal time.

THE HOUSE OF ATTILA

The team gathered at the side of the pitch drinking from bottles of water. Herr Shoemaker said to Nico, 'What do you think?'

Nico gestured to the players to gather round. He shouted, 'Do you want to win this game?' He got a lot of 'Yes' replies. Now that he had their attention he went on. 'Zach with his big heart has helped us by going in goal even though he is not a regular goalkeeper. We must do our best to protect him and stop them having shots on goal. Keep to the same game plan, there are signs that they are tiring from playing so long with only ten men. We conceded that goal by relaxing from our game plan and they just sliced through us. Keep to the game plan.'

Finally he shouted for the third time. 'Are we agreed?' They responded as before in unison. They ran on to the pitch looking like a united organisation and took up their positions.

The first half of extra time was bogged down in midfield but the Harold Szirtes team definitely had most of the possession and pressed their opponents back into their half.

The Partizan team were now visibly tiring and when their right back went down with cramp and was receiving treatment, Nico ran back to Zach, the goalkeeper and said, 'Zach, when you get a chance give me a long ball down the left wing.'

The game started again and Partizan attacked down their right wing, crossing the ball into the penalty area. Their striker met the ball perfectly and sent a header goal bound. Zach surprised everyone with a beautiful save. Almost before anyone had got over their surprise he ran out to the edge of his area and launched a long kick down the left wing beyond Nico.

The full back was physically done and started a limping run, but Nico darted past him and on to the ball. He ran to the line and then in towards the goal. The keeper came out to meet him, leaving the goalmouth completely open. Nico waited until the last minute then cut the ball back across the goalmouth into the path of Diminshie who had made his run when he saw Nico break away.

It was the easiest goal Diminshie had ever scored.

This time as they ran back to prepare for the other team to centre the ball and restart the game, Nico shouted at every player, 'Concentrate and keep to the game plan.' They turned round for the second half of extra time with Nico telling them, 'Keep to the game plan and protect our goal as far up the park as we can.'

With the opposition now struggling to keep going, the referee finally blew for full-time and the end of the game.

The celebrations on the park were overwhelming. Ever aware of his opportunities, Harold Szirtes got the attendant to unlock the dressing-rooms and sneaked in and got Imri up and out into the celebrations. As the initial high spirits died down, first Partizan paraded to be presented with their individual runners-up league medals. Then the Harold Szirtes boys were paraded with Imri leading and were presented with their individual league winners' medals. Then Imri stepped forward to pick up the league cup. Harold Szirtes shouted from the side. 'Imri, hold it up high, hold it up high.' The press photographers took many photographs of Imri and Harold holding the cup.

It took ages for the boys to quieten down in the dressing-room; Partizan had left the ground before the Harold Szirtes team started to shower. Finally, in various stages of dressing, they made their way out and on to the bus.

On the team bus Harold Szirtes announced, 'We are going to party tonight at the Harold Szirtes Hotel; everyone must come back to the Hotel.'

Harold phoned ahead and arranged for the pre-booked brass band to be playing in the town square in front of the hotel. He also arranged for the local press and three politicians to be at the hotel for the arrival of the team bus.

By the time the bus arrived there was a big crowd gathered in the town square.

The team cascaded out of the bus and into the cheering crowd. Herr Shoemaker was getting carried away and got the team to form into a conga dance. He ran alongside, shouting, 'Three steps forward, kick, two steps back, kick. Three steps forward, kick, two steps back, kick.'

Nico watched from the shadows at the side of the hotel front door, waiting on his chance to slip round the back to see his sister Maria. He thought to himself, 'It's ironic that Herr Shoemaker, a modern day people trafficker, is teaching a dance originated by the slaves in Cuba who danced when they were shackled in a line by chains.'

Soon the conga became a giant conga, snaking itself randomly and rhythmically round the town square with the brass band responding with one Latin American rhythm after another.

Nico waited until the chaos provided the diversion he needed to slip up the side of the hotel to the back of the kitchen. Maria saw him through the window and let him in. They hugged then Nico said, 'The team will be celebrating in the hotel tonight, so I will be here for a few hours. 'We must be careful no one suspects that we know each other. These are dangerous men we are working for. I must join the team before anyone notices that I am missing and come looking for me.'

Nico made his way back to the crowded square the same way that had come.

Eventually the team were herded together and posed for various photographs with Harold Szirtes and the politicians holding the cup in various poses.

Then they were all shepherded into the hotel bar for pre-dinner drinks and speeches by Harold Szirtes. Then on into the dining-room for dinner and more speeches by Harold and two of the politicians; the other one was already too drunk to say anything discernible.

Then it was on to the lounge dance hall where a section of the brass band was playing popular tunes.

Nico found Herr Shoemaker and said, 'Is there a job I could do? I don't want to drink.' Herr Shoemaker thought for a moment and then said, 'The only thing I can think of is that you could collect empty glasses and wash them to keep the bar stocked with clean ones.'

Nico said, 'Thank you, I will do that.'

Herr Shoemaker said, 'Come, I will introduce you to Freda, the hotel manager.'

Herr Shoemaker took him to Freda and said, 'Freda, this is Nico, he is too young to drink and wants a job collecting and cleaning glasses.'

Freda said, 'What a find, someone who wants to work, well I can keep him busy.'

Nico quickly settled into the role and often got the bonus of seeing Maria working in the kitchen through the serving hatch.

The evening quickly drifted into alcoholic comradeship stimulated by the popular music supplied by the brass band and occasional ambitious singers from the audience.

About ten o'clock Karl shepherded two of the hotel cleaning girls on to the stage and instructed them to strip in time to the music. Behind his instructions was an implied threat and his reputation. But first he had to demonstrate his party piece.

He stood at the side of the stage and announced, 'Let me give you a word of warning.' He pulled a free-standing spiked pole with a raw cabbage impaled on the top. He picked up his cat-o'-nine-tails and whipped the cabbage with a single blow, decimating about a third of it. He then shouted, 'If anyone approaches this stage while the girls are performing they will be met with this deadly whip, which will take your face off.' Karl aggressively prompted the girls to perform encore after encore, encouraged by a now wild audience.

After the performance Karl took the girls back upstairs and he rounded up all the other cleaning girls and said, 'Quickly get dressed for a party and then come down and join us.' The girls did not need inviting twice and were soon integrated into the general celebrations.

Imri did not last long; with a head start from the night before, he soon collapsed over his table.

Herr Shoemaker spotted him and helped him up to an empty bedroom, dumped him on the bed and covered him with the duvet.

Eventually Harold Szirtes, who was drinking heavily with the politicians, got tired and said to Herr Shoemaker, 'Get a taxi, I want to go home.'

Herr Shoemaker said to Nico, 'Nico here are some coins, phone a taxi for Harold to go to the House of Attila. The phone numbers for taxis are displayed on the wall at the telephone.' Nico noticed the league cup lying on the floor near Harold's table; he picked it up and gave it to Freda for safe keeping.

Nico phoned the taxi company and they said, 'A taxi will be there in five minutes.'

He quickly found Maria and kissed her on the cheek and said, 'I have to go now. God bless you and keep you safe.'

The taxi arrived. Nico told Herr Shoemaker, but Harold Szirtes was in a drunken conversation with one of the politicians. It took Herr Shoemaker fifteen minutes to get him out to the taxi. Nico was relieved that Harold went into the passenger seat beside the taxi driver. Herr Shoemaker and Nico got into the back seats.

Harold instructed the driver, 'The House of Attila as fast as you like, I am ready for my bed.' He then fell asleep. When the taxi arrived at the gates, Herr Shoemaker got out and identified himself and the gates opened. He got into the taxi and it drove to the front door.

Herr Shoemaker paid the driver and went round to help Harold. He said, 'Come on, Harold, we are home.' He helped him out of the taxi and, with Nico running ahead opening doors, they got him up to his room. When they got him into his bedroom Herr Shoemaker said, 'Thanks, Nico, I can manage now.'

Nico was glad to get away and quickly ran downstairs; he locked the front door and made his way out through the kitchen and round to his boiler house.

He quickly checked the boiler and put more logs on the fire and closed the fire doors to let the logs smoulder away for what was left of the night.

He quickly knelt and raised a prayer for the continued safety of his sister Maria.

26

The Second Gathering

The Sunday after the league-winning celebrations was relatively quiet. Imri surfaced about lunchtime but did not want any food and quietly left the hotel to go for a walk.

At the House of Attila Harold Szirtes was also conspicuous by his absence, spending most of the day in his room, then getting a taxi into town with Imri, saying that they wouldn't be back until Monday.

Herr Shoemaker phoned Felix Hiennman and asked him to meet him at seven o'clock for dinner at the Harold Szirtes Hotel.

Not so with Nico, who was up at his usual time. He checked the boiler and banked up the fire with logs and closed the fire door tight shut. The mild spring weather meant that the boilers needed much less fuel. Nico was now building up a good reserve of logs behind the boiler house and he was keeping them dry with a tarpaulin cover tied down to a few logs on the outside.

Nico then had breakfast with the girls and then attended to his two horses. He decided to give them the freedom of the paddock. He took Charlie out first and let him into the paddock and closed the gate. He went back for Annabel, the replacement horse for Prince, but she was very stroppy. He tried to back her out but she wasn't having any of it. Nico, with some difficulty, fitted a training halter to her head and eventually got her out of the stall and into the paddock.

She went straight over to Charlie who was cropping some grass and peed right in front of his face. Then she went for a gallop round the paddock.

He shook his head, puzzled about what was up with Annabel, and went back to his boiler house. He put his laundry in the washing machine located in the pump house, primed it with washing powder and turned it on.

He changed into his running gear and ran out to the forest cabin where he spent the rest of the morning tidying up and preparing his equipment for the week ahead.

He ran back to the House of Attila and went to the boiler house. He changed into his work clothes and went towards the stables. As he approached he saw Miljana standing on the bottom rail of the paddock fence holding on to the top rail and looking over the top at Annabel and Charlie. Annabel was standing in front of Charlie sort of crouching and Charlie was certainly aroused. Nico ran forward towards the gate shouting, 'Stop it, Charlie, you dirty devil.'

Miljana jumped down from the fence and blocked his path, saying, 'It's not dirty, it's beautiful, let them do it, they are going to make a foal.' She held him back although he could have easily broken away. Charlie mounted Annabel, probed about and gently inserted his huge member, then began to thrust rhythmically. Miljana applauded clapping her hands, shouting 'Go on, boy; go on, boy, more, more.'

Nico started blushing and walked away back towards the mansion house kitchen, leaving Miljana encouraging the horses.

He entered the kitchen to find Senca and said, 'Hello, Senca, what time are you girls eating tonight?' Senca said, 'Come around about six o'clock, I am making a delicious Hungarian goulash. There is a pot of soup and bread to keep you going just now.' Nico helped himself to a plate of soup and two thick slices of bread.

He finished eating and went back to the boiler house, glancing at the paddock, things seemed to have quietened down, but he did not look too long for fear of seeing Miljana.

He went into the pump room, retrieved his laundry and hung it on a clothes horse to dry, thinking, 'This pump house is perfect for drying clothes with the hot water pipes giving off plenty of heat.'

He then thought, 'OK, let's get these horses in.' He went to the paddock and noticed thankfully Miljana wasn't there. The two horses were calm and perfectly compliant and let him lead them one at a time to the stalls in the stable.

He decided that it was a good idea to wash both of them down and spent about an hour washing and grooming the two horses.

He gave them fresh food and water then washed and disinfected the grooming implements and hung them up to dry.

He went back to the boiler house room and selected some dry underpants, socks, T-shirt, a track suit, a towel and his toilet bag.

He went to the stables dressing-rooms and started running a shower. He stripped off his work boots, and clothes and stepped into the hot shower. He luxuriated in its cascade. His back was to the door and he could not see Miljana quietly sneak in.

She quickly kicked off her shoes, slipped out of her clothes, dived into the shower, grabbing him from the back round the waist, saying, 'Miljana wants you just like Annabel wanted Charlie.' She washed him down with deft, well-practised hands. When they had finished she quickly left the shower and, using Nico's towel, dried herself off. She quickly dressed saying with a laugh, 'See you at dinner, don't be late.' Then she disappeared through the door, leaving Nico completely mesmerised with a silly grin across his face.

Nico dried himself using the slightly wet towel; though he wasn't bothered about that, he felt ten feet tall. He combed his hair, put on the clean underwear, track suit, socks and trainers and collected up his dirty working clothes, boots and towel. He went back to the pump room and put the dirty clothes and towel in the laundry basket. He went to his room and checked the time and got a shock; it was six o'clock.

He made his way over to the kitchen and found the girls were just finishing preparations for dinner. Valda said, 'Good, Nico, perfect timing.'

Miljana acted perfectly naturally and said, 'Sit down at the table and I will be mum and pour the tea.' She made the tea in a big teapot and refilled the kettle and put it on the stove to boil again.

The girls set large plates of Senca's Hungarian goulash at each of the place settings and Miljana poured five mugs of tea. She emptied the teapot and made a fresh pot of tea saying, 'I have a special use for that when it cools.'

Milinka said, 'Please don't start yet, can someone say grace first.' There was a long silence. Then Milinka said, 'You are religious, can you please say grace, it is very important.'

Nico felt guilty about what had just happened in the shower and was a bit unwilling to be hypocritical. Milinka, sensing his uncertainty, pleaded with him, 'Please, Nico; I want you to say grace.'

Nico still felt guilty but he bowed his head and an old school thanksgiving grace came into his head.

> 'Bless us,
> O Lord,
> And these your gifts,
> Which we are about to receive from your bounty.
> Through Christ our Lord.
> Amen.'

The girls whispered, 'Amen.'

Then all five of them got stuck into the goulash with groans of deep satisfaction.

When they finished Senca got up from the table and brought the big cooking pot over and despite protests, spooned small but equal portions of second helpings on to everyone's plate.

As she was doing that Miljana spooned the tea bags out of the teapot.

They finished eating and Valda said, 'Nico, tell us about the football.'

Nico told them the highlights of the game, getting great laughter as he explained how Imri unwittingly managed to get their centre half sent off, finishing by saying, 'He probably couldn't have done it if he was sober.' Which triggered another bout of laughter as the girls visualised Imri staggering about and bumping into the big centre half.

Miljana said, 'Tell us about the party at the hotel. We heard that the cleaners were doing striptease. Tell us about that.' Nico blushed bright red and the girls really laid it on, winding him up about the strippers for about half an hour. Eventually they wound down, having exhausted every possible avenue to keep Nico blushing.

Miljana got up and felt the teapot. She said, 'That's good, it is quite cold, now for some ice,' and she got some ice from the fridge, broke out some ice cubes and put them in the teapot. Senca could not contain her curiosity and said, 'Miljana what are you doing?' Miljana went over to one of the cupboards under the sinks and pulled out a full bottle of vodka. 'Herr Shoemaker brought a bottle of vodka back with him, which he confiscated from Imri when he flaked out at the hotel last night. He told me to get rid of it, saying that Imri would not remember anything about it. Girls, we have to obey orders and get rid of the vodka so we will mix the vodka with the iced tea in case anyone surprises us and comes in while we are drinking.'

She opened the top of the vodka bottle and emptied it into the big teapot.

She then said, 'Pass your tea mugs and I will give you a top up and this is the most refreshing tea you have ever tasted.' The girls passed their mugs which Miljana filled with iced tea from the teapot. She said, 'Nico, give me your mug.'

Nico said, 'No, Miljana I am only fourteen.'

Miljana threw up her hands in a gesture of horror. 'You are not only fourteen are you? Oh no! I thought you were at least sixteen.' Miljana immediately left the room.

Senca said, passing out some sheets of paper, 'I have made up a song sheet of some of the favourite old songs, so let's have a singsong.'

Senca led off the singing and the others followed enthusiastically. Miljana quietly rejoined the group and soon engaged in the singing.

The iced tea with its added vodka added to the sense of comradeship and nostalgia, occasionally causing a few tears to flood the eyes. Although Nico was not drinking the vodka-laced tea he was enjoying the singing. The time just flew and no one noticed that it was eleven o'clock until Herr Shoemaker came into the kitchen. He said, 'No don't stop! I heard the singing and I just came in to see what was going on. I wonder if I could have a cup of tea please, I have been busy all evening at a meeting in town.' The girls froze momentarily, looking at the big tea pot.

Valda was quickest to respond and said, 'Let me make you fresh tea, this is iced tea in the pot and will be well stewed by now.' She quickly made a small pot of tea and placed it on the table at the end furthest away from the big teapot. She placed a cup with a small jug of milk and a sugar bowl beside it. She said, 'Sit down here, Herr Shoemaker while I make you some buttered toast.' She quickly put bread into the six-slot toaster; she picked up the big teapot and emptied it equally into the girls mugs, then took the teapot to the sink and rinsed it out. With her back to Herr Shoemaker she expelled her breath in a silent 'Phew!'

Valda buttered the toast, replacing each slice as she took it out of the toaster, and soon had a large plate of toast.

She placed the plate of toast on the table and everyone helped themselves.

The girls took great delight in sipping their vodka-laced iced tea in full view of Herr Shoemaker.

When they finished eating, Herr Shoemaker said, 'Sing me a song before I go to bed.'

Senca passed him a song sheet and said, 'You can join us in the singing.'

Senca led off with an old Russian Slavic folk song:

> 'Once upon a time there was a tavern
> Where we used to raise a glass or two;
> Remember how we laughed away the hours,
> And dreamed of all the great things we would do.
>
> 'Those were the days, my friend,
> We thought they'd never end,
> We'd sing and dance forever and a day;
> We'd live the life we choose,
> We'd fight and never lose
> For we were young and sure to have our way.
>
> 'Then the busy years went rushing by us,
> We lost our starry notions on the way,
> If by chance I'd see you in the tavern
> We'd smile at one another and we'd say,

'Those were the days, my friend,
We thought they'd never end,
We'd sing and dance forever and a day;
We'd live the life we choose,
We'd fight and never lose
For we were young and sure to have our way.

'Just tonight I stood before the tavern,
Nothing seemed the way it used to be,
In the glass I saw a strange reflection,
Was that lonely woman really me?

'Those were the days, my friend,
We thought they'd never end,
We'd sing and dance forever and a day;
We'd live the life we choose,
We'd fight and never lose,
For we were young and sure to have our way.

'Through the door there came familiar laughter,
I saw your face and heard you call my name,
Oh, my friend, we're older but no wiser,
For in our hearts the dreams are still the same.

'Those were the days, my friend,
We thought they'd never end,
We'd sing and dance forever and a day;
We'd live the life we choose,
We'd fight and never lose,
For we were young and sure to have our way.'

Herr Shoemaker joined in enthusiastically and when it was finished he cried, 'Bravo, bravo.'

Valda took the opportunity to say, 'Come on now it won't be this in the morning when we have to get up. Let's get these things washed up and put away.'

THE HOUSE OF ATTILA

As the girls washed up the dishes Nico slipped away to his boiler house.

The Monday morning came quickly and Nico went about his well practised working week routines easily and contentedly in the warm spring weather.

Herr Shoemaker was making preparations for the next gathering of franchisees, like the last one a mixture of newcomers and slightly experienced hotel brothel operators. Felix Hienmann (in charge of intelligence) ran the contact details and invitations from his growing business database. He collected the most detailed intelligence profile of every franchise area.

He visited every franchise and made up a list of all local politicians including all regulatory enforcing officers, ranging from police, taxation, fire, health and safety, to environmental, licensing, newspaper reporters and so on. More importantly he made a list of any competition operating in the areas. His database included personal information on every one of these key individuals.

This gathering was oversubscribed but Herr Shoemaker had trimmed the list down to twenty-one, which was simply based on the fact that there were twenty-one guest bedrooms in the mansion house. Also Felix was structuring invitations to gatherings strictly on ethnic and religious lines. Felix understood the power structures in every geographical area.

The Friday evening of the gathering arrived and all the preparations and ceremony went largely as before, except instead of the man hunt, this Saturday's bloodletting involved the elimination of a rival gang in another part of the country.

27

Elimination

The leader of the rival gang had over a number of years purchased and developed an old run-down hotel into a really plush night-club and brothel.

He had developed the habit of running a big poker game every Saturday in his night-club. The game started at noon on Saturday and finished at noon on Sunday. It had become famous in gambling circles and gamblers came from hundreds of miles away to play. The players were scheduled by strict ticket number order and sometimes had to wait for several weeks for their next likely game at the table. There was always a waiting list of players in the bar ready to step in as soon as a player dropped out of the card game in the rear of the building. What the ordinary players did not know was that ten of any weekend's allocation of tickets were for gang members who could join the game as and when needed. Players at the end of the waiting list could spend some time with the ladies or play the gaming machines or pool, or could drink their time away. However, such was their desire to play, they would wait all night and through the Sunday morning even to play a few hands near the end.

As they became richer, the gang members were beginning to believe that they were highly skilled at poker. The gang leader was deluding himself, because he and his close associates had simply become highly skilled in collusion.

THE HOUSE OF ATTILA

They used one of the most common and easiest methods for cheating at poker, by involving constantly changing partners. Two of them would form a secret partnership and strategically sit at opposite ends of the table. They would raise and then re-raise one another, hoping to trap other players in between during the process. They also employed a range of sophisticated signalling methods to exchange information about each other's hands and eventually identify who would play on.

There were ten of them working together in such a way. As such, a different one ended up winning the bulk of the money each week, making it difficult for other players (who could only get a game several weeks apart). The winnings averaged 100,000 Czech Crowns per week for the night-club.

Such was his increase in confidence that the gang leader believed he could expand his empire by starting new night-clubs and brothels.

He had purchased a two star hotel in one of the House of Attila's franchise territories and had even had the impudence to try to recruit one of their best prostitutes. When the franchisee complained to Felix there was no option.

The opening ceremonial for the twenty-one franchisees was as impressive as before. However, when Harold Szirtes spoke, he changed the tack at the end slightly.

He said, 'Gentlemen, you have all bought a franchise from the House of Attila, the seven of you sitting across from me are about to begin your businesses, the fourteen of you sitting at the sides of the hall are all very recent franchisees, but you have returned to the source to learn again the basic principles of success.

'The final fact of life that you have to learn is that no one goes against the House of Attila and gets away with it. In this regard every franchisee needs to be absolutely ruthless. One act of weakness or mercy by you in your local area will come back tenfold to haunt you. In some cases we need to join together to defeat powerful foes when they arise, and arise they will.

'Gentlemen, a foe has arisen in one of our franchisees' areas. Tomorrow we will act collectively to protect our interests. Be ready to rise to a new level of commitment.'

This time the Friday evening did not end with a ritual humiliation. Herr Shoemaker simply announced, 'We are now going to retire for dinner followed by some musical entertainment before you retire to bed. We have a very busy day tomorrow and you need to be fresh and alert.'

The Saturday morning started with breakfast at nine o'clock when the franchisees assembled in the dining-room.

When they had all finished eating, they were led into the great hall where they found their places and sat down. When they were all seated Herr Shoemaker strode into the centre of the hall, ascended the small stage and announced loudly. 'Today we are going to act in unison against a foe that has foolishly tried to muscle into one of our franchise territories.

'The first thing to notice is that our foe does not pick the time or the place. Felix has been assembling the intelligence and preparing the battlefield. He will now present his plan of action.'

Felix came forward into the open end of the U-shaped seating arrangement. He switched on the photographic slide projector.

When he was satisfied with the sharpness of the image he turned to face the audience. 'Good, good, morning,' he said nervously, 'I am not used to being the centre of attention.'

Felix moved the slide show to the next slide. It showed the face of a relatively young man and Felix said, 'This is Andrija Milošević, a small-time gangster who is beginning to flex his muscles. He has foolishly tried to move into one of our franchise areas.' Felix got visibly excited and said, 'He, he, he, shouldn't have done that. He, he has bitten off more than he can chew and he is going to lose more than his false teeth. Ha, ha, ha.' Felix laughed at his joke.

The audience responded sympathetically.

Felix cut their laughter short, using both hands to give the hand signal 'Cut!'

He said very loudly, 'What sets the House of Attila apart is the way we wage war. We don't take chances; we pick the time, the battlefield and the weapons.'

The next slide showed the night-club building with a long elegant front elevation set back from the pavement with well kept gardens. In the middle of the building, splitting the gardens, was a large reception hall, which extended out from the building right on to the pavement, including a drive through drop-off and pick-up lay-by.

Felix explained, 'This reception hall not only extends from the building to the roadway but opens out into a large central atrium inside the building, extending the three floors to the glazed roof.' The next slide showed this atrium with two stairways each side of the reception hall with balconies leading to numerous rooms on the upper two floors. He continued, 'The most important feature to note is the extensive ornamental timber balustrades and panelling.'

Felix brought up the next series of three slides each, showing emergency exits with their panic bars chained and padlocked.

Felix explained, 'Because security is the priority in this night-club, they chain and padlock all the emergency exits except the main entrance.'

Felix carried on by saying, 'Gentlemen, this building design, coupled with their practice of padlocking all the emergency exits makes the owners very vulnerable to fire in the main reception.' He continued, 'Not only is this their only escape route but the reception hall opening out into the large atrium will exacerbate the rapid spread of fire throughout the building.'

By this time in the presentation Felix was now quite confident and said, 'A further factor is that most of the security personnel are alcoholics, and on the Saturday of the big card game they drink discreetly but steadily throughout the day.'

He continued, 'There is a security shift change at midnight on the Saturday so the best time to hit them is about ten o'clock at night. Three of our experienced people have managed to buy ticket numbers thirty-two to thirty-five for the card game. These numbers will not be expected to play until the early hours of Sunday morning, which means we can have three of our people in the reception area just before ten o'clock on Saturday evening.'

Felix was getting excited now. 'Just before ten o'clock our three men inside the night-club will disable and hide the security personnel and take their place wearing their uniforms. Cones will be placed to block the drop-off lay-by. Three vans will arrive with seven men in the back of each. Each man will carry a large single ignition, multi-barrage display firework, and these will be quickly transferred into the reception hall and atrium. Starting at the furthest firework from the exit, the first man will ignite the fuse and retreat towards the exit. As he passes the next man, he will ignite his firework and retreat and so on until we are all clear of the building. We will get into the vans and speed off.'

Felix continued. 'About three miles along the riverside there is a footbridge across the river, the seven men in each van will get out and run across the bridge and board a bus hidden in the small wood. The bus will bring them back here.

'The van drivers will drive away from the river and the town and deliver the vans to an isolated location where they will burn them and the drivers will be brought back by car.'

THE HOUSE OF ATTILA

Felix could not contain himself and finished by making a joke. 'Gentlemen, it is a pity that you cannot stay to watch the display.'

Instead of laughter there was shocked silence.

Harold Szirtes moved to the centre of the assembly and said aggressively, 'If you think you are beaten, you are. If you think you'll lose, you're lost. History favours the brave. Believe you will win and you will.' He continued. 'The House of Attila will always come to your assistance but you must bite the bullet and fight for your territory.

'If we stand together no opposition will beat us. In this case the opposition is too much for our franchisee to take on his own so the House of Attila will come to his aid. This is also your opportunity to show your commitment to the organisation.'

Harold Szirtes lowered his voice so that they all had to strain their ears to hear. 'You have a decision to make, to fight or not to fight. You can try to walk away but you need to consider the risk that will entail.'

The room descended into a deathly silence, which Harold let continue for a full minute. He then said, 'I take it no one wishes to leave.' Again he let the silence continue for a full minute and the tension became electric, but no one in the room moved. Then he said, 'I guess the hunting hounds will go hungry tonight.' He let out a loud laugh and the whole room followed suit, relieving the pent-up atmosphere.

When the laughter subsided he said, 'Good, we are all united in the House of Attila. Bring in the Bikavér and let us drink to our lifelong partnership.'

Harold told them the story of the Bikavér, the best known of the Hungarian wines, while three men with trays of large wine glasses appeared and dispensed them to each of the men present. Harold, holding up his glass, said loudly, 'To our lifelong partnership in the House of Attila, may only death separate us.'

The assembled company concurred and threw back their heads and swallowed the wine.

Harold stepped back and let Felix continue.

Felix said, 'Gentlemen, we will now go over to the stables where you will strip and shower. Then you will dress in new underpants, socks, track suits and trainers to minimise the chance of personal evidence being left at the scene. When you reach the target you will wear gloves and balaclavas.'

The entire group made their way from the mansion house to the stables and into the changing rooms. Their names were on labels on the seats and the clothing was hanging on pegs above the seats and the trainers were under the seats. Felix said, 'Now strip off, shower and change in to the operational clothing.' Herr Shoemaker went to his own room to change.

When they were ready they were taken outside to three vans that were parked outside the stables. Felix told them, 'It is now half past twelve, the journey will take about five hours; we will stop for a one hour break at three different service stations. Sort yourselves out into three groups of seven and get into the back of the vans; the experienced men who will infiltrate the night-club will ride in the drivers' cabs. We have booked a football pitch at an all weather sports centre near the target, where we will play a game of football, shower and change before heading for the target.'

They got into the back of the vans and settled themselves as best they could, sitting on two bench seats running along the length of the two sides of the van.

In the middle of the floor were two cardboard boxes with big display fireworks. Each box contained three or four assorted hundred-shot barrages containing multicolours and effects including falling leaves, bombettes and spinners.

There were also two boxes of wrapped sandwiches, one box of apples and three crates of bottled water. There was also a bag of football strips in each van.

THE HOUSE OF ATTILA

The three vans set off at five minute intervals and also took slightly different routes so as not to draw attention by running in convoy.

The journeys went as planned and each of the vans passed the front of the night-club, carried on for about one hundred metres and dropped off an estate worker who had been riding in the drivers' cabs. They then carried on and arrived at the football facilities at various times between a quarter to seven and quarter past seven. The drivers were careful not to park near the other vans. They had booked the football pitch for half past seven to nine o'clock as Felix thought it best to keep them busy right up to the last minute.

They got ready and started playing at quarter to eight. Herr Shoemaker was the referee and blew for full-time exactly at quarter to nine. They showered and changed, then completely cleaned the shower and dressing-rooms, taking all their kit and litter with them.

They got back into their vans and waited. In the back of each van each group played Felix's recorded instructions twice over.

'Three vans will arrive with seven men in the back of each van, each man will carry a large firework, and these will be quickly transferred into the reception hall and atrium. The first man in will go to the furthest point in the atrium; the second man will place his firework a little less far and so on and so on. Starting at the furthest firework from the exit the man will ignite the fuse and retreat towards the exit. As he passes the next man, he will ignite his firework and retreat and so on until we are all clear of the building. We will get into the vans and speed off. About three miles along the riverside there is a footbridge across the river, the men in each van except the drivers will get out and run across the bridge and board a bus hidden in the small wood. The bus will bring you back to the House of Attila.'

* * *

At the night-club the three experienced estate workers who had bought the tickets for the card game had arrived separately and were sitting apart in the bar slowly sipping beers and watching television reports on the day's sports or playing the large variety of gaming machines. They were also quietly watching the habits of the two security guards in the reception.

They soon noticed that the security guards were heavy drinkers and were consuming at least a half litre of beer each every hour. They also noticed that they took turns to go to the bar and presumably the toilet and were away from the reception for about ten to fifteen minutes each time. This left only one guard on reception every time they replenished their drink. Felix had instructed them to watch for such patterns and they had all come to the same conclusion without speaking to each other, that twice in every hour one of the two guards would be away from the reception for at least ten minutes.

As it approached ten o'clock, one of the guards stood up and made his customary way towards the bar, which was a separate room off the ground floor of the atrium. As soon as he was out of sight one of the House of Attila men, who was playing by himself at pool, walked slowly into the reception area carrying his pool cue. The security guard was not sitting at the reception desk; he was sitting at a table playing patience with a pack of cards and did not look up as the House of Attila man approached.

The pool player who had been carrying his pool cue suddenly lifted it, and with a two-handed back hand, struck the security guard hard on the side of the head with the heavy end of the cue.

He quickly dragged the unconscious guard across the floor and laid him out of sight behind the reception desk. One of his two colleagues who had slowly sauntered out of the bar area immediately went out through the main doors and removed one of the cones that he had previously placed to block the drive-through drop off and pick-up lay by.

THE HOUSE OF ATTILA

Felix led with the two other vans following. The vans arrived at the night-club at two minutes to ten. The man who had removed the traffic cone blocking the drive-in lay-by signalled him to drive in. The three vans drove into the lay-by outside the main entrance and stopped.

The men in the back of the vans quickly spilled out, each carrying their firework, with the words of the recorded message embedded in their brains.

The process of laying the fireworks took less than one minute and no one had discovered them. The process of lighting the fuses and progressively retreating was accomplished in about half a minute, as they reached the main entrance door the first firework began its barrage.

They quickly piled into the vans and were away. Although the adrenaline was pumping, the drivers controlled their urge to speed. They reached the river footbridge in about five minutes. All the men except the drivers spilled out and walked across the footbridge. They followed a path, running now, for about half a mile into a wood until they suddenly came to a single deck coach with the driver in his seat, engine running and the door open. They quickly boarded the coach and sat in their seats. Felix counted the passengers and when he was satisfied everyone was on board he instructed the driver to go.

The night-club by now was an absolute inferno. The design of the night-club was very much conceived for the discretion of its customers, and the grand reception and atrium areas were merely open facades, leading to private suites of secrecy, excitement and passion. None of the occupants of the night-club knew anything was amiss until the first firework barrage started, followed by more fireworks seconds later. It was only thirty seconds before all the fireworks were cascading their flares and bombettes off the walls and the panels of the glazed roof.

All the ground-floor windows were fitted with security

grills and all the emergency escape exits at the rear of the building were chained and padlocked for security reasons.

The firework barrage lasted for a full two minutes. The atmosphere was so smoke-logged that it was impossible to see anything, or even attempt to breathe. All the wood panelling and balustrades in the reception hall and atrium were now a real inferno; glass objects and windows were beginning to shatter as the bombettes exploded against them and with the rapid rise in heat. The resulting inrush of air only increased the intensity of fire.

The big poker game with eight players was on the ground floor and a number of players waiting for their turn at the table were in the large ground-floor lounge bar. A few clients were also dancing with hostesses to a three-piece band in the lounge bar.

Most of the prostitutes were entertaining clients in rooms on the first and second floors of the night-club.

As the fire rescue services arrived, those on the first and second floors were able to break windows and were rescued by being helped on to and down the extending ladders deployed by the fire engines.

Those on the ground floor perished in the fire, which totally consumed every combustible element of the building. Such was the intensity of the fire that after rescuing those through windows on the first and second floors, the fire rescue services could only stand back and protect adjacent buildings with their water sprays. The roof began to collapse less than one hour from the start of the fire. In the early Sunday morning light only the thick stone walls of the building remained as a smoking ruin.

The bus run back to the House of Attila was uneventful on the empty roads late on a Saturday night, and they only stopped once to let the men relieve their bladders. They arrived back at the House of Attila at half past one on the Sunday morning.

THE HOUSE OF ATTILA

They were all led into the stables to shower and change clothing. All their used clothing was bagged and one of the estate workers quickly found Nico and brought him to the stable shower rooms.

Herr Shoemaker said to Nico, 'I want you to take these plastic bags to the boiler furnace and put them into the fire chamber and burn them one by one without opening the bags.'

The cleaned-up franchisees and the three estate workers were escorted back to the dining-room with the tables expanded to take the three estate workers who had infiltrated the night-club.

Harold Szirtes said, 'Please be seated, gentlemen.' When all the audience were seated he said, 'I congratulate you on your success tonight. You have learned tonight that the House of Attila is a very capable organisation. More than that, you have learned that the House of Attila does not tolerate opposition in its territory. You have also learned that you must be ruthless in your territory, secure in the knowledge that you have the support of the House of Attila behind you.

'Finally, gentlemen, the House of Attila has a constant supply of illegal immigrants. The poorest countries or where ethnic tensions prevail and cause conflict is an insatiable source of free labour to the House of Attila. There is nothing to stop you growing your business with your franchise in the House of Attila.

'Now, gentlemen, Herr Shoemaker has prepared something to eat and drink and then we can have some real fun.'

After the franchisees had eaten at the cold finger buffet, Herr Shoemaker said, 'Before you get carried away with the naked wrestling, which is your chance to select and buy a girl to work for you as a prostitute, please remember this, tomorrow morning you will assemble for the final briefing at noon. Before you do, send your girls down to the kitchen where they will be given some breakfast and taken to shower and change into clean clothing for travelling.

'Now let us go through to the great hall for the naked female wrestling.'

The usual naked wrestling matches took place and the auction process until every franchisee was matched with a girl whom they took to their rooms.

Only the servants and Nico appeared for breakfast on the Sunday morning. The gathering had gone on until four o'clock in the morning and none of the guests appeared until about twelve o'clock for the final briefing. Lunch was scheduled for two o'clock and then departure at three o'clock.

After breakfast Freda got the girls to tidy up the function rooms; she delegated two girls to be available in the kitchen to meet requests for tea, coffee and food as guests and their purchased girls slowly gathered before the final briefing.

Freda had overheard Karl and Felix discussing the arrangements for the gathering at a meeting at the Harold Szirtes Hotel. Although she did not deliberately eavesdrop, she learned about the twenty-one girls, the naked wrestling and the auction. Freda was a good woman and the information had upset her, so she had spoken very firmly to Herr Shoemaker to register her disapproval. She said to him, 'I do not agree with this immoral behaviour, naked wrestling, buying and selling human beings.'

Herr Shoemaker had replied, 'Freda, dear Freda. I do not agree either, but like you I am powerless. I cannot tell you the details, but I am compromised by past indiscretions and Harold Szirtes holds these over me. I have to do as he wishes.'

Freda realised that she had Herr Shoemaker's sympathy and had said, 'Help me by agreeing that the girls be allowed to eat in the kitchen and be allowed to shower before they are transported away by their brothel masters.'

Herr Shoemaker had said, 'I will give you an extra 21,000 Czech Crowns on the budget for the gathering. You can spend that on the girls, but lose it in the general expenses, if it is discovered I will not know anything about it.'

She had decided to cut the really expensive food and drink budget for the weekend. She went to the usual general wholesale warehouse where she usually bought food and household goods for the hotel.

She had arranged to have a warehouse salesman list all her items and have it delivered to the House of Attila on the Friday afternoon of the gathering weekend.

When she had finished buying all the food, drink and household goods she still had 25,000 Czech Crowns left.

She had gone through to the clothing section of the warehouse and selected a complete range of assorted sizes of women's underwear, T-shirts, track-suits, training shoes and socks.

A plastic wrapped pallet of mixed women's shoes caught her eye. The sales assistant was quick to say, 'This is a real bargain as there are one hundred pairs of shoes in that pallet.'

Freda had said, 'Done.'

Then she had gone into the pharmacy section and ordered a range of hygiene, skin and hair care products.

The delivery was made on the Friday afternoon and Herr Shoemaker had been at the House of Attila ready to receive it. He'd instructed the delivery driver and his mate, 'Take your delivery round to the stables dressing-rooms and I will show you where to stack it.' He'd gone round and supervised the stacking of the delivery neatly in a corner of the dressing-rooms and then instructed the delivery men, saying, 'Get a large tarpaulin from the stables.' When they brought the tarpaulin he'd said, 'Cover it neatly, tuck in all the loose edges, that's good, that's fine.' Herr Shoemaker had tipped the men, giving them 500 Czech Crowns, saying, 'Here, get yourselves a beer for doing such a good job.'

When Nico appeared for breakfast on the Sunday morning Freda said, 'Nico, I know you are Maria's brother, she pointed you out to me after the celebrations after your football team won the league.'

Nico was a bit startled but recovered his composure. She continued. 'Nico, I want you to look after twenty-one girls at twelve o'clock today.' He was even more startled and lost his composure. He said, 'What, what!'

Freda intervened. 'Nico, listen to me, there are twenty-one poor girls in the mansion house, they were abused all last night and will need to wash. When they come downstairs to the kitchen and have had breakfast, take them over to the stables dressing-rooms to let them strip and shower.

'There is a big tarpaulin covering boxes of clothes and goodies; take the tarpaulin off and open the boxes. Let them choose clothes that fit them and share all the toiletries equally. Take plenty of plastic bin bags from the kitchen to give them something to carry their clothes and toiletries in.

'You will stay with them at all times in case anyone tries to escape. If anyone does escape the hunting hounds will be set loose. When the girls have finished dressing bring them back here to the kitchen.'

Freda walked over to Nico and put a hand round his shoulder and said, 'Nico, these girls are very young girls with a bleak future. Most of them will be on drugs within a year and dead within twenty years. It is as much as we can do to treat them kindly while we have the chance.

'After you bring them back here return to the changing rooms and take all their old clothes and burn them in your boiler furnace.'

THE HOUSE OF ATTILA

Nico found a corner of the kitchen and sat down to wait for all the girls to assemble.

Slowly and shyly, the girls started to come into the kitchen. They were all very dishevelled and gaunt looking. Some were crying.

Valda, Milinka, Miljana and Senca were on kitchen duty and had egg sandwiches and big mugs of tea ready as they came in.

Nico watched the girls eating and tried to work out their ages. He compared them to his sister, who was thirteen, and despite their different nationalities they did not look much older than her. When they had all finished eating, Freda came through and counted them. She said, 'Twenty-one, good you are all here. Now Nico,' she pointed to Nico, 'will take you over to the shower room where you can have hot showers and put on new clothes. You must discard your old clothing and Nico will bag it for disposal. It is now coming into summer and your new sports clothing will be comfortable to wear. When you have finished, Nico will bring you back here.'

Herr Shoemaker came into the kitchen and said, 'A word of warning, do not try to escape, this is a hunting estate and if you try to run they will just let the hunting hounds loose. It is not a good way to die.'

Nico led the girls over to the stables and into the shower room. He stripped back the tarpaulin and lifted down the boxes, spreading them out.

One of the girls stripped and turned on one of the showers, then the others followed suit. Nico noticed that most of the girls were badly bruised and he started bagging all the discarded clothing.

As they dried themselves, the girls started to find underwear of the right size and tried it on, then they found T-shirts and track suits and finally trainers.

Eventually they were all fully dressed and there were still

boxes of stuff left. Nico gave them the plastic bin bags and said, 'Share all the remaining stuff equally, ensuring it fits you and put it in these bags.'

Eventually they were all satisfied with their selections and with considerable relief Nico led them back to the kitchen.

Freda counted the girls and said, 'Well done, Nico.' He took the opportunity to escape, saying to Freda, 'I need to go and clear up the shower room and dispose of the old clothing.'

Nico ran back to the shower rooms and lifted the first two bags of discarded clothing and shoes. He took them to the boiler room and put them into the boiler furnace. He went back for the next two and repeated the process, then went back for the final two bags. The bags burnt quickly. He went back to the shower room and gave the whole place a thorough clean.

About a quarter to three the franchisees came out of the great hall and came through the kitchen to collect their newly purchased girls.

Freda watched sadly out of a window as the girls got into their brothel masters' cars and were slowly driven down the drive towards an unknown future. As the last car disappeared out of sight she said angrily, 'Bastards, bastards, bastards.' She broke away from her depressed anger and went to the kitchen. Most of the servants had gathered in the kitchen to keep out of the way while the gathering broke up. Freda said, 'Well done all, now the last thing we need to do is strip all the beds and clean up the rooms. Let's break into our teams and try to be back here for half past four.'

They all gathered back in the kitchen at the agreed hour. Freda saw the bus coming to take the Harold Szirtes Hotel girls back.

She shouted, 'Well done, girls, thank you for all your help

over the weekend. The bus is here; make sure you haven't left anything.'

The hotel girls boarded the bus and it drove off with the girls waving out the back window.

Herr Shoemaker arrived back from town with a collection of Sunday papers. A couple of the late editions had the photographs and the story of the night-club fire. Herr Shoemaker called a meeting of Harold Szirtes, Karl Stonier and Felix Hienmann to read the newspaper reports.

After digesting the reports Harold Szirtes said with a big grin, 'I don't think they will even think of us. It looks like they think it was disgruntled gambling losers. The newspapers are saying that there were rumours of cheating and connections with the mafia.'

Harold carried on, 'Gentlemen, this is as good a time as any to start our move west. Our lawyers have completed the purchase of the hotel in Oban, Scotland. Martin, you will select a small team to decorate, furnish and start operating the hotel in Scotland. Felix, you will work with Martin to see that all the identification papers and passports for the girls Martin is going to take with him are procured. You will also train them in their new identities. I would like this to happen as soon as possible.

'Martin, you will go to the lawyers and get two sets of duplicate copies of all the title deeds and all records pertaining to the purchase of the hotel in Scotland.

'You must make sure you have a complete understanding of all the legal and planning conditions applying to the hotel in Scotland. You need to know how to run perfectly legally before you start to engage in illegal activity.' Harold pondered for a minute. 'I believe that's a contradiction in terms.' Harold erupted into a fit of laughter at his own cleverness. Affected by his laughter, the other three followed his lead and collapsed into a fit of prolonged hilarity.

When they finished laughing, Herr Shoemaker said, 'I

would like to take Senca and Valda from the House of Attila, and Maria from the Harold Szirtes Hotel.'

Harold Szirtes said, 'That's what I like about you, Martin, positive thoughts and positive actions. Felix, now you know the names, you can get started on the fake identity papers and passports. Martin, as soon as Felix has the names of the new identities, you can book your travel arrangements and get your team over there as soon as you can.' Harold added, 'I don't want to come in winter to see my new hotel.'

28

Visit to Grandmother

Freda arrived back at about tea time and quickly assessed the situation at the hotel. Everything was running smoothly so she said to Maria, 'Well done, Maria, can you hold the fort for a little longer? I need to lie down for an hour to get my strength back, it was a very late night last night and I didn't get any sleep.'

Freda went to her room and got into bed and immediately fell asleep. She woke from a nightmare about nine o'clock drenched in sweat. In the nightmare she was trapped in a maze. She tried path after path but she was always confronted by Karl. She began to run but it was no use, he was always there. She ran faster and faster but he always blocked her path.

Freda believed in the power of dreams and she tried to analyse the meaning but after a few minutes she gave up.

Her mind went on to questions about the weekend. 'Where had all these very young girls come from? Where had they been taken by their new brothel masters? What was their future? What right did these men have to treat them so cruelly?'

Freda got out of bed and went to the toilet, and then she went into the shower and tried to wash off her depression. She slowly put new make-up on, dressed and went out to face the world.

* * *

It was a typical Sunday evening. The customers had left early, preparing for their work in the morning. The girls were just clearing up, putting things away and cleaning.

She went into the kitchen and helped Maria finish cleaning and disinfecting all the work surfaces and finally the floors.

When they finished they sat down for their customary tea, toast and a chat.

Freda said, 'Well, how did the weekend at the hotel go?'

Maria said, 'Everything went very smoothly and everybody worked very hard. I have something very special to show you.'

Freda was curious and said quickly, 'What is it?'

Maria said, 'Wait here and I will show you.' She got up from her seat, unlocked the pantry door, retrieved an envelope from a drawer and gave it to Freda.

Freda opened the envelope, took out a letter and read it. Her face broke out in a big smile.

She said, 'Dmitar Hrvat, Breeding Manager at the Al Quoz Stables in Dubai, wants you to join him at his grandmother's home to have lunch next Sunday. Ooh la la!'

They both burst out laughing at Freda's exclamation of surprise with its strong sexual connotations.

Freda looked thoughtful for a moment then said, 'We will have to ask permission of Harold Szirtes. Leave that to me, he is coming tomorrow to check over the hotel accounts for the last month with me. The accounts show very good profits especially from the restaurant, so he should be pleased.'

This little chat with Maria had cheered Freda up and they both went to bed in a happy mood.

As Freda expected, Harold Szirtes was very happy with the hotel accounts for the past month. Freda pointed out, 'This improvement has been since Maria took over Milo's place as head cook.'

THE HOUSE OF ATTILA

Freda pulled Maria's letter from her smock pocket and gave it to Harold Szirtes, saying, 'It would be good to recognize her good work for the hotel restaurant.'

Harold Szirtes carefully read the letter and said, 'I know Dmitar Hrvat, I sold him that white horse. Yes that will be all right if you can get suitable cover for the cook's job on the Sunday.'

Freda said, 'I will cover for the cook on Sunday.'

Harold Szirtes said, 'That's fine; tell her I am pleased with her work.'

Freda was so excited to give Maria the good news she rushed out without waiting for Harold Szirtes to give her back the letter. He shouted loudly, 'Freda.' She sheepishly returned. He said. 'You forgot this letter. You also forgot who is boss, you wait until I dismiss you. Do you understand?' Freda nodded. He handed her the letter and said, 'You may now go.'

Freda gave Maria the letter and said with a big smile, 'It's OK for Sunday, I nearly made a mess of it, but Harold Szirtes agreed that you can go if I cover your job in the kitchen.

'Here is the letter and here is the key to my office, go lock the office door and phone the telephone number on the letter and tell him you will be delighted to lunch with his grandmother if he picks you up here at the hotel on Sunday.'

Maria said, 'No I can't do it; I am frightened to phone him. I won't know what to say.'

Freda said, 'Here, give me that letter. I will write it down on the back exactly what you have to say. Just read it out to him.' Freda wrote a few words on the back of the letter and said very sternly, 'Maria, in the short time you have been here, you have seen several people bruised and cut from being cruelly beaten, you have heard some of the girls say that they have been raped and you have seen some of their injuries, you have noticed that some people have just disappeared, in fact you and I had to clean up Milo's blood when he disappeared.

'Now go and do exactly what I told you, I never had the chance to marry and have children.' Tears came into her eyes. 'I think of you as the daughter I never had and I want you to have a happy future if it is at all possible.'

This shocking confrontation with the truth seemed to have a significant effect. Maria took the letter and the office keys and quietly left the kitchen. Freda busied herself looking after Maria's job while she was away.

Maria came back with a smile on her face and said, 'It was easy; he's picking me up at half past twelve on Sunday.'

Freda gave Maria a big hug and said, 'Do you have anything decent to wear?'

Maria's face fell and she said, 'Oh! I didn't think of that.'

Freda said, 'Well, we'll need to do something about that, I have to go to the big wholesale warehouse on Wednesday and I could take you with me to help me carry all the things. Do you still have some of your share of the tips left?'

Maria said, 'Yes, most of it, I have nearly 6,000 Czech Crowns.'

Freda said, 'That's more than enough. Bring it with you on Wednesday and ask Lette and Mary to cover the kitchen while we are away.'

Wednesday came and Lette and Mary were happy to be in charge of the kitchen so Freda and Maria set off in the hotel minibus.

After they had filled two big warehouse trolleys with items for the hotel they quickly found the womenswear section. With Freda suggesting many items, Maria finally decided on an outfit in lime green with suitable underwear and shoes.

When they totalled up the cost her full outfit only came to 3,900 Czech Crowns and they were both amazed. So Freda said, 'Get yourself a light coat to go with your dress and a head scarf just in case it rains.' They left the wholesale warehouse feeling very pleased with themselves.

THE HOUSE OF ATTILA

* * *

Sunday soon came and it was difficult to know who was more excited. Freda, Lette or Mary. Maria cooked the breakfasts, withstanding the constant pressure from the others to go and get ready. Freda came in with a bottle of bath salts and shampoo and said, 'Go and take a good long bath.' So taking the bath salts and shampoo, she relented and went through to her bathroom and ran a bath. When she came back to the kitchen Lette said, 'Let me do your hair, I was practising to be a hairdresser when I was at home with my mother.'

Maria said, 'We can't do hair in the kitchen, let's go into the toilet.'

Lette said, 'I will need the electric extension cable.' Mary fetched the extension cable and plugged it into an electrical socket. Maria sat on the toilet seat while Lette blow dried and combed her hair, wetting it in places over and over again until she was satisfied.

Finally, Maria was ready and she went downstairs with Lette. When they entered the kitchen both Freda and Mary said together, 'Who's that beautiful girl! You are gorgeous!'

Freda said, 'I have a small bottle of Chanel No. 5, which I was keeping for when my Prince Charming comes along, but he seems to be very late. So you can have a couple of dabs.' She produced the small bottle of perfume and unscrewed the top; she wetted her finger with it and said, 'Girls you want to smell that perfume, no man can resist that fragrance.'

They all had a sniff and a good laugh, then Freda dabbed a few drops on to each side of Maria's neck.

One of the cleaning girls came into the kitchen and dramatically announced, 'Dmitar Hrvat, is at the front door requesting a Miss Maria Sokota.'

Freda held Maria's coat out for her and then escorted her out to the door. Dmitar bowed to the ladies and said, 'Good afternoon, ladies, it is a fine afternoon for a drive in the country.'

He held open the passenger door of his car and Maria got in. He closed the door and walked round to the driver's side and got into the car.

Initially the conversation was a bit strained, but when he started to tell Maria about his grandmother the atmosphere warmed. Dmitar said, 'As you know, my grandmother is eighty years of age. She has lived on a little farm all her life even through the Second World War. My parents were killed in ethnic troubles in 1983 when I was nine years of age and I came to stay with my grandmother. She got me a job right away at the horse breeding stables next to her farm and I got on very well at the stables. I was looking after several young race horses by the time I was sixteen. The manager of Al Quoz Stables visited our stables two years ago and bought the string of horses that I was looking after. He said he wanted me to go with them and I have been working in Dubai ever since.'

They arrived at Dmitar's grandmother's farm and she met them at the door of her little house and welcomed Maria with a big hug.

She said, 'Come in and take your coat off and I will hang it up. The dinner is just ready, so we can start just as soon as we wash our hands; the toilet is just at the end of the hall.'

Maria went to the toilet and washed her hands, then walked back along the hall to the front door. She coughed to signal her presence and Dmitar appeared and invited her into the main room, which was a combined living-room and kitchen. Some of the furniture had been pushed back to allow a dining-room table to be set up with three chairs. The table was covered with a beautiful linen tablecloth with three place settings.

Dmitar's grandmother said, 'Sit yourself down, dinner is ready to be served.' She filled soup bowls and placed them at each of the three place settings and sat down. She said, 'Dmitar, please give thanks for our food.'

Dmitar bowed his head and said, 'Dear Lord, thank you for our lives and all our blessings and sustenance. Amen.'

Dmitar's grandmother said, 'Thank you, Dmitar.' She carried on, 'I hope you like this vegetable soup, Maria, most of the ingredients come from my farm.'

Maria said, 'Yes it's lovely.'

Dmitar's grandmother talked and talked through the whole meal; she seemed to be delighted to have a guest visiting her and was making the most of it. However, she was a homely person and Maria liked her.

After the meal they went out into the small farm and inspected all the neat rows of vegetable crops, fruit shrubs and fruit trees in the fenced off vegetable garden and orchard. She then showed them another small fenced area, which was her herb garden. Dmitar's grandmother said, 'Is there anything you can think of that I am not growing?'

Maria laughed and said, 'No, I am just completely amazed.'

She then took them into a large field where chickens and geese ranged freely along with her single cow, which was contentedly grazing.

Finally she took them to her trout pond where she threw some seed grains on to the water, resulting in a flurry of activity as trout competed for the seeds.

The afternoon flew by and soon it was time to go. Dmitar's grandmother reached up into a cupboard and retrieved a jar of home-made raspberry jam. She handed it to Maria and said, 'This is for you, remember me every time you use it and may it bring you good luck.'

Maria did not know what to say. She just said, 'Thank you, I have so enjoyed meeting you in your home,' and then she started crying. Dmitar's grandmother put her arms around her and hugged her very tightly.

* * *

Karl came into the hotel late in the afternoon, still really drunk from his all-night session at a local night-club, and ordered more drink. No one in the hotel could deal with Karl when he was drunk so everyone humoured him, serving him as he demanded and trying not to upset him because he could be really violent.

When Maria came back from her visit to Dmitar's grandmother's farm, Dmitar dropped her at the door and drove off with a cheery wave.

She went into the kitchen and Freda said, 'You're back, how did you get on? Let me make a pot of tea and you can tell me all about it.' Freda filled the kettle and switched it on.

At that moment Karl spotted Maria through the serving hatch. He shouted through the hatch, 'Who's that beauty in there? I am coming to get you.' He made his way round and staggered drunkenly in through the kitchen door, loosening his belt and unzipping the front of his trousers as he approached.

'Oh! It's our Maria all dressed up and what a beauty she is.' He grabbed her wrist and pulled her hard towards the kitchen door saying, 'Yes, it's time I broke you in, you beauty.' Maria struggled to break free, pulling Karl off balance, and in his drunken state he staggered and bumped into Freda. She was holding the kettle ready to pour it into the teapot. She turned and poured it straight into the front of his open trousers. She didn't think about it; she just did it. Karl fell on to the floor screaming and trying to brush off the boiling water with his hands. Freda dropped the kettle on the floor and said with venom, 'You won't do much damage with that for a few weeks, you evil bastard.'

Maria ran into the hall and phoned for the local doctor.

Staff in the hotel came running in response to the screaming, which had now reverted to shouting, swearing and wailing.

The local doctor arrived within minutes. He took one look,

opened his doctor's bag, selected a disposable morphine-filled syringe and injected into Karl's arm.

Karl almost immediately relaxed and drifted into unconsciousness. He was carried out to the doctor's car and taken to the hospital.

29
Journey to Oban

Felix came to the hotel immediately when he heard about Karl's accident. He interviewed everyone in the hotel, but only Freda knew what had happened and she was not offering herself up to the executioner. The others knew that Karl had been really drunk. They knew that Karl often exposed himself when he was drunk. They knew that Karl often raped young servant girls. They knew that Karl had barged into the kitchen and had grabbed Maria. They believed that in the struggle he had knocked the kettle out of Freda's hand. They saw Karl lying on the kitchen floor with his trousers and underpants at his ankles. They saw the kettle lying on the floor.

Everyone gave the same general story based on what little they knew and conclusions they had reconstructed in their minds.

Felix visited Karl in hospital on the Monday but he could not even remember being in the hotel on the Sunday.

Felix reported to Harold Szirtes on the Monday evening and said, 'It was Karl's own fault. He was blind drunk and when he saw Maria looking so pretty, he fancied her. He barged into the kitchen dropping his trousers and grabbed Maria. In his drunken condition he tripped on his trousers and crashed into Freda who was making a pot of tea. He fell and the kettle landed in his lap scalding his exposed private parts.'

Harold Szirtes was furious and shouted, 'Why do I get

imbeciles working for me? Tell him he is off wages until he is fit to work again. I do not deserve this. Tell him it will take a long time to gain my confidence again, if ever.'

Felix slowly retreated, walking backwards until he reached the door, which he quietly closed behind him. He ran out of the front door of the mansion house glad to get away from Harold Szirte's wrath and fearful of hearing a shout.

On Tuesday, Felix and Herr Shoemaker met at the hotel to progress the preparations for the journey to Oban.

Herr Shoemaker opened the meeting by saying, 'Harold says that you, Felix, should get started right away on the fake passports and identity papers. I am to get the travel tickets booked and get over there as soon as I can. I asked Harold if I could take Senca, Valda and the cook Maria and he agreed. So we will need full sets of identity papers and passports for the three of them and I already have mine, which you supplied for the exploratory trip.'

Felix said with a smile, 'I have already started the process. Let me explain. When you enter the United Kingdom you will need to show your passport or national identity card. You should use the separate channel marked "'EEA/EU" where it is available. Immigration officers will check your passport or national identity card to make sure that it is valid and belongs to you.

'As a German you are part of the European Common Market and you have a right to live in the United Kingdom; your family may join you, Senca is eighteen, Valda is sixteen and Maria is fourteen; they are sufficiently similar to pass for sisters and you are racially similar to pass for their father, and they are still dependent on you.

'I will have German passports, national identity cards and birth certificates prepared for each of you as father and three daughters. You are going to Oban to set up a local branch of the Harold Szirtes Hotel Group; people perceived as legitimate business travellers are not questioned to the same extent.'

Herr Shoemaker said, 'I prefer to travel by train.' Felix said, 'It is a long haul by train from Serbia to Scotland and your passport and papers will be checked more times as you leave and enter various countries. However, the passports and national identity cards are of the highest quality. You should have no problem. I will put you and the girls through training in being questioned by customs and police officials until you are used to all their tricks. I will get photographs of you and each of the girls and have the passports ready by the end of the week. You will need these to book your train journey; however, you should go to the travel agent and get them to work on booking your seats. You want to ensure that on each train you have four seats together, and where you book overnight sleeper accommodation you want your own cabin or cabins.

'The family name will be Shoemaker; it is very common in several European countries. We will get the girls to practise saying their new name over and over again. Book your tickets from Belgrade, we have a franchise hotel there.'

When the time came to travel, the girls got no warning; Felix arrived at the House of Attila in a large Mercedes. Senca and Valda were working in the kitchen. Herr Shoemaker came in and said, 'Senca and Valda, come with me.'

He led them outside and put them in the back seat of the Mercedes. He got into the front seat with Felix and they drove off. Valda said, 'Where are we going?' Felix snapped, 'Be quiet, you will soon find out.'

They drove to the Harold Szirtes Hotel and Herr Shoemaker went in. He came back out minutes later with Maria and put her in the back seat of the car. He got into the front with Felix and they drove off.

Herr Shoemaker turned to face the girls and said, 'You

and I are going to start a new Harold Szirtes Hotel in the United Kingdom.' He paused to let the information sink in. 'If you work to help me things will be very pleasant. But if you work against me your time will be short and unpleasant. When we get to Belgrade I will explain more to you.'

Felix arrived in the main square in Belgrade. Then he drove a short distance up a hill to a hotel. He parked outside and said, 'Get out and book in, you are expected. I will need to park this car somewhere secure and then I will join you.'

Herr Shoemaker led the three girls into the hotel. There was a man and a woman behind the reception desk. He said, 'My name is Herr Shoemaker and these are my three daughters. We have two adjoining rooms booked with a total of five single beds. My friend who will arrive later, and I, will stay in one room and my daughters will stay in the other room.'

'Yes, Herr Shoemaker, we are expecting you, please sign in and I will need to take your passports,' said the male receptionist. Herr Shoemaker was wearing a traveller's bum bag to keep his passports and money safe. He took out the four passports and handed them over, saying, 'I hope these will be safe.'

The man said, 'Yes, I will put them in our safe and you will get them when you leave.'

The receptionist said, 'Here are the two room keys – the room numbers are on each fob and the first number indicates the floor level; the lift is over in the far corner.'

The rooms were both a good size and they soon settled in with the adjoining door open.

When Felix arrived he quickly sorted and put away his luggage and spare clothes and then he said, 'We should go down to the main square and get lunch and then find a shop to get you and the girls suitable travelling clothes and luggage.'

The five of them walked slowly down the hill to the main square and found several cafés on one side of the main entrance to the railway station. They selected the best looking one and sat at a table pulling five seats round. Valda said, 'What is going to happen to us?'

Felix replied, 'Don't talk about anything important here, there are too many ears listening and some that you can't see. The large public building beside the station is also the police station and some of the people serving these tables will be undercover informers, wait until we go back to our rooms and I will tell you everything.'

They ordered and ate.

When they finished, Herr Shoemaker paid for the meals and then Felix led them to a large department store.

Herr Shoemaker said, 'We are going to be travelling for three days and two nights. There will be no chance to have a bath or a shower until we get to Glasgow. You need to have two to three changes of underwear and a set of clothes for travelling, plus a spare set in case of some unexpected accident. Pick lightweight shoes at least half a size too big for travelling and one spare set of trainers. Select a shower-proof but lightweight jacket for weather protection. Get yourselves toilet bags and toiletries and make sure you have everything you need for personal care. Oh! I almost forgot. Include a small towel and a packet of baby wipes each; they are very good if you can't get a shower. You will need suitable luggage such as a reasonably sized rucksack. Finally get a good strong bum bag to keep your passport and identity papers safe.

'The first rule of survival is to learn to keep your valuables safe and with you at all times. I now regret handing over our passports to the hotel reception. I will ask to have them returned.'

When they had finally selected and Herr Shoemaker had paid for their purchases, they each packed them away into their rucksacks and carried them on their backs.

When they reached the hotel, Herr Shoemaker went to the reception and said, 'You have had time to check our passports, may I have them back now?'

The receptionist said, 'Most guests leave them until they check out.'

Herr Shoemaker said, 'We are not most guests and I want our passports.'

The receptionist said, 'Please wait while I enquire about this.' He came back ten minutes later and handed Herr Shoemaker the passports.

They went up to their rooms and Felix then gave each of them a card with the essential information about their individual new identities. He said, 'Go into a separate corner using the two rooms and learn what is on the card. I will only give you ten minutes to complete the task because the amount of information you have to learn is very little.'

After approximately ten minutes he gathered them all in the girls' room and said, 'I am going to call you one at a time into the other room and I am going to ask you questions about what you have learned.'

They completed the session and Felix said, 'You have all done well. We will repeat it again in half an hour.'

Herr Shoemaker said, 'While we are waiting, I will tell you what is going to happen. Harold Szirtes has bought a hotel in the United Kingdom. It is located in a beautiful town named Oban and you three girls and I are going to open and run it for Harold Szirtes. We start the train journey tomorrow morning at six forty-five and we will be two nights and three days travelling by train.'

Felix said, 'In reverse order this time, come in one at a time for another interrogation and this time it will be a little more severe.'

They repeated this twice more and at the end of the final session Felix declared, 'I am impressed and satisfied with all four of you. I have been much tougher than the police or customs officers will be, so you have nothing to worry about.'

Herr Shoemaker said, 'The time is now seven o'clock and it's time to eat. We will eat in the hotel and have an early night because we will have to be up at five o'clock to catch the train.'

They had a leisurely meal, which took them to nine o'clock and then Felix said, 'Come on now, it is time for bed if we are to get up at five.'

Herr Shoemaker awoke and looked at his alarm clock, it indicated a quarter to five. He immediately rolled on his back to prevent him falling asleep again, then he pushed back the duvet and swung his legs over and off the side of the bed, using them as a counterweight to help propel his body into a sitting position.

Felix said, 'What time is it?'

Shoemaker replied, 'Quarter to five.' He opened the connecting door to the girls' room and said, 'Get up, girls, and have a quick shower, remember we will not get another shower for three days.' The alarm call came in at exactly five o'clock.

They were all ready with their bags packed by six o'clock.

Felix said, 'Everyone check their bum bags to see that you have your passports and identity papers safe, and make sure you zip the pockets tight shut.' He did not really have to worry because the girls had identity papers for the first time and as displaced persons they knew how important they were. Felix said, 'Let's go.' They all went into the corridor, and then he said, 'Wait while I check that we have not left anything behind.' He went back and searched the two rooms including their *en suite* bathrooms. He reappeared and said, 'That's fine, let's go.'

They checked out at reception and the receptionist said, 'Will I phone a taxi?' Felix said curtly, 'No.'

THE HOUSE OF ATTILA

They left the hotel at ten past six and began walking slowly down the hill towards the railway station. They reached the station at twenty-five past six. Felix quickly checked at 'Information' and was told the train left from platform one. People were already boarding and Herr Shoemaker said, 'We are looking for coach 409.' They made their way along the train. Felix pointed out the buffet car and said, 'You will be able to get meals in there.' Their coach was just two along from the buffet coach and their seats were four together with a table between. Herr Shoemaker said, 'Perfect, just what I asked for.'

The train was not very crowded and they did not have many people sitting near them. They put their luggage on the rack above their seats. Felix said, 'I will need to go before the train starts moving so I will keep my farewell brief. I will come over in a few months' time to see how the hotel is working.' As he turned, the train made a little shudder so he quickly ran to the door and got off. Almost immediately the train began to move forward and did not speed up until it was clear of the station.

Herr Shoemaker said, 'Girls, we have a long way to go and we are not due to arrive in Vienna until eight minutes past six tonight. We have to concentrate very hard when we have to make train changes.' He lifted down a plastic bag from the rack and said, 'I bought this little book of games for travellers to play, which will keep us amused. We must make a rule that two of us will stay here in the seats at all times to guard the luggage and our seats.'

The girls nodded their agreement. He said, 'I will go and check with the buffet coach what time they will serve breakfast.' He got up and went towards the buffet coach.

Valda said in a whisper, 'Girls, this is exciting, let's look on this as a big adventure.'

Senca said, 'Herr Shoemaker is not as bad as Felix or Karl; compared to them he is positively decent.'

The three girls nodded in agreement, smiling for the first time since leaving the Harold Szirtes Hotel.

Herr Shoemaker came back with a small menu and four bottles of water, which he handed round. He said, 'The buffet is very good, they will make and serve food any time passengers want it. I suggest we hang on another hour, then we will go in pairs to have breakfast. How do you feel about that?' The girls nodded their agreement.

The ticket inspector came round and inspected their tickets.

By this time the train was well out in the country and there was flat farmland on either side as far as the eye could see. Where they passed small farms and villages, they could see that the standard of housing was very poor and consisted of a lot of small holdings growing a mix of vegetables, fruit, grains and vines, with chickens, geese, cows, goats, horses and pigs all sharing the limited areas on the small farms. In between these small communities there were other obviously large and mechanised farming operations.

The girls quickly settled down and began to have quite animated whispered conversations. It was clear that they were aware of the hostile world around them, but they were beginning to bond together including Herr Shoemaker.

At eight o'clock Herr Shoemaker said, 'Senca, you are the oldest, and Maria, you are the youngest. You two go to the buffet coach and get some breakfast, take this 500 Czech Crowns, have a look at this menu and select your choices before you go.'

The girls went towards the buffet coach. When they came back they gave Herr Shoemaker the change and then he and Valda went through and had their breakfasts.

Everyone felt better after breakfast and they played some games from the book. The train came to a big town called Novi Sad, and a few people got off and a few people got on.

THE HOUSE OF ATTILA

The journey was uneventful until they came to the border between Yugoslavia and Hungary. The train stopped and Yugoslavian police came on and asked to see everyone's passports. They examined them very carefully, checking that photographs matched faces, but said nothing.

Then the train moved on and stopped just inside Hungary. Here the Hungarian police came on and checked everyone's passports. When they came to Shoemaker and the girls, two of the police examined the passports very thoroughly. They asked to see their identity papers, then one of them asked Herr Shoemaker, 'Where are you going, and what's the purpose of your journey?'

He replied, 'I am a hotel manager and I am going to open a new hotel in the United Kingdom. These are my three daughters.' This answer satisfied the police and they moved on. However, the train was held up for over an hour as customs officials checked all the internal and external voids in the train structure.

Herr Shoemaker said, 'I hope this delay does not cause us to miss our connection at Vienna. Even if we are on time we only have a time slot of about two hours before the train leaves.' He took out a small map of Europe and peered at it intently. The train started to move again and this time it seemed to be going a bit faster. The ticket inspector came round and inspected their tickets. The train stopped at a couple of stations before coming to the city of Budapest. Herr Shoemaker studied his map again and seemed to be relieved. He said, 'We are probably about two thirds of the way to Vienna.' The train started to move again and Herr Shoemaker said, 'In case we are late and are rushed when we get to Vienna we will have a good dinner now. Senca and Maria you go now, here is another 500 Czech Crowns, that should be enough.'

Senca and Maria came back and gave Herr Shoemaker change, then Herr Shoemaker and Valda went through to the buffet coach.

At the border with Austria there were more ticket and passport checks.

Herr Shoemaker said, 'The train is going much faster now, I think the track is much better in Austria, however, I still think we are going to be late.'

The train finally arrived at Vienna (West) at half past seven in the evening and the train to Frankfurt was due to leave at eight-thirty five: Herr Shoemaker said, 'Make sure your bum bags are fastened securely.' He checked that they had not left anything and they made their way to the main station information centre. They checked the departure board and saw that the train was leaving from platform 8. But Herr Shoemaker was a bit confused as one half of the train was destined for Stuttgart and one half of the train was destined for Strasbourg. They went to platform 8 but the train was not open for boarding. The two train staff on the platform that he asked were less than helpful. He was beginning to panic and they rushed back to the information centre. He found an information kiosk and asked the information clerk, 'How do I know which part of the train at platform eight is going to Frankfurt?'

The attendant checked his computer and said, 'Which coach number is on your ticket?'

Shoemaker said, 'Coach 269.'

The information clerk said, 'That's fine, that coach goes to Frankfurt.'

They rushed back to platform 8 and found coach 269. The train was still closed for boarding so they found four platform seats, sat and waited.

When the train opened, the attendant showed them to a four-person sleeping cabin with couchettes. He said, 'You have this to yourselves; there are WCs and washrooms at either end of the coach. There is a buffet coach next to this one in that direction. I need to take your passports and tickets for the border crossing.'

Herr Shoemaker said to the girls, 'Give me your passports and tickets.' He collected them and gave them with his own to the ticket collector.

They stowed away their luggage and settled into their space and soon the train was moving.

Herr Shoemaker said, 'I will go to the buffet and bring back some water and sandwiches. Girls, go one at a time and familiarise yourselves with the WCs and washrooms. Remember, two people must remain here in the sleeping cabin to guard the luggage at all times.'

Herr Shoemaker was very relieved to be on the right train, the last hour had been very stressful for him. He decided he needed a drink and he ordered up a double vodka and tonic.

After drinking the vodka and tonic he ordered four bottles of water and four packets of mixed sandwiches.

When he returned to the sleeping cabin Senca was naked and busy rubbing herself down with baby wipes. She said, 'You can't really wash properly in the small WC compartment.'

Herr Shoemaker said, 'Good, that's what I bought the baby wipes for, they are very good. You should all try them.' Senca finished washing and pulled on a new pair of knickers and a T-shirt.

Herr Shoemaker handed out the sandwiches and water and said, 'Well it's been a full day, but it is even busier tomorrow, this train gets in to Frankfurt at six o'clock in the morning and we have an hour and twenty-eight minutes to catch the Brussels train.

'I have arranged for the attendant to wake us at five o'clock in the morning and he will return our passports. Girls you must remind me in the morning to get our passports. Now I will go to the buffet car to have a couple of beers, then we need to sleep.'

After Herr Shoemaker left, Maria said, 'Senca that was terrible letting Herr Shoemaker see you completely naked like that and for all that time.'

Senca laughed and replied, 'Maria, didn't you know? Herr Shoemaker is gay, and in his job for Harold Szirtes he sees me naked often. He used to be a fashion designer specialising in sexy lingerie, and Harold Szirtes entered a local lingerie competition and he won with Herr Shoemaker's designs and with me as his model.

'Sometimes, when Harold Szirtes invites politicians or business associates to the House of Attila, Herr Shoemaker has to organise a show for after dinner, which often involves me modelling his sexy lingerie. It usually ends with them shouting, "Take them off", which I have to do. However, I must give credit to Herr Shoemaker. He has always stepped in and diverted them from abusing me when it begins to get out of hand. It usually ends with other servant girls being used for their amusement. But I have to say, Martin Shoemaker has always protected me.'

Maria said, 'How terrible that is.'

Senca looked at Maria tenderly and said, 'Maria, for girls like us, we have no rights, and men rule the world, and rich and powerful men are the worst of all.'

Herr Shoemaker went to the buffet coach; it was fairly busy and noisy. He ordered up a beer and stood by himself at the standing tables, leaning on the bum rest. He thought to himself as he sipped at his beer, 'It is good to be away from Harold Szirtes, Karl and Felix.'

The brutality now developing in the organisation was completely against his compassionate and sensitive nature. He had been sickened by the ruthless murder of the simple farmers in the hills above Sarajevo. He had been revolted by the scourging and manhunting of Fredrick the boiler man, and he couldn't rid himself of the image of the dogs tearing him apart.

He now thought, 'Scotland is a long way from the Balkans, perhaps I can be my own boss so far away.'

THE HOUSE OF ATTILA

He ordered another beer and a large vodka, and continued his day-dreaming. He ordered another large vodka, drunk it and finished his second beer. He looked at his watch; it was ten o'clock. He thought, 'Time to get some sleep.'

Herr Shoemaker visited the WC and then returned to the cabin. The girls were already in their couchettes. He set his alarm clock, switched off the lights, stripped to his underpants and lay on his couchette, pulling the light duvet over himself. He thought, 'Oh! It's so good to lie down.'

Herr Shoemaker woke, realising that the train had come to a halt. He looked at his alarm clock and saw that it was only half past four. He quickly got out of bed and pulled his clothes and shoes on. He opened the cabin door, looking to see if he could find one of the attendants. He followed the passageway until he found one and asked, 'Why have we stopped?'

The attendant replied, 'We are just separating the two parts of the train, the other half goes to Stuttgart; this half will stop at Frankfurt before going on to Strasbourg, though we are running forty minutes late at the moment.'

Herr Shoemaker said, 'That's terrible, forty minutes late; we have to catch the Brussels connection at seven twenty-eight.' The attendant just shrugged her shoulders and walked away.

Herr Shoemaker was stressed again and thought, 'We need to be ready to move when this train gets into Frankfurt.' He went back to the cabin, reached into his rucksack and pulled out the plastic bag he had prepared the night before, containing fresh underpants, socks, shirt, packet of baby wipes and his toilet bag.

He made his way to the washroom where he used the WC, stripped off, brushed his teeth, shaved, washed his face and under his arms, then he took a few of the baby wipes and gave himself a thorough body wash.

He applied deodorant then quickly dressed in his fresh clothes, putting the soiled ones in the plastic bag.

He returned to the cabin just as the train started moving again. He looked at his alarm clock and saw that the time was five to five, he deactivated his alarm clock and put it in his rucksack.

He wakened the girls, saying, 'We are running more than forty minutes late, you must be ready to move when the train arrives at Frankfurt, if you get up now the washrooms are empty.' He added. 'I am going to get our passports, get ready and we will go for breakfast before it gets too busy.'

He made his way to the coach attendant's cabin and asked for his passports. The attendant said, 'We are only fifty minutes late at the moment; you should still have plenty of time to catch your connection. Here are your passports and have a pleasant breakfast in the buffet coach.' Herr Shoemaker checked each of the passports, but he didn't say thank you as he was annoyed that the train was running late. He went back to the cabin where he found the girls ready and waiting. He gave the girls their passports and they all put them securely in their bum bags.

They made their way to the buffet coach and ate their continental style pre-packed breakfasts with cups of coffee.

Herr Shoemaker checked his watch every five minutes, looking out of the windows on both sides of the train, trying to get some clue as to where they were. When it was quarter to seven he said, 'Right, girls, let's go and get our bags, we are cutting it very fine, and we need to find the connection to Brussels as soon as we can.'

They went back to their cabin and got their rucksacks on and stood in the corridor next to one of the doors.

The train finally arrived at Frankfurt at seven o'clock; Herr Shoemaker was panicking and saying, 'We only have twenty-eight minutes to find the Brussels train.'

THE HOUSE OF ATTILA

They made their way to the main station concourse and found the departures information board, then followed the information signs, which led them to the train. They quickly found coach 33 and their seats; there was only one other passenger on their coach at the time. They stowed their luggage above their seats and settled down. Herr Shoemaker looked at his watch and said, 'We cut that a bit fine; only eight minutes to spare.'

Apart from the ticket collector waking them to check their tickets they slept all the way to Brussels.

They had a two hour wait in Brussels so they decided to waste an hour walking round the station partly for exercise and partly to pass the time.

They spotted a reasonable place to eat and spent a leisurely hour having lunch, they then made their way to the Calais-Ville train.

They left the train at Calais-Ville and boarded the shuttle bus from the station to the ferry terminal. They passed through customs quite easily and made their way to the ferry waiting room. The weather was wet and windy and the small group pushed each other to get up the gangway to the ship.

They found four seats together near a luggage rack and sat down to wait for the ship to sail. Crossing the English Channel was very rough and they were all glad to disembark at Dover. They boarded the train for London Victoria Station with collective sighs of relief.

Herr Shoemaker said to the girls, 'We are in England now, you have done very well. It is half past four and the Glasgow train does not leave Euston Station for another seven hours.'

Seven hours later, after what seemed like an eternity of waiting, Herr Shoemaker announced, 'At last, girls, our train is on the departure board.'

Half an hour later they got their rucksacks on and went down to the station concourse and followed the signs to platform 9.

They found their seats and stowed their rucksacks and jackets on the overhead racks. Herr Shoemaker went on to the platform and walked a bit along the train and he noticed that the buffet coach was next to their coach.

He boarded the train again and sat with the girls. They heard a whistle being blown and the train began to move. There were only two other passengers in their coach.

They slept for much of the journey.

The train arrived at platform 2 at Glasgow Central two minutes early at seven fifteen. Herr Shoemaker checked to make sure that they had not left anything and then they disembarked from the train.

After a good breakfast, showers in the public toilets, and several cups of tea each, Herr Shoemaker said, 'We have nearly three hours until our connection to Oban. A friend told me that there is a great shop on Sauchiehall Street where we can get very cheap clothing. I have a map here and the store is near to Queen Street Station where we get our train for Oban. Come, we will get a taxi to take us there and then we can walk to Queen Street Station. We can spend seventy pounds each to get essential clothing.' The girls' attention suddenly sharpened up and they started to follow the signs for taxis.

The taxi dropped them at the store at quarter to ten. Herr Shoemaker said, 'Now I want us to be leaving this shop at quarter past eleven at the latest, is that agreed?' The girls said in unison, 'Yes.'

They left the shop laden with their rucksacks on their backs and bags dangling from each arm.

With Herr Shoemaker checking his map at almost every road junction, they got to Queen Street Station at quarter to twelve.

They looked up at the departure board and saw that the train for Oban was leaving from platform 7. They boarded the train and found their seats, which were marked 'reserved'.

The train started on time and made its way out of the station; it soon cleared the outskirts of Glasgow and was running along the edge of the River Clyde. Maria and the others were captivated with the scenery. The River Clyde soon opened out into the Firth of Clyde, a massive body of water with large ships engaged in their business. Then the train was climbing up the side of the mountains with a long narrow sea loch far below on the left-hand side. Maria heard another passenger say, 'That's Loch Long.' Maria thought, 'That's a very good name for it.' They left Loch Long behind as the train climbed through a mountain pass and suddenly she saw another loch on the right-hand side. She heard the same passenger say, 'That's Loch Lomond.' Maria felt a sense of ownership because 'The Bonny Banks of Loch Lomond' was one of the songs they sung over and over again in her English classes at school. She stood in the passageway to get a better sight as they only got glimpses of the loch through the trees. She thought, 'This country has a lot of trees.'

Maria noticed the hillside on the left of the train had little groups of Scots pines and she thought, 'This is the prettiest scenery I have ever seen; these little Scots pines look like they belong here.' Shortly after this the loudspeaker in the train said, 'We are approaching Crainlarach and the two front coaches will go to Oban and the rear coaches will go on to Fort William and Malaig.' The train stopped at Crainlarach and some of the local travellers got out of the train and stretched their legs on the platform, some used the opportunity to smoke a cigarette. The locals knew that the front coaches were being separated from the main train here and they had a few minutes. The train soon started again after further warnings to passengers to make sure that they were on the right part of the now separated train.

The approaches to Connel Ferry were so beautiful that

Maria fell in love with the place and soon the train was spiralling down the hillside into the town of Oban.

They waited until the train was completely stopped and then gathered up all their bags, with Herr Shoemaker checking to ensure that they had not left anything.

The first sight of Oban as they came out of the station was impressive with McCaig's Folly dominating the skyline. They stopped and looked at the town for fully a minute, taking in the whole harbour front with its two piers. It was without doubt a very beautiful place.

30
Freda Pays the Price

No one knew the girls had been taken, and it was a few hours before people started to wonder why they were missing. Freda was the first to act by confronting Harold Szirtes when he arrived at the hotel that evening. She asked him direct, 'Do you know where Maria is?'

Her directness caught him off balance and he said, 'Yes, she has gone to Scotland with Herr Shoemaker and two girls from the House of Attila to open a hotel there.' Then he regained his composure and shouted, 'It's none of your business, how dare you question me?' He stamped off towards the bar, mumuring loudly to himself.

Freda realised that she had taken a big chance as no one usually got away with insubordination with Harold Szirtes. She retired to the kitchen where Lette and Mary were cooking. She said, 'How are you doing girls?'

Lette cheerfully replied, 'OK, we are doing OK, Mary, aren't we?'

Mary repeated, 'Yes, we are doing OK.'

Freda said, 'Can you manage for a bit, I need to go to my room to think for a while?'

Freda went to her room, she was worried about herself but relieved that Maria was all right. She thought, 'Yes, Lette and Mary are doing OK; there are always young people to take your job as soon as you flounder. You have to keep going, to keep going.'

She knelt down in front of her bed with her arms resting on the bed. She began to pray. 'Dear Father, I am getting into trouble because I love Maria like the daughter I never had. I don't know what came over me when I scalded Karl and just now when I challenged Harold Szirtes. I think my card is marked now, but, because I trust in my Lord Jesus and I know that He is awaiting me, I am not afraid of them or even of death. Please place your angels around Maria to protect her. In Jesus' name I ask this of you.' She rose up feeling much better and made her way back to the trials and tribulations of the hotel.

At the House of Attila it was the second day before the servants began to ask what had become of Senca and Valda and it was the third day before Nico knew they were missing. It worried Nico because he had become very friendly with Valda. Several weeks went by before Nico got the opportunity to go to the Harold Szirtes Hotel. One Saturday night Harold Szirtes said to Imri, 'I want to read the Sunday papers to see if I am mentioned in any articles about a charity event I attended today and I want you to get up early tomorrow morning and cycle to town and get me the Sunday papers.' Imri was not keen to cycle the forty kilometres to town and forty kilometres back. Instead he went over to the boiler house, pushing his bicycle and found Nico. He said, 'Nico, tomorrow morning as early as possible take this bicycle and go and get father the Sunday papers in town and bring them back as soon as you can; take this money, it is more than enough for the papers.'

The following morning Nico woke as usual at five o'clock. He just had a quick wash, dressed in a track suit and mounted the bicycle. It was a lightweight sports bike and once on the road Nico had it really moving along quite effortlessly. He reached the town and the paper shop at seven o'clock. He then rode a little detour to the Harold Szirtes Hotel. He went

THE HOUSE OF ATTILA

to the back door and saw Freda through the kitchen window. He waved to her and she let him in the back door. He said, 'I hoped to see Maria.'

Freda said, 'Maria has gone to open a new hotel. She had no warning, she just disappeared, but I asked Harold Szirtes and he told me that she had gone with Herr Shoemaker and Senca and Valda to start a new Harold Szirtes hotel in Scotland.'

Nico's disappointment showed in his face. Freda said, 'Sit down and I will make you a cup of tea and something to eat.' She gave Nico a plate of porridge with honey and sliced banana, and a large mug of tea.

Nico finally said, 'What can I do?'

Freda said, 'I don't know but I am praying for your sister and I will pray that you find her. Let's pray together just now.' She laid her hand on Nico's head, bowed her own head and said, simply, 'Lord, You said, "For where two or three are gathered together in my name, there am I in the midst of them." Nico and I are gathered in Your name now. We ask You that Nico can find and rescue his sister Maria. Amen.'

Freda said, 'Nico, believe that you will and you will.' She added, 'Do not let anyone know that you know where your sister is. Now get on your bike before anyone sees us, and God bless you.'

Nico got on his bike and rode away.

Freda worked away at the usual hotel routines until late afternoon. Just as things quietened down, and she was thinking of going for a quick nap, Harold Szirtes, Felix Hienmann and Karl Stonier walked in. Karl said, 'Hello, Freda, I am out of hospital now and I have been looking forward to this moment.'

Freda's stomach and chest constricted as if a steel band had tightened round them.

Harold Szirtes said, 'Freda, do you have the key to the wine cellar?' Freda just walked over to the key board and took down a big brass key; it was the spare key to the wine cellar, as the key borrowed by Harold Szirtes when Nataša disappeared was never returned.

Felix said in his high-pitched, steely voice, 'You can come quietly or we will drag you.' Freda just walked slowly out of the back door and made her way towards the wine cellar. Harold Szirtes ran ahead and opened the door. Karl went to a parked van, opened the door and took out his specially designed whip, a length of rope and a roll of heavy polythene sheet.

They entered the wine cellar and Karl rolled out the polythene sheet covering the centre of the floor. Felix took the length of rope and threw one end over the ceiling beam above the polythene sheet. Karl said, 'Freda, do you have anything to say?'

Freda looked him straight in the face and said, 'No, just get on with it.'

Karl said, 'Take your clothes off, or we will forcibly strip you.'

Freda quietly took her clothes off, folding them and laying them neatly in the corner of the cellar.

Felix said, 'Over here.' Freda walked over to where Felix held the rope. He took a large plastic cable tie and fastened her wrists tight together in front of her. He then fed the end of the rope through between her arms and the cable tie and tied the rope firmly. He then pulled the other end of the rope, which was dangling down from where it hung over the ceiling beam. He hung his weight on the rope, which lifted Freda's arms high above her head until she was standing on her toes.

The tension in the room was electric, Karl was pouring with sweat and his breathing was fast and laboured as if he couldn't get a breath. He gasped, 'You know what this is for?' Freda did not hear him; she was deep in silent prayer. He carried on, 'You have ruined me and now it's time for you to pay and you will pay dearly.'

Karl began to circle Freda, obsessed with revenge, just as when he whipped Fredrick the boiler man.

He said to Felix, 'Take the tension off and let her down a bit to relieve the strain on her toes.' As the upward tension and strain eased so she opened her legs. Seeing his opportunity Karl drew the whip sharply upwards, lashing her between her legs with the ends of the thongs in a whip-like motion. One of the metal rivets lacerated a main artery. The trio of murderers were shocked and stunned for a moment; they had not expected so much blood. Harold Szirtes shouted, 'Stop it, stop it.' Slowly Felix let Freda collapse to the ground. Although the pain was excruciating, it was all over for Freda in just over three minutes. As she slipped into unconsciousness she closed her eyes and a smile broke across her face.

Harold Szirtes began to panic; he shouted at Karl, 'You were supposed to contain any blood on the polythene sheet. Now it is all over the cellar floor and wall. You cannot get rid of traces of blood easily. This is Sunday and most places are closed, tomorrow you two will have to hire a steam cleaner and clean the whole of this cellar.'

Harold Szirtes calmed down a bit and began to think clearly. He said, 'OK, we need to be careful, I haven't got any blood on me, and I will go to the hotel and get some bed sheets and some towels.' He came back with a big bundle of sheets and towels.

He said to Karl, 'Take this towel, fold it several times and place it over the wound to try to stop more blood leaking out.' He took one double bed sheet and said, 'Roll her on to this sheet.' They did as he asked. He laid another sheet on an uncontaminated part of the floor and said, 'Now pick up the roll and place it on the edge of this sheet and roll her up again in the second sheet.' They did so, and with a third and fourth bed sheet.

'Now go to the door and clean your feet on this towel and then reverse the van up to the ramp.' They carried the heavy roll up the ramp and placed it in the van and locked the van doors. They returned to the cellar and cleaned up all the debris. Harold Szirtes said, 'You must hire a steam cleaner and come back tomorrow. Clean the entire cellar, take this key and don't lose it.' He handed Felix the key to the wine cellar and Felix locked the door, taking the key with him.

They drove out to the House of Attila and parked at the boiler house.

Harold Szirtes saw Nico working with the horses in the paddock and he went over and said loudly, 'Nico, I do not want you to go near the boiler house for the next four hours, do you understand, do not go near the boiler house for any reason during the next four hours?' Nico nodded and said, 'Yes.'

Harold Szirtes, Felix and Karl entered the boiler house and loaded four logs into the fire chamber, they left the fire door open and soon the fire was roaring. Harold Szirtes said, 'Now make sure no one is watching and get the wrapped up body out of the van and into the boiler house.'

The three of them quickly carried Freda, still rolled in the sheets, into the boiler house and carried the bundle up to the upper fire door and rolled it into the fire chamber on top of the burning logs. They then carried another two logs up to the upper fire door and dropped them carefully on top of the now raging fire beside the burning body. They fed the fire continually in this way, keeping the draught at maximum for a full hour. They let the fuel burn completely. When the heat was just bearable they raked out the fire bed and retrieved all the bones by filtering all the ash through a mechanical sieve. They put the bones in a polythene bag and Felix took them away to put them through a stone crusher up at the estate quarry. Karl and Harold Szirtes put two new logs in the fire to self ignite from the still red hot refractory brick.

They closed the fire door and swept the entire boiler house clean, throwing the sweepings into the fire.

Felix drove Harold Szirtes and Karl back to the hotel; he loaded a container of petrol into the van and drove out to a remote place with Karl following him in a car. He doused the interior of the van with petrol and set it alight. He watched it for a few moments, then he got into the passenger seat of Karl's car.

Karl drove Felix back to the hotel and they joined Harold Szirtes for a drinking session.

31

The New Hotel

Herr Shoemaker pointed to a hotel across the harbour and said, 'That's our new hotel over there, however, we are booked into a self-catering three-bedroom apartment with a bathroom and a nice view of the harbour, we will stay there for a week while we make the hotel suitable for us to move in.'

He led the way to an apartment block just beside the station. He rang the door bell marked 'Caretaker.'

A few minutes later a door opened and a woman said, 'Come in and I will show you the apartment.' She showed them round, instructing them in how everything worked, getting them to try each piece of equipment in turn for themselves. She said with a laugh, 'At least one of you will remember how to work everything.'

As she left the apartment she said, 'Come to the door and I will show you the way to the supermarket.' She pointed along the road and said, 'You just follow that road for about five to ten minutes and you will come to it. 'Don't hesitate to contact me if you have any problems.'

Herr Shoemaker took the smaller of the bedrooms and left the girls to sort out who was occupying the other two rooms, both of which had twin single beds.

Herr Shoemaker came back into the living room and shouted to the girls, 'Let's go to the supermarket and get some provisions.'

THE HOUSE OF ATTILA

After stocking up at the supermarket, Herr Shoemaker said, 'Come on, we should go look at the town.'

They walked along the south pier looking at the fishing boats and the huge passenger ferry. They turned near the end and walked back along the pier, looking across the water to the north pier. Maria said, 'This is a beautiful place.' Everyone indicated their agreement. Herr Shoemaker said, 'That is our hotel over there, I will go to the lawyer and get the keys at nine o'clock in the morning and we will go and see what we need to get done to make it operational.'

They walked over to the building but the windows were boarded up at ground level so they could not see into any of the rooms. They made their way over to the north pier and looked around. Maria pointed and said, 'That's a very large church over there; I haven't been to church since I was captured.'

Herr Shoemaker coughed nervously and said, 'It has been a long journey, we have been travelling for two nights and three days and I think we all deserve an early night and a good sleep, let's go back to the apartment.'

Herr Shoemaker was up at seven o'clock; he had a shower and dressed in clean clothes. When he came out of the bathroom Senca was already making breakfast.

Soon they were all sat at the table tucking into a lovely cooked breakfast.

Herr Shoemaker said, 'I will go to the lawyer and get the keys and check the title deeds and see what more formalities need to be completed. Then I will come back here and we will go together to our hotel.' He took half a dozen brand new notebooks and pens that he had purchased in the supermarket.

* * *

Herr Shoemaker returned at ten fifteen with the lawyer. He locked the apartment and then the five of them made their way to the hotel.

The lawyer opened the front door and led them inside. The lawyer was a practised talker and showed them round the hotel, exaggerating every feature as if he was trying to sell it. Eventually Herr Shoemaker said, 'Stop. What I want to know is where are the essential utility controls such as water, electricity, gas, telephone connections and so on? I need to know how they work and what I need to do to activate them.' Valda giggled until a frosty look from Senca silenced her. Herr Shoemaker spent about an hour with the lawyer checking all the services in turn, writing the details and contact information in one of his notebooks.

He finished by saying, 'Where will I get a phone book for local trades and services?'

The lawyer replied, 'I will go back to the office and get you a Thomsons Local directory and a Yellow Pages directory.'

Herr Shoemaker said, 'Good I will appreciate them today.' The lawyer left to get the directories.

When he was gone, Herr Shoemaker said, 'The design of the hotel previously satisfied the tourist board and local environmental health inspectors and we will consult them early to get their thoughts, but I want you girls to have an extra input from the hotel management perspective. Maria, will you look at the kitchen and make a list of what you think we need to do to make it efficient. Here is a notebook and pen.

'Valda, will you look at the dining-room and make a list of what you think we need to do to make it run efficiently, including converting the kitchen annexe into a dish-washing facility. Here is a notebook and pen.'

Finally he asked Senca to look at the laundry room and make a similar list.

Herr Shoemaker finished by saying: 'You work on your

ideas while I go and telephone some companies in this Yellow Pages directory. Towards the end of the day we will exchange ideas.'

The three girls shared their notes and agreed the best ideas for each work area, and at the end of the day presented them to Herr Shoemaker, who said, 'I am very impressed and I agree with all your ideas.'

'I have found an electrical company who will come and test and repair all the electrical systems and will start next Monday. A plumbing company will also start on Monday to check and service the plumbing and so on. After they have finished a good painting and decorating company will decorate the whole hotel. We will need to make the staff quarters habitable by a week today and we will do it ourselves as we will have to vacate our apartment then.'

They then discussed and shared their ideas for fitting out and improving the hotel.

The three girls were impressed with the way Herr Shoemaker incorporated all their ideas into his clear specifications. They discussed everything from kitchen layout to the bar and lounge and finally bedrooms and sitting-rooms.

Finally, satisfied that everything was covered, Herr Shoemaker said, 'Let's go and if the library is open. We can do some more research and type up our notes with their computers.'

They locked up the hotel and walked to the library. Herr Shoemker explained to the librarian who they were and their short-term need to use the library computer services. The librarian was very helpful, and after filling simple application forms, she gave them membership cards. Herr Shoemaker picked up a leaflet for the Highland Theatre, Oban's local cinema. Herr Shoemaker said, 'Let's go for a walk and find the cinema.' He took out the cinema leaflet and said, 'I think we will go to the cinema on Saturday evening.'

They found the cinema and had a look at the coming

programmes and then went back to the apartment and Valda started to make cottage pie for their meal.

During the meal Herr Shoemaker said, 'I am very pleased with the hotel and I think we can make a success of it.' They watched television for a while then went to bed.

Herr Shoemaker and the girls cleaned, decorated and furnished the staff quarters before their week's booking in the apartment ran out, and they moved in. It was now mid summer and Herr Shoemaker had been talking to the tourist board about his hotel reopening. In the conversations, he said, 'I miss running my under sixteen football team back in Serbia.'

The tourist board representative replied, 'Did you run an under sixteen team? We are working with the Scottish Football Association, trying to get an international football tournament for under sixteen teams in the highlands during the third week in July. We are trying to attract teams from less developed countries to make up half the entries, but because of the cost of accommodation, the response has been poor. We have just three Romanian teams who have entered, so the SFA has chartered a bus from Bucharest passing through Arad. The bus is only half full and if you could get your team to Arad there will still be more than enough seats. The extra team would balance the competition, making it four Scottish teams and four foreign teams.'

Herr Shoemaker replied excitedly. 'Yes, I think my boss would jump at the chance to bring the boys over, they can stay in the hotel as our first guests and he can see the hotel at the same time. I will speak to him by phone tonight.'

The tourist board representative said, 'Why not phone from here now, time is running out for us to complete all the bookings for the tournament and we are keen to finalise the arrangements.'

Herr Shoemaker phoned the House of Attila and fortunately Harold Szirtes was there. He quickly updated him on the progress of the hotel refurbishment and then told him about the opportunity to play in the football tournament during the third week in July.

Harold Szirtes replied, 'International football tournament, yes, I like the idea of winning that, second week in July, yes, that suits, we will come, send us the travel details and Felix will arrange all the paperwork,'

He continued, 'Listen carefully, this is very important, I have two prostitutes coming in on a Spanish fishing boat and I want you to hire a small local boat that you can use yourself, I don't want any locals involved. You must meet the boat ten kilometres west of the island of Iona, which is outside the three mile international limit. At midnight on the fourteenth of July transfer the two girls to your boat and bring them to the hotel where you can put them to work.'

Herr Shoemaker replied, 'No, I don't want them, I can run a profitable hotel here just on the potential tourist market.'

Harold Szirtes exploded. Herr Shoemaker held the telephone tighter to his ear, frightened that the tourist board representative could hear. Harold Szirtes forced himself to calm down and said very coldly, 'You will do what you are told. Get a pencil and paper and write down what I have told you. I will repeat it once to make sure you have understood. You know that I do not suffer fools gladly, in fact I do not suffer fools at all.'

Herr Shoemaker asked the tourist board representative for some paper. He then spoke into the telephone and said, 'Yes, I have paper and pen.'

Harold Szirtes said very slowly to allow time for writing, 'I want you to arrange a small local boat to meet the Spanish fishing boat on your own ten kilometres west of the island of Iona at midnight on the fourteenth of July and transfer two girls to your hotel where you can put them to work. I don't want any locals involved. You will also receive ten onekilogramme sealed packages of cannabis resin; check that they are still properly sealed and weigh them, because you will have to account for every gramme. Do not pay any money, everything is already paid.'

Harold Szirtes hung up the telephone without waiting for a reply.

Herr Shoemaker wrote the message down and folded the paper and placed it in his wallet. The tourist board representative said, 'Are you all right, you have gone very white, can I get you a drink of water?'

Herr Shoemaker replied, 'No, I am OK, it's just my boss, he is very difficult at times.'

It was the tourist board representative's turn to panic now. He said, 'Is the football team still coming?'

Herr Shoemaker replied, 'Yes, the football is still OK.'

The tourist board representative said, 'Good I will complete the arrangements and get back to you.'

When Harold Szirtes slammed down the telephone handset he said to Felix, who was sitting in the office beside him, 'Herr Shoemaker has gone soft; we will need to deal with him.'

Herr Shoemaker walked slowly back to the hotel, he knew that he had made a big mistake.

The weeks went by and the hotel suddenly began to shape up. The decorators began to move out and the carpet fitters moved in. Soon the hotel was ready for the furniture to be delivered. Herr Shoemaker decided to open the bar and restaurant and then progressively open the hotel to tourists. He involved the tourist board and the environmental health officers from the start and they were helpful and also complimentary on the practical design features.

32

The Boat

Herr Shoemaker made enquiries of the local fishermen at the south pier as to where he could hire a seaworthy boat. They told him of a fisherman named John Kelly who had had a stroke and was now unable to use his lobster fishing boat; they added that it was a good seagoing boat. They also gave him the fisherman's address and phone number. He phoned and arranged to go out and see him the following morning.

Herr Shoemaker got a taxi to the fisherman's house and asked for a card with the taxi company's phone number as he paid the driver.

The fisherman's wife answered the door and when he explained what he had come for, she invited him in. The fisherman was sitting in an armchair. His wife said, with an emphasis on the 'e' in Meester, 'This is Meester Shoemaker and he wants to hire your fishing boat.'

She continued, 'My name is Jean; John, my husband, lost his speech with the stroke, but he can understand everything you say. I can answer your questions for him. The boat is a good boat and it is a simple boat to handle. You will need to pump it out as it has been lying for a couple of months.' John murmured and gesticulated with his hands. Jean said, 'He says the diesel tank is half full and you can fill up at the Railway Pier in Oban.' John made a few more sounds and hand gestures and Jean said, 'You need to take the battery out and charge it; there is a battery charger in the workshop behind the house.'

John made a few more noises and began to push himself off his chair, reaching for his three-wheeled walking frame.

'This is his sports Zimmer; it is so fast that it is fitted with brakes.' John made gurgling noises as if laughing at his own joke and Jean laughed loudly with him. Herr Shoemaker wasn't sure whether to laugh or not. Jean said, 'He will show you what to do with the boat.'

Herr Shoemaker said, 'Wait a minute, we have not discussed a price.'

John made some more noises. Jean said, 'He asks you, are you an honourable man?' Herr Shoemaker was caught unawares and a bit unsure what to say. John made more sounds and Jean said, 'Why do you hesitate with that question?' Herr Shoemaker blushed and was speechless. John then made more sounds and Jean said, 'John says that because you couldn't answer that question, it's money in advance. It will be two thousand pounds deposit, returnable with the safe return of the boat, undamaged and one hundred and fifty pounds per day for the hire. How long do you want it for?'

Herr Shoemaker was so flabbergasted with the directness of the attack, he could only agree.

John made more noises and Jean said, 'Do you have the money with you?'

Herr Shoemaker nodded his head and took out his wallet. He counted out the money and said, 'I would like to hire the boat for one week.'

Jean took the money and disappeared into another room.

Herr Shoemaker had a sudden thought and shouted, 'Come back.' Jean came back. He said. 'Ask John how much to buy the boat?'

John looked at him and said, 'It is a bargain at seven thousand pounds.'

Herr Shoemaker said, 'Done.'

Jean threw her arms round her husband and shouted, 'John, you spoke! You spoke!'

John started to go towards the door and Herr Shoemaker followed him. He led Herr Shoemaker to the back of the house and down a paved path to a pontoon floating on the sea. John's boat was tied to the pontoon and there was a gangway leading from the pontoon to the work deck at the back of the boat. John reached the gangway and abandoned his three-wheeled walking frame, and by holding on to the two handrails, he made his way down on to the work deck. Jean caught up with them and carried the three-wheeled walking frame down on to the work deck and gave it to John.

John made more noises, but now Herr Shoemaker could discern key words and Jean said, 'John says, take the battery out of its sump under that hatch cover.'

Herr Shoemaker unscrewed the wheel-shaped hand nuts securing the hatch cover and lifted it off. John pointed to the cover, making speaking noises. Jean said, 'Turn the cover over.' There was a screwdriver and a shifting spanner clipped to the underside of the hatch cover. Herr Shoemaker soon had the battery out and John passed the walking frame to Jean and made his way up the gangway. Jean returned the walking frame to him and he led the way to the workshop.

With directions from John through Jean, Herr Shoemaker connected the battery to the battery charger and switched it on.

They returned to the boat with John making the big physical effort required, and speaking through Jean, he instructed Herr Shoemaker how to pump out the boat by auxiliary hand pump.

Jean and John made a very effective team, and with John's voice improving, between them they instructed Herr Shoemaker in all the aspects of the boat including the fact that the twin diesel engines gave the boat a good turn of speed when required.

They made their way back to the house for lunch where Jean dished up two large smoked haddock and poached eggs with two large slices of bread each.

After that she served large mugs of tea. When they had finished John said, 'The battery will be charged enough now, let's go and fit it in the boat.'

When the battery was fitted and the hatch cover fastened down John said, 'OK, try to start it.' The engines started immediately.

Jean went on to the pontoon and pulled the gangway up. She cast off the retaining ropes and jumped back into the boat. With John instructing him, Herr Shoemaker slowly made away from shore and turned toward Oban.

They tied up alongside the fuel point and Herr Shoemaker went ashore to get the rest of the money to pay for the boat and a receipt book. John shouted, 'Remember to get enough money to pay for the fuel.' Jean hugged John, excited by the way he was recovering his voice. Herr Shoemaker came back about half an hour later and gave Jean the balance of the payment and got John to sign a statement of sale and receipt of the money. He went back ashore and paid for the fuel and returned to the boat.

They cast off and John said, 'Let's take the boat round the island of Kerrera and you will get a better feel for it.' They headed north and round the headland of the island where they were exposed to much stronger wind and waves. John showed Herr Shoemaker how to radio the coastguard's office and tell them the name of the boat and where they were going. He said, 'It is very important that you contact the coastguard. The coastguards know this boat and they know that I fish lobster from Oban along the south coast of the island of Mull.' John said into the microphone, 'Fishing boat *Mermaid* to coastguard.' The radio responded. 'Coastguard

THE HOUSE OF ATTILA

to *Mermaid*, receiving you.' John said, '*Mermaid* to coastguard, sailing round Kerrera, due to arrive Oban at seventeen hundred hours.' The radio responded, 'Coastguard to *Mermaid*, understood, over and out.'

They ran down the west coast of the island, feeling the roll of the boat with its side on to the waves. Suddenly Herr Shoemaker gestured to John to take the wheel and he lurched over and grabbed hold of the side rail and was sick over the side. He held on to the rail for the rest of the trip until John returned to the pontoon and Jean tied up. John spoke into the microphone, '*Mermaid* to coastguard.' The radio responded: 'Coastguard to *Mermaid*, over.' '*Memaid* arrived Oban, over,' said John. The radio replied, 'Coastguard to *Mermaid*, message understood, over and out.'

Herr Shoemaker said, 'I would like to keep the boat here for a reasonable rent.'

John said, 'Twenty pounds per week for the mooring and any advice you need. I think we need to sail again tomorrow before you are ready to take the boat out yourself.'

Herr Shoemaker said, 'OK, I will come back tomorrow.'

Herr Shoemaker phoned for a taxi and returned to the hotel. The girls were running the bar and the restaurant perfectly. When he came in Senca said to him with a big smile, 'Come in to the restaurant and be a guest for tonight.'

He replied, 'Let me go up to my room and shower and change first.' He went to his room, brushed his teeth to remove the residue of his sickness, gargled with water, then drank a glassful of water. He showered and put on fresh underwear, shirt, jogging pants and socks, and a soft pair of slip-on shoes.

Feeling a lot better, he went down to the restaurant and realised he was hungry.

Senca met him at the door and said, 'Is it a table for one, sir? I have kept one of the window seats especially for you, sir.'

She led him over to a window table and held out the chair for him. She said, 'Would you like something to drink, sir?'

He said, 'Yes please, I would like a cold beer.'

Senca returned with a cold lager and a glass. She said, 'Would you like me to pour it, sir?'

He said, 'No thanks, I like to pour it myself. What's the chef's special tonight?'

She replied, 'Ujhazy chicken soup, Hungarian goulash, and strudel pastries.'

Herr Shoemaker said, 'That sounds delightful; yes I will have that, and please bring me another cold beer while I wait.'

He very carefully poured his lager down the inside of the tilted glass, ensuring that the minimum head was generated. He took a mouthful and swilled it round his mouth before swallowing and thinking to himself. 'Nectar.'

He looked round the restaurant and noticed that all fifteen tables were occupied; he counted the number of people including himself and it came to twenty-nine. He thought, 'Very impressive, this is before we open the hotel for residential guests.'

Senca arrived with the 'Ujhazy chicken soup' and bread.

He savoured every drop. He looked out of the window at the busy harbour as one of the large ferries came in to dock. He thought to himself, 'If only this could last.'

Senca came and removed his bowl, then she brought the goulash. He sampled the soft meat, wet with gravy and heavily flavoured with paprika. He almost let out a moan of pleasure.

Senca noticed that he had almost finished his second beer and brought over a third unobtrusively.

He took his time finishing the goulash, thinking about the prospect of meeting Harold Szirtes, Felix and Karl.

Senca came over with another beer as she collected his plates and said, 'That's unlike you, putting the beers away like that.'

He said, 'Yes, I know, but that's how I feel tonight.'

THE HOUSE OF ATTILA

Senca brought the pastries and another beer.

As the beer began to take effect, Herr Shoemaker thought, 'I am glad I bought the boat, we have done really well with the project, the costs of refurbishing the hotel are only two thirds of what we estimated and the time taken is three quarters of what we allowed. Already the girls are bringing in profit from the restaurant and bar weeks before we thought it would, so the cost of the boat will not be noticed when I tell him we have not spent all the budget.'

Tomorrow was July 13 and he knew he had only one more day to learn as much about the boat as possible. He would need to sail to meet the Spanish fishing boat early on the fourteenth.

Herr Shoemaker was up early as usual in the morning and he told the girls at breakfast that he would be away all day again, but he did not tell them about the boat. He returned that evening satisfied that he could handle the boat and went to bed early after telling the girls that he would be away for a couple of days and asking them to run the hotel.

In the morning, Herr Shoemaker got up at seven o'clock. He finished breakfast at eight and asked Maria to make him two standard loaves of mixed sandwiches wrapped in cling film and packed in a box.

He went outside to the waste recycling store and found two big plastic containers that had previously contained bulk orange juice. He washed them out several times and filled them with drinking water.

Maria finished making and packing the sandwiches at half past eight. Herr Shoemaker phoned for a taxi. When the taxi came he put the sandwiches and two containers of water in the boot of the taxi. He said goodbye to the girls and left in the taxi. He arrived at the fisherman's cottage at nine thirty, paid off the taxi and carried the sandwiches and water in two journeys to the front door.

Jean opened the door and said, 'Come in, John's in the kitchen having his breakfast, I will make you a cup of tea and some toast.'

Herr Shoemaker said, 'A cup of tea will do fine; I have just had my breakfast.'

Herr Shoemaker entered the kitchen carrying the box of sandwiches and said, 'Hello, John, I am going to take the boat out today.' He returned to the front door and got the water bottles.

John managed a discernible, 'Where are you going with all that?'

Herr Shoemaker said, 'Iona,' trying to sound casual. John tried to speak but got tied up. Jean came rushing through saying, 'John says, "do you realise that's the Atlantic Ocean out there, not some duck pond?"'

Herr Shoemaker said, 'It's OK, I've brought a box of sandwiches and two big bottles of water.' John tried to speak but he was so worked up he stood up but merely spluttered. Herr Shoemaker said, 'John, I have no choice, I have to go and I must be there by midnight, the people I work for are ruthless.'

John sat back down in his chair and said, 'I should have guessed. Smuggling.'

Herr Shoemaker said nothing.

After an age John said, 'You had better take my oilskins and wellington boots, come on, they are in the workshop.' Herr Shoemaker quickly got his box of sandwiches and then went back for the bottles of water. John had pulled out an assortment of wellington boots, oilskins and life jacket. He said, 'Get that barrow and we will take the lot to the boat.' Prompted by John, Herr Shoemaker took three barrowloads of wet weather gear to the boat. When Herr Shoemaker was ready, Jean and John made their way ashore; Jean threw a large bottle of Irn-Bru to him and pulled up the gangway, then cast off the mooring ropes, which Herr Shoemaker quickly coiled on to the cleats. He started the engines and slowly edged away from the pontoon. He made his way back to the Railway Pier at Oban and tied up alongside the fuel point.

After fuelling the boat and feeling very vulnerable he set off down the Sound of Kerrera.

Crossing the Firth of Lorn from Rubha Seanach, he glanced behind to notice Gylen Castle, thinking how beautiful it looked, like something out of a fairytale. As he approached Mull, he kept well out from the towering cliffs along the south-east coast of the island. Despite his apprehension about being on the edge of his capability, he tried to take in his surroundings: the mighty cliffs, the goats, seals, red deer and much birdlife that he glimpsed. He looked on the chart supplied by John. He passed Carsaig Arches – spectacular eroded sea caves adjoining the high cliffs. Thankfully the wind calmed as the day progressed and after a long sail of approximately twenty odd miles, he passed the end of Mull and saw what he concluded was the south-west tip of Iona. He was immediately alarmed at the broken, rocky profile. He thought, 'How can I possibly risk sailing round there in the dark?' He veered into the Sound of Iona. He stopped the engines and went below, but he soon panicked when he noticed that the boat was drifting on a strong current. He started the engines and sailed out of the Sound and round the southern end of the island of Iona, keeping well out from the rocky tip. He sailed up the west coast of the island, looking at the chart. He thought, 'There are sandy beaches on this side and if I anchor in shallow water, when it gets dark it is just a matter of sailing west for ten kilometres and then there are no rocks to worry about.' After a while he spotted an isolated mooring buoy and managed to get a line on to it.

He switched off the engines.

Herr Shoemaker relaxed for the first time since sailing. As

well as being on the edge of the great Atlantic Ocean, he was really on the edge of his capability and he knew it. He thought, 'If I get lost out here it is three thousand miles to America.' He went below and lay on one of the two bunks and promptly fell asleep.

He woke in a sweat, dreaming about falling through space. Unsure where he was he was, aware of the rolling movement of his bed. Then he remembered he was in a boat and quickly looked at his watch; it was twenty past nine. He thought, 'If I start at ten o'clock and sail slowly due west I will get to the fishing boat about twelve o'clock.' He got up and went to the afterdeck. The sea was relatively calm and the sky was a mass of stars with a full moon shining. He thought, 'I don't know anything about the stars and how the moon moves across the sky.' He looked around for any landmarks to use as reference points and saw that the land and sea were indistinguishable in the dark. He decided to use two distant lighthouses away to the north west as his references and also try to use the boat's compass.

He went into the wheelhouse and checked the compass, the bow of the boat was straining on its mooring and was pointing due west. He dipped the fuel tank and it indicated three quarters full.

He waited until exactly ten o'clock, then, heart pounding he went to the bow. He pulled the mooring rope until the bow was touching the mooring and unhitched the figure of eight windings. Pulling the rope aboard, he coiled it on to the rope hooks and ran back to the wheelhouse.

He checked that the gears were set at medium and started the engines. They fired immediately. He said out loud, 'Good on you, John Kelly, you have kept this boat well.' He opened the throttle levers to about a third full and the boat gently made way into the slight swell. There was a speedometer but it was marked in knots. Herr Shoemaker knew knots were more than kilometres and had an idea that a knot was nearly two kilometres per hour. So he set the throttles to show a speed of four and a half knots and switched off all the boat lights.

The sea was calm and the early part of the voyage went by quickly with some porpoises racing alongside the boat, splashing as they jumped and distracting Herr Shoemaker from constantly checking his watch. As it approached five minutes to twelve Herr Shoemaker began to panic. He thought, 'What if I miss them?' He stopped the engines and peered into the darkness, listening intently for any sound.

He looked at his watch; it was twelve o'clock. Suddenly his eye caught the merest glimmer of light, someone was smoking a cigarette. He peered into the darkness, the light glowed again briefly. He quickly started the engines and steered towards the position. Suddenly a voice shouted, 'Identify yourself or I will shoot.'

He quickly replied, 'The sword.'

The voice replied, 'Of Attila.'

He replied, 'Rules.'

The voice replied, 'Come, friend.' He edged his boat *Mermaid* alongside a large ocean-going fishing boat and threw up his bow mooring rope then his stern mooring rope, which were quickly tied on to the fishing boat. One end of a hinged stair with handrails was dropped on to the deck of the *Mermaid*.

Two men led a young girl to the edge of the fishing boat and prodded her to climb down the stairs; then another young girl was brought and similarly encouraged to follow. Even in the darkness Herr Shoemaker could see they were dishevelled and distressed. Herr Shoemaker gestured to them to go inside the boat. Then one man came down the stairs carrying a simple sports bag. He opened the bag, took the ten sealed packages of cannabis resin and laid them carefully on the deck. Herr Shoemaker took out a spring laboratory balance and a torch. He carefully examined each package to see if it was intact, then weighed each package and recorded the weight in a small book. When he finished he returned the packages to the bag.

Business done, the man turned and ran up the stairway. As soon as he was aboard, two deckhands pulled up the stairway and cast off *Mermaid*'s securing ropes. The big fishing boat got under way and quickly sailed into the darkness.

Herr Shoemaker took the bag of cannabis resin into the boat and, using the torch for illumination, stowed it in a cupboard. He locked the padlock and hid the key in the wheelhouse.

Herr Shoemaker returned below decks and switched on the torch. He shone its beam on the two girls. It was obvious they had been abused by the crew of the fishing boat and were a sorry sight. He said, 'Do you speak English?' They both nodded. He remembered the two loaves of sandwiches and the water. He had been too terrified and occupied to eat and had only drunk the bottle of Irn-Bru.

He found three mugs in a cupboard above the sink and filled the mugs with water. He opened the box containing the sandwiches and said to the girls, 'Eat, drink. I am sorry but I need to switch off the torch.' He did so. They ate in silence in the darkness. When they finished eating he went on to the deck and looked around. He could only see the distant lighthouses so he returned below deck and switched on his torch again. He showed them the toilet and said, 'It is all right to switch on the toilet light when the curtain is closed.' He then showed them the two forward bunks and said, 'Lie down here and try to sleep.'

Herr Shoemaker went back to the wheelhouse, he looked at his watch, it was quarter past two. He listened to occasional routine conversations between ships and the coastguard as he thought.

He was very worried in case he was drifting away but he could not do anything until daylight. He also had to think

THE HOUSE OF ATTILA

about what to do with the cannabis resin. Senca would look after the girls until Harold Szirtes arrived.

That thought really worried him, he knew that he had made a big mistake in rebelling against Harold Szirtes' instruction; he knew that Szirtes had built his power on his reputation for never tolerating dissent in any form.

They say that four o'clock in the morning is the lowest level of your energy and Herr Shoemaker looked at his watch which indicated that hour. He thought back to Fredrick the boiler man. Fredrick wasn't a bad man; he had just been lazy and had forgotten to clean Harold Szirtes' riding boots at the weekend of the gathering. For that omission he was set up and found to be disloyal, he was humiliated, hunted down and killed by the wolfhounds. A terrible shiver went through Herr Shoemaker and he let out a loud groan.

He got up and went out on deck to shake off the demons. He looked to the east and he could see the sky lightening and he could see the skyline of Mull with the distinctive Ben More silhouetted against the light. Seeing that he had not drifted away from his position cheered him up, but he decided to wait until daylight.

As it got lighter he went below and found the girls sitting and they smiled at him. He said, 'Let's eat some more sandwiches and drink some more water.' They shared his food. Then he said, 'I think it is time to get going.'

He went back to the wheelhouse and started the engines. He opened the throttles and headed compass bearing due east.

Soon they saw the outline of Iona and he headed for the southern point, keeping well to seaward of it to avoid the submerged rocks.

He stuck his head down into the doorway to below decks and shouted, 'You can come up here if you wish.' The girls appeared smiling.

The run back was uneventful and Herr Shoemaker progressively increased speed as his confidence increased.

He went back to the mooring at the fisherman's cottage and tied up.

Herr Shoemaker put the padlock key in his pocket. Carrying the remaining food, he led the girls to the fisherman's cottage. John met him at the door and said, 'Well you managed it, well done.'

Herr Shoemaker said, 'Can I phone a taxi?'

John said, 'Help yourself.'

The taxi arrived and they went back to the Harold Szirtes Hotel.

Herr Shoemaker took the two girls to Senca and said, 'Senca, please look after these girls, Harold Szirtes has sent them to us for customer entertainment. I am going to bed now, I have not slept for two days. Remember the football team is arriving tomorrow night.'

Senca nodded and said, 'Yes, the hotel is prepared for them.'

33

International Football

The bus arrived at the hotel at six o'clock and Herr Shoemaker supervised the unloading of the luggage. Maria grabbed Nico and pulled him into the kitchen, hugging him tightly with tears running down her face.

The girls in the hotel booked everyone in and showed them to their rooms, informing them that dinner was to be served at half past five.

Harold Szirtes came over to Herr Shoemaker hugged him, kissed him on the cheek and said, 'Is everything arranged for the football tomorrow?'

Herr Shoemaker said, 'Yes, everything is arranged.'

Harold said, 'Martin, show me the harbour before dinner.'

They walked out and along to the north pier. There was no one about. Harold Szirtes said, 'Martin, did you meet the Spanish fishing boat?' Martin, realising that Harold Szirtes would already know because payment would have been collected, repied, 'Yes.' Harold Szirtes continued: 'I have arranged for the cannabis to be collected tonight at nine o'clock in the Corran Halls car park, do you know where that is?'

Herr Shoemaker said, 'Yes, I can be there with the cannabis at nine o'clock.'

Harold Szirtes replied, 'Good. Now are you sure everything is arranged for the football?'

Herr Shoemaker replied, 'Yes, a bus will pick us up at the hotel at eight o'clock tomorrow morning and take us to Fort William. We play one game in the morning and one game in the afternoon. Then it is the same on Sunday.'

Harold Szirtes said, 'Good, Martin, you know that I expect to win this competition.' They made their way back to the hotel in silence.

Herr Shoemaker went up to his room in a panic. He lay on top of his bed trying to work out what to do. He thought, 'I will need to get a taxi out to the boat, pick up the bag of cannabis and get the taxi to take me to Corran Halls before nine o'clock.' He began to work out the time and thought, 'If I go down to dinner and read out the arrangements for the football before the meal, I can start my meal then slip out about six o'clock before the meal finishes.'

Satisfied that he had a plan, he quickly got his football arrangement notes and went down to the dining-room. The team were all already seated. He went to the kitchen and asked Maria, 'When will you be ready to start serving?'

She replied, 'In ten minutes.'

He went back to the dining-room and picked up a knife from a plate and struck the plate several times to get attention.

He announced loudly, 'Welcome to Scotland. We are here to try to win an international football competition.'

Harold Szirtes interrupted. 'Correction, we are here to *win* the competition.'

The boys gave a big cheer. Herr Shoemaker continued. 'A bus will pick us up at the hotel at eight o'clock tomorrow morning and take us to Fort William. We play one game in the morning and one game in the afternoon. Then it is the same on Sunday, two games. Remember the bus will be here at eight o'clock each morning and you all need to be on it with your football gear.'

Martin noticed that there was a space at one of the boys' tables near the door and he sat there.

THE HOUSE OF ATTILA

Senca had looked after the two girls from the Spanish fishing boat and they looked much better and were dressed in clean waitress uniforms and were serving the food.

Herr Shoemaker quickly ate his soup and main course and slipped out of the hotel at six o'clock to find his prearranged taxi was waiting.

The taxi took him to the fisherman's cottage and he asked the driver to wait. He knocked on the cottage door but there was no one at home so he went round the back and down the path to the boat.

He retrieved the bag from the cupboard, checked the contents and returned with the bag to the taxi. He said to the driver, 'I want you to take me to Dunollie Road, near to the Corran Halls.'

The driver replied, 'You don't want to be going near to the Corran Halls tonight or tomorrow, as there is a big motor bike convention on there this weekend.'

The driver dropped him where he indicated. He made his way to the gable end of a group of guest-houses across from the Corran Halls and leaned on a wall pretty well out of sight. He recognized Felix and Karl walking along the pavement and going towards the Corran Halls. He looked around and saw three bins parked conveniently outside one of the guest-houses. He quickly opened their lids and discovered one was empty and put his bag of cannabis in it. He watched Felix and Karl approach the Corran Halls. Two motor bike men confronted them and they stopped. Herr Shoemaker quietly walked across to them. A big Hell's Angel approached and said, 'Do you have the stuff?'

Karl said, 'We want to see the money first.' The big Hell's Angel said loudly, 'Don't mess with us, get the stuff.'

Karl said, 'No money, no see.'

The Hell's Angel pulled out a knife. Karl went for him but forgot that the Angel was wearing a crash helmet. The Angel stabbed Karl in the shoulder. Herr Shoemaker kicked the angel hard in the balls. He grabbed Karl's good arm and shouted, 'Follow me, run.'

The three of them ran across the road in front of three tour buses, which blocked the pursuit of the motor bike men. They ran along Dunollie Road until Herr Shoemaker spotted a hiding place behind a motor repair garage and they hid behind the buildings. Not too soon, as the roar of dozens of motor cyclists trying to find them assailed their ears and continued for about an hour and then slowly died away.

They waited for a further half an hour, then Herr Shoemaker hailed a passing taxi and the three of them got into the taxi. Herr Shoemaker said, 'Take us to the hospital.'

They arrived at the hospital at about eleven o'clock. The hospital staff treated Karl's wound and gave him an anti-tetanus injection.

They got a taxi back to the hotel at half past one in the morning.

Harold Szirtes was waiting and furious about having to stay up so late. He became even more furious when Felix told him what had happened. Adding that he did not think the Hell's Angels had the money.

Harold Szirtes said, 'What about the cannabis?'

Everyone looked at Herr Shoemaker, who said, 'The cannabis is safe.'

Harold Szirtes replied, 'I want it here, now,'

Herr Shoemaker said, 'I will go and get it.'

Harold Szirtes said, 'Felix, you go with him.'

Karl said, 'I will come too.'

Harold snarled, 'No, you have done enough harm for one night.'

Herr Shoemaker led Felix to the gable end of the guest-houses and said, 'You need to be quiet and not be seen.'

Felix whispered, 'That's my business.'

THE HOUSE OF ATTILA

The Corran Halls were really bouncing with heavy metal music. Herr Shoemaker retrieved the bag of cannabis from the bin and they crept away and returned to the hotel. Harold Szirtes carefully examined the contents in his room.

Satisfied, he dismissed Herr Shoemaker by saying, 'You can go now; I will keep the cannabis here where I can keep my eye on it.' Herr Shoemaker left the room and closed the door, leaving Felix and Harold Szirtes in the room. He went to his room, stripped off and lay on top of his bed to think.

He thought to himself, 'Things look bad. It is clear that I am being frozen out, normally I would be left to look after the safety of the cannabis. Karl and Felix have hardly spoken to me, and I have received Harold's Judas Kiss. He lay on his back, letting the importance of these thoughts sink in. He concluded, 'They will let me run the football team before they move against me. Harold Szirtes desperately wants to win the international football competition for all the publicity it will give him when he returns home.'

He lay quiet for a few moments then thought, 'The last football match will finish about a quarter to five on Sunday, then there will be the presentation of trophies, then the boys will get changed. After all that the bus will probably arrive back at the hotel about seven o'clock at the earliest.'

He decided, 'I can't wait until they have the initiative; I will need to move as soon as we arrive back at the hotel when Harold Szirtes, Karl and Felix will want to go to their rooms to freshen up after the long day.'

Satisfied that he had a plan, he got under the duvet and went to sleep.

The Saturday morning came and the team and supporters boarded the bus at eight o'clock. The competition was simple: the four Scottish teams played the four overseas teams once each and the team with most league points won the competition.

The Harold Szirtes team won both of their games on the Saturday, giving them six points. One of the Scottish teams also won two games, giving *them* six points.

They arrived back at the hotel at quarter to seven with dinner arranged for eight o'clock.

While everyone retired to their rooms, Herr Shoemaker got a taxi and went to the fisherman's cottage. Jean Kelly invited him in, saying, 'I have just boiled the kettle for a cup of tea.'

He went into the living-room and said, 'Hello, John.'

John replied, 'Hello, you are still alive then.'

Herr Shoemaker said, 'I am glad to hear you have regained your speech, but what do you mean?' Jean interrupted by bringing in a tray of mugs full of tea and some egg sandwiches. She sat down, placing the tray on a small table. John said, 'I can see the tension in your whole being, you are running scared and for it to show like that it must be an imminent life threat.'

Herr Shoemaker was staggered. Jean interrupted: 'Eat your sandwiches and drink your tea.'

Herr Shoemaker ate one of the sandwiches and took a drink of tea, then said, 'You are right. Let me eat another of these lovely sandwiches and I will tell you the story.' Jean went through to the kitchen and brought back a fresh pot of tea.

Herr Shoemaker finished the story and then said, 'If I don't escape tomorrow night between the time the bus returns to the hotel and dinner, I will be a corpse by midnight.'

Jean exclaimed, 'Mercy me, we can't have that.'

Herr Shoemaker added, 'I would like to take my three girls and young Nico with me.'

There was silence for a minute and then John said, 'I was all crocked up before you came along and now I have my voice back and a bit more mobility. Give me the money to fuel up the boat and I will have it ready to go, at the north pier, at seven o'clock on Sunday night. Now you had better get back before they miss you.'

Herr Shoemaker slipped in through the kitchen and said to Maria, 'Has anyone come down yet?'
She replied, 'No, it is still all quiet.'
He slipped up stairs to his room and stripped off for a shower.
Everyone gathered about ten to eight for dinner; they were all hungry after the long day. Herr Shoemaker arrived at eight o'clock and noticed that there were no spaces at Harold Szirtes' table. He found a table space with the boys.
Harold Szirtes ordered up a bottle of wine for every table and instructed the waitresses to pour it. When everyone had a glass he stood up and said, 'Well done, boys, if you do the same tomorrow we will be winners. I propose a toast. To the Harold Szirtes Under Sixteen Football Team.'
Everyone responded by raising their glasses and saying: 'The team.'
Herr Shoemaker took a menu, it was a small book type menu and it had a blank inside back page. He carefully wrote a message on the blank page.

> *Senca,*
> *Get the girls – yourself, Maria and Valda – to pack all your clothes into a bag each. We are going to escape at seven o'clock tomorrow night and you will need all your clothes and toiletries with you. Don't forget your bum bags with your identity papers and passports.*

When Senca came over to clear dishes from the table he let her read the message. She whispered, 'I understand.'
He tore the menu into tiny pieces and put them in an empty teacup.

As the meal was finishing, Herr Shoemaker stood up and said loudly, 'Boys, we need to have a short team talk about tomorrow's games.'

Harold Szirtes said loudly, 'I have had enough of football for one day, let's retire to the bar.'

Herr Shoemaker said, 'Boys, come up this end of the dining-room to let the waitresses clear the tables.'

They all gathered round and Herr Shoemaker said, 'Well played today, boys, you made a lot of chances and scored in both games. I watched bits of the Scottish team who won both games today and they have one player who is a class act. When we play them it will decide the competition and according to the games schedule we play them last. What I am going to do is rest Nico as a substitute in the morning game to allow him to have all his energy to mark the class player out of the game in the afternoon.

The room fell silent as they digested the implications. Herr Shoemaker said, 'Are there any injuries from today's games?' There were no replies. He said, 'OK, that's it. Nico, can you wait behind to talk about how to mark this super player.'

When the other players had left the room, Herr Shoemaker told Nico the plan. He said, 'Pack your bag, including your passport and identity papers, tonight ready to grab when we return here tomorrow.' Nico nodded and left the room to pack his bag.

Herr Shoemaker strolled into the bar and ordered an orange juice and lemonade. He walked over to where Harold Szirtes, Karl and Felix were sitting. Their conversation suddenly stopped. After an embarrassing pause Harold Szirtes said, 'Well, did you sort out the boys for tomorrow?'

Herr Shoemaker said, 'Tomorrow is not home and dry; the best Scottish team have a real class player. We play them last and I am going to rest Nico as substitute in the morning so that he is fresh to mark him out of the game in the final game when we play them.'

THE HOUSE OF ATTILA

Harold Szirtes said, 'So long as we win the competition; if we do not win, your head is on the block.' Karl and Felix went into knots of laughter. Harold joined in the laughter, which went on and on until Herr Shoemaker stood up and left the room. The laughter continued even louder as he walked along the passage to the kitchen.

On the Sunday morning the bus turned up at eight o'clock and the team and their supporters got on.

The first game was a dreary battle and the Harold Szirtes team did not make the breakthrough until the eighty-fifth minute to win by the only goal.

After lunch Herr Shoemaker took the boys to the changing rooms an hour before the time for the final game. He reviewed the position and said, 'We are tied on points with the top Scottish team, but they are better by ten goals on goal difference, so we have to beat them to win the competition. This morning the Scottish team won seven nothing with their star player scoring a hat trick and he was significantly involved in the other four goals. So make no mistake, with this exceptional player they are favourites; their huge goal difference compared to ours proves their superiority. But I believe team work can beat individual brilliance.'

He continued, 'Their star player has played in all four games and I have rested Nico this morning in the hope that he can nullify this outstanding player. After four very physical games in two days it is likely that he will begin to fade in the second half, so it is important to keep them from scoring early in the game and we might just spring a surprise near the end. Is everybody happy with our game plan?' There was a unanimous roar of approval.

Herr Shoemaker then led the boys through a thorough loosening up regime.

He then carefully timed the preparations and left the

dressing-room to check what the position was outside. He returned and said, 'Now get your football strips and boots on, the game is being televised by one of the Scottish regions and it has to start exactly on time. The Scottish team is only just arriving; the way they are strolling about they seem to think they have the competition won already.' The referee came in and inspected the boys' boots and said, 'The game is being televised and I will not tolerate bad language or any dissent so you have had fair warning.'

About three minutes to kick-off a florid-faced official came into the dressing-room shouting, 'Come on, come on, this game is being televised, get on to the park, get on to the park.' They ran out and on to the park as one unit. The Scottish team came out in dribs and drabs with officials pushing them along.

The game started with Nico marking his man. He soon understood why this player was so effective, he had great ball skills with all sorts of stepovers, side steps, back heels, in fact the whole bag of tricks normally only seen at the highest level of football.

Nico decided, 'The only way to play this guy is not to look at his feet, which he uses to mesmerise, but look at his head, which indicates the way he is really going.'

Nico adopted this technique and hung in close to the great player, completely nullifying him through the first half. So much so that for the last quarter the great player ran all over the park trying to get free of Nico.

They came off at half-time and Herr Shoemaker was delighted. He said, 'They are not a good team; they are all over the place. Nico, you are playing that class player right out of the game. Now I can see signs of exhaustion creeping into their game so keep doing the same thing and they will crack before the end. It is important you keep going.'

The second half started as the first had ended, with the class player trying to run all over the park to get away from

Nico. The game had been going for about seventy minutes when the class player cracked. He suddenly said, to Nico, 'Get away from me, you wee bastard, or I will break your leg.'

Nico laughed and said, 'I can run like this all day.'

When the next ball came their way the class player held back and let Nico get it, then he viciously lunged in with his foot high, striking down on Nico's left leg. Fortunately Nico sensed the danger and jumped just before the impact; with his foot off the ground the impact was much less severe. However, the referee had seen the intent and blew his whistle immediately. He pulled out his book to record the booking when the booked player exploded. 'What are you booking me for, you specky wee bastard? With those beer bottle specs you're wearing, you canny see anything anyway.'

The referee had no option but to send the player off.

While the disgruntled player was reluctantly leaving the field Herr Shoemaker came running round the side of the park shouting to Nico, 'I want you to play wide on the wing, with them down to ten men we must keep them wide and stretch them as much as possible; I am going to put Diminshie on as centre forward.' He ran round to the other side of the park and shouted the same instruction to the other winger.

By this time Imri was limping and glad to be substituted by Diminshie. The game restarted with fifteen minutes to go. The opposition's ten men were finding it difficult to cope with the wide wingers and for about ten minutes the Harold Szirtes team kept possession for most of that time, playing the ball from one side of the park to the other with the opposition chasing backwards and forwards.

Diminshie made the breakthrough with four minutes to go. The ball was played out to Nico wide on the left wing and he ran at the rapidly tiring full back. He now realised that Herr Shoemaker had been right to rest him in the morning; he pushed the ball past the full back and sprinted, leaving him helplessly behind. Now he was running down the line, there was no one else to stop him, so the goalkeeper had to come to him. Nico waited until the goalkeeper was nearly on him and slipped the ball back to Diminshie who simply walked it into the open goal.

The celebrations were ecstatic. The Scottish team could hardly reassemble for the restart. The game eventually restarted only to allow the full-time whistle to be blown.

Harold Szirtes was jubilant and as usual Imri was presented with the trophy. However, Herr Shoemaker was not concerned about the celebrations, his mind was now on life or death.

34

The Escape

The bus journey back to Oban was exuberant. When they got back to the hotel the boys immediately wanted to party. Herr Shoemaker shouted, 'No, go to your rooms and shower and change for dinner at eight o'clock and then you will party.'

Harold Szirtes interrupted and said, 'It has been a hard, long weekend and I need to relax and freshen up, we will all meet in the dining-room at eight o'clock.'

Herr Shoemaker breathed a sigh of relief; he had not anticipated the party mood. He looked at his watch and it was quarter to seven.

Harold Szirtes, Felix and Karl were already upstairs so he encouraged the stragglers to go to their rooms. When the downstairs area of the hotel was clear he quickly went to his room. He looked out the window and saw the bow of his boat sticking out past the end of the north pier. He put on his bum bag, got his bag and carried it down to the kitchen. Senca, Valda, Maria and Nico were waiting there with their bags hidden in the pantry.

Herr Shoemaker said, 'Come, let's go, we have no time to spare.'

Carrying their bags, they left by the back door and ran across the road and along to the north pier. Jean was on the pier and said, 'Throw your bags down on to the deck and climb down the ladder, I will cast off.'

At that moment Felix came out of his shower and looked out of his window. He opened his bedroom door and ran into the corridor naked and banged on Karl's door and Harold Szirtes' door. They eventually opened their doors and Felix shouted, 'Herr Shoemaker is escaping.' He then ran back to his room to get dressed.

When they were all on the boat Jean Kelly cast off and quickly clambered down the ladder to the afterdeck. John Kelly eased the throttles back and the boat began to move slowly away from the pier. He steered the boat out into the middle of the channel, keeping the boat speed down so as not to draw undue attention, and proceeded south down the Sound of Kerrera.

Harold Szirtes, Karl and Felix rushed out of the hotel and over to the north pier. They watched the *Mermaid* sail away. Harold Szirtes said, 'We need a boat.' Felix pointed to a man preparing to leave the pier in a sports runabout with its engine already running. It was an open boat much like an open-topped car. It had two bench type seats, one behind the other, taking up to six people. Karl went to the ladder leading down to the boat and shouted down, 'Can you help me?' The boatman looked up puzzled and shouted up. 'I am about to cast off.'

Karl said again, 'Can you help me?'

The man said, 'I don't know what you want me to do.'

Karl said, 'I will come down and explain.' He clambered down the ladder and stepped into the boat. Karl said, 'Have you enough fuel in the tank?'

The man said, 'Yes, it's a full tank.'

Karl suddenly struck the man hard on the side of the head, knocking him over the side of the boat and into the water.

Harold Szirtes and Felix clambered down the ladder and into the boat. They looked at the man who was now lying face down in the water against the pier.

THE HOUSE OF ATTILA

Karl took out his knife and cut the mooring rope; he took the boat controls and powered away from the pier, but quickly throttled back and slowed down as there was a strong wind blowing, whipping up the waves. He followed the *Mermaid* as fast as he dared and did not seem to be losing ground.

Meanwhile on the *Mermaid* Herr Shoemaker said to John, 'What do you think, can we outrun them?'

John said, 'Yes, we can outrun them, but that doesn't solve your problems. We must somehow neutralise these dangerous people.'

The two boats sailed down past Easdale Island and on past the island of Luing. As they headed along the west coast of the island of Scarba they were exposed to serious waves but the mood in the two boats was quite different. In the *Mermaid* they had their sea legs, while Harold Szirtes, Karl and Felix were holding on to parts of their boat absolutely petrified with fear. However they were slowly overhauling the *Mermaid* and were now only a hundred metres behind.

John shouted to Herr Shoemaker, 'Come here.' Herr Shoemaker walked over beside him.

John smiled a wicked smile and said, 'I have an idea. With the strong wind in this direction the huge tidal flow, which runs between the islands of Jura and Scarba, is at its peak today. It causes a giant whirlpool in the Gulf of Corryvreckan. As the flood proceeds up the Sound of Jura it is squeezed by the narrowing of the Sound and this increases the flow to a point where it passes through the Gulf of Corryvreckan at eight and a half knots on a full spring tide. When there is any serious wind strength, particularly from the west like today, the waves can get pretty big. In gale force conditions, standing waves can reach up to fifteen feet high.'

By this time the two boats were passing the end of the island of Scarba, and looking into the Gulf of Corryvreckan.

John said to Herr Shoemaker, 'Tell the others to hold on to something strong, I am going to take you through the Corryvreckan Whirlpool.'

John drove the *Mermaid* forward into the mêlée, steering this way and that way to avoid the worst of the waves. Herr Shoemaker looked back to see the chasing boat veer away. Everyone was holding on for dear life as the boat rose to the heights of a wave and then fell into what seemed like a bottomless pit only to rise again with water cascading off the boat. After what seemed an age the seas calmed in front of the boat and they all let out sighs of relief and released their steel-like grip on the boat.

They looked back but no one had followed them through the ancient and terrible maelstrom.

John said, 'Your pursuers will go back to the hotel in Oban now.'

Herr Shoemaker said, 'It is time to alert the coastguard about the cannabis hidden in the hotel.'

Herr Shoemaker lifted the microphone and switched on the radio. He said, 'Calling coastguard, calling coastguard, over.' The radio crackled and responded: 'Coastguard receiving you, over.'

Herr Shoemaker said, 'I am reporting illegal drugs and two women trafficked against their will into this country. The gang masters are at sea in a stolen boat heading for Oban and will arrive approximately at midnight. Their base is the newly opened Harold Szirtes Hotel on the esplanade where the women and the drugs are hidden. Over and out.' The radio spluttered but Herr Shoemaker switched it off before any message came through. He looked at John and John said with a big smile, 'Check mate.'

John steered the boat to a mooring he knew and Jean tied up to it before it got dark.

Jean called them all on to the quarterdeck for tea. When

they had their tea mugs in their hands Herr Shoemaker said, 'What do we do now?'

John said, 'We need to make ourselves comfortable until daylight, then we will sail to Port Ellen.'

Maria, the youngest one, spoke up, 'I have a friend, Dmitar Hrvat, if I phoned him he might help us.'

Herr Shoemaker said, 'You can phone from Port Ellen. Tell him there are seven of us and that we have money. I drew the balance of the project money out of the bank just in case and I have it in my bag.'

Maria looked up the phone number on the card Dmitar had given her, then she said, 'The last time we met he told me that Dubai is four hours ahead of the UK, which means he will be sleeping.'

John said, 'We will phone him first thing tomorrow.'

They all made themselves comfortable and slept until daylight.

There was no food on board so Jean made some more tea. When they got to Port Ellen, Maria phoned Dmitar and he answered. She told him in concise terms their situation.

He said, 'Maria, I need you and Nico to come and look after Prince, he misses you so.' Maria's face lit up in the biggest smile imaginable.

He asked to speak to Herr Shoemaker and he confirmed that they had the paperwork that would be required to let them land in Dubai. Dmitar said, 'I have quite large savings and have always had an idea of opening a hotel in Dubai, perhaps I could be your partner, but I would want Nico to come and work at the stables.'

John cast off and started the engines, saying, 'Let's go to Dubai.'

Jean gave John a big hug, and said, 'It's a miracle, you've recoverd.' She held up her handbag and said, 'It's a good job I brought our passports!'

Herr Shoemaker said, 'Yes, John, set a course for Dubai.'

Maria looked at Nico and said with a smile, 'Our Mother always said that everything was possible with God.'

Author's Note

£1 from the author's royalty for every book sold will go towards planting trees in the world's poorest communities. As well as providing a good read, each book sold will thereby help women in poor countries to plant and nurture at least ten trees, providing fruit, food, medicines, firewood, shelter and building materials.

For more information, please see www.planttreesaveplanet.com